THE COMO FALCON

JEFF CARSON

CROSS ATLANTIC PUBLISHING

ALSO BY JEFF CARSON

THE DAVID WOLF SERIES

Gut Decision (A David Wolf Short Story)– Sign up for the new release newsletter at http://www.jeffcarson.co/p/newsletter.html and receive a complimentary copy of the David Wolf story.

Foreign Deceit (David Wolf Book 1)

The Silversmith (David Wolf Book 2)

Alive and Killing (David Wolf Book 3)

Deadly Conditions (David Wolf Book 4)

Cold Lake (David Wolf Book 5)

Smoked Out (David Wolf Book 6)

To the Bone (David Wolf Book 7)

Dire (David Wolf Book 8)

Signature (David Wolf Book 9)

Dark Mountain (David Wolf Book 10)

Rain (David Wolf Book 11)

Drifted (David Wolf Book 12)

Divided Sky (David Wolf Book 13)

In the Ground (David Wolf Book 14)

High Road (David Wolf Book 15)

**NEW! Dead Canyon (David Wolf Book 16)

THE ALI FALCO SERIES

The Como Falcon (Ali Falco Book 1)

1

Ali stood on the cobblestone street, inhaling the fragrance of freshly baked bread and potted oleanders in summer bloom, squinting against the morning light streaming between the medieval buildings. Grass poked from some of the ancient pavers, a product of the wet weather the Tuscan countryside had been showered in recently, giving the small piazza a fairytale aura. The beauty of Siena in July was on full display, but she ignored all of it.

Instead, her attention was fixed on the man walking a half-circle behind a group of tourists, his dark, bloodshot eyes locked onto the unsuspecting group of elderly Germans like a lion watches gazelles at a watering hole.

Two of the male tourists argued loudly in their native tongue, poking at a map, the heavy Swiss watches affixed to their wrists reflecting the sunlight like two beacons advertising their wealth. If that weren't enough, they wore pressed Bogner outfits—pastel polo shirts, khaki pants with knife-like pleats—with billfolds bulging in rear pockets.

Five other people of similar age, one man and four women,

stood quietly a couple of meters away, as if waiting for a familiar argument to conclude.

The man lurking behind them ignored the Rolexes of the alpha males, his eyes flicking between the two women that stood farthest from the group, and the Prada handbags hanging loosely off their shoulders.

Ali kept her gaze locked on the unfolding scene, her feet moving instinctively toward the action.

Potential action, she reminded herself. The man looked like he was on the hunt, but he wasn't one of the usual suspects she had plucked off the narrow streets of Siena before.

But he fit the bill: young, wearing Levi's and a Puma tee-shirt, both of which hadn't been washed in days or weeks, head shaved short on the sides, a flop of greasy hair on top, face covered in smoky-looking stubble, athletic shoes that were gleaming white and laced tightly, like he was prepared to run at a moment's notice.

And it didn't take a special gift to see those eyes bouncing between those handbags, which meant he was thinking criminal things.

She turned to the bar she had been waiting outside of for the last five minutes. She couldn't see inside. Only her reflection stared back at her, showing a slim thirty-year-old woman of average height, long black hair pulled into a ponytail and hidden beneath an official Polizia di Stato cap. Her eyes, as dark brown as the espresso served within the cafe, were large with excitement. Or was it fear? She glared at herself, forcing the doubt from her appearance, letting the sight of her uniform, with its dark jacket, blue pants, tie, and most importantly the holster stuffed with a Beretta FS92, fill her with the confidence an authority figure should exude in a situation like this.

She eyed the man again, the striated muscles rippling on his arms, the skin slick and dirty. He looked fast and strong. And even though it was mid-morning, those bloodshot eyes signaled that he might be high or drunk.

She didn't have to consult her reflection again to know she was outmatched if it came to a physical confrontation, no matter how much training she'd had at the academy. And there was no way she was pulling her weapon—she had yet to do so in her six years in the department and wasn't about to start now, not with all the tourists funneling through these narrow streets.

The smart decision would be to go inside and get Basso before trying to engage this man alone.

No. The man looked like a cat ready to pounce. There was no time. Basso was here with her now because she had proven to be a woman of action.

"Excuse me!" she called out, taking another step toward the man.

His red eyes swiveled to her, narrowing, his body tensing to a stop. He looked back at the handbags, then back to Ali. Assessing his odds.

Ali continued walking forward, keeping eye contact, putting a hand on the butt of her Beretta. *I see you, asshole.*

If the man grabbed and dashed now, he would have a serious head start on her.

She continued walking, and the man stood straight, his demeanor shifting to nonchalance.

"Falco? Where are you going?" Basso's voice came from the bar behind her. He was back outside.

She slowed and looked at Basso, holding up a hand, then turned back to the man just in time to catch a blurred glimpse of the would-be-criminal's white sneakers disappearing around the corner, lost in the maze of Siena's medieval streets.

A few of the German tourists looked at her, oblivious as ever. The argument continued.

She turned around, waiting for Basso.

"Where were you going?" he asked, a bag dangling from his hand and a copy of *Corriere Della Sera* tucked under his arm.

She shook her head, thumbing in the direction of the tourists. "That man was about to do something."

"That man?"

"No. He went around the corner."

Basso assessed her, glancing again at the Germans still arguing at the map.

He started walking, joining the tail end of a group of passing tourists. "You know, you don't have to try and impress me. As far as I'm concerned, you are inspector material. I've told Ferrari as much... but don't tell him I said that."

She walked next to him, shaking her head.

"I'm serious," he said. "With this next week spent with me, you are to act normal. Do as you would normally do. I know what it's like to be a patrol officer. Some days, most days, you work on your blisters, walking circles around town."

"And some days you chase assholes who steal purses," she said under her breath.

"Excuse me?"

"Nothing." She gestured to the bag and newspaper. "Time for a break already, is it?"

He flared his nostrils, defensive. "I haven't read the paper yet today. Getting up so early to meet you threw a wrench in my routine."

She held up her hands.

"That's another great thing about being inspector. No more of this dawn shift thing. You'll be able to sleep like a normal human being. I can't function unless I read at least the first few pages. I'm walking around blind otherwise."

Her father used to say the same thing, reading Italy's oldest newspaper religiously every morning in the kitchen before work, as if digesting the news was more important than breakfast. *What would I talk about at work?*

Ali remembered her response: *You could talk about work.*

Basso opened the bag and tilted it toward her, revealing two brioches inside.

"Chocolate?"

She shook her head, any appetite she may have had, vanishing with the thoughts of her father.

She broke off from Basso as they passed the German tourists. Using formal Italian, she said, "Buongiorno. Do you need help with directions?"

The two men were facing opposite ways, the map still opened between them, startling at the sight of the uniformed woman talking to them.

"Uh. Mi scusi," one of them said. "Non parlo Italiano."

"English?"

"Ja-- Yes." They both nodded.

She smiled and switched to English. "Can I help you?"

"Uh...we are trying to find z' Piazza del Campo."

Ali swiveled and pointed down the road in front of them. "It's down that way. See the tower?" She pointed at Torre del Mangia jutting up between two long rows of ancient buildings, with its orange bricks rising to meet a white marble square balcony and bell tower on top. "Head towards that. Continue straight for ten or fifteen minutes and you'll run right into it."

The two men looked at one another, one of them wearing a triumphant smile, the other huffing defensively.

"There are no signs!" the losing man said.

"There will be signs down there if you stay on this street. And please keep vigilant with your belongings." She pointed at the women behind the two men, speaking to them now. "I would recommend zipping up your bag, signora, and pulling it higher, onto your shoulder."

The woman looked at her, confused, and when one of the men translated, she looked down at the bag, frowned, and did nothing.

"Thank you. Grazie," one of the men said, leading the group away.

She switched to Italian and spoke under her breath. "But what do I know? I've only been patrolling these streets for the last six years of my life."

"See what trying to impress me gets, Falco?" Basso began walking again.

She stepped in line with him. "If I wanted to impress you, I'd show you how to tie a tie."

He blinked, looking down. He was dressed in one of his Armani suits, purchased off the rack from the Arezzo factory store before Ali had met him.

"What's wrong with my tie?" Basso's name literally meant *short*, and as fate would have it, he was shorter than average, standing just about Ali's height, so he often tilted his head back when she said something controversial. She suspected it gave him the satisfaction of looking down on her even though they stood at the same height.

"Ask Marta when you get home," she said. Nothing was wrong with his tie.

"You'll make a good inspector," he said, "if only for your banter."

Basso walked in silence for a bit, stuffing his face with brioche. He finished chewing and said, "Ferrari has a notion that you couldn't care less if you stayed on patrol duty for the rest of your life."

Her face flushed, feeling violated to learn of talk behind her back. She kept her face carefully neutral, taking a deep breath and shrugging. "If things don't work out with becoming inspector, life will go on. If I'm patrolling all my life, then..." she ended the sentence with a shrug.

Basso chuckled, looking at her again. "Then what? What do you mean, Ali? If you don't get assigned to inspector, and you're stuck patrolling the streets of this small city, then what?"

"What's wrong with the streets of this small city?" she asked. "You don't like Siena?"

"I love Siena. It's my home. I grew up here, in case you forgot. I'm merely making a point. I'm saying you are good, and your boss thinks you don't care enough about the job to move up."

"I care." Her voice rose.

Basso's eyes flashed. He seemed entertained by the emotion he was wringing out of her.

"But there's no sense getting worked up about it," she said, subduing herself with the flick of a switch. "People who get too invested in an idea make bad life decisions when things don't go exactly as planned."

Like her mother had.

"Believe me," she said. "I know."

"You don't want to get too invested in the idea of becoming inspector?" Basso asked.

"What is this? Part of your screening process?"

"Yes." He held her eye.

Her gaze fell to the stone cobbled street in front of them. They walked in silence for a beat.

"Sometimes it's good to fight on your own behalf, Ali."

She frowned, looking at the man next to her. Basso had been kind to her since the first day she had shown up on duty, fresh out of the academy. He had shown her the city, with all its beautiful hidden places, and the evil lurking within, introducing her to the influential people in the neighborhoods, showing her how to stay out of trouble with the powers that be, and how to keep cretons, like the would-be purse-snatcher from a few minutes ago, at bay.

Watching him be a father to his two young boys made her choke back tears every time she saw it in action, reminding her of what she once had in her own life. He was a good man.

But he was also an ass, with his constant unsolicited advice and life-isms. It had all started the day he was promoted to inspector three years ago.

"I'm just saying," he continued. "If you don't fight for yourself, who will?"

"I once got expelled from school for fighting," she said.

"You know what I'm saying."

"I'll do the job the way I see fit and let that be my way of fighting."

"If that were enough, we wouldn't be having this conversation. You have to speak up. Let Ferrari know you're ready to have the new position. Tell him you're ready to step up. That you want the responsibility. Do you want the responsibility that comes with inspector, Ali?"

You have to make your own fate, Ali.

That's what her father had told her once—the man who knew something about tinkering with fate to disastrous effects.

"I get it," she said.

"Do you?"

She pulled out her phone, pretending she'd just received a message.

Basso waved his hand dismissively, stepping a few paces in front of her.

She followed, pocketing her phone, hanging back, certain she wasn't doing well on this part of the review process.

And what was her problem? Basso was right, she wasn't exactly showing enthusiasm. She had put herself on the path to becoming an inspector. Why was she pushing back now that the prize was within reach?

I want to be just like you someday, Papà. The words she had once told her father rose to the surface, telling her the answer. She wanted to become an inspector, but the last thing she wanted to do was be like her father.

Basso led them up the road and through the arched fourteenth-century Roman fortified gateway of Porta Romagna, one of the portals out of the walled medieval city of Siena. He made an immediate right, heading in the direction of a favorite pair of benches.

Sunlight streamed through the tall trees, shooting shimmering solar coins on the ground. They sat down in the shade of a trio of huge cypresses, so old they had probably seen people sitting in their shade for more than a thousand years.

She was roasting in her wool uniform. A breeze flitted past, licking some of the heat away, but the asphalt, the cobblestone walkway, and the ancient stone bench they sat on carried a store of the day's warmth, making her break out in a sweat.

"I would be happy to be rid of this uniform," she said, trying to break the ice.

Basso sat down next to her. He dug into the bag, pulling out another brioche but presented it to Ali. "Are you sure?"

Her mouth watered as she stared at the chocolate-filled pastry. "You only got two, right?"

He handed over the brioche with such force she had to take it, then produced another one out of the bag. "Two? Who gets only two brioche? I got three."

She smiled. "Most people get one."

They ate in silence. At least, Ali did. Basso breathed heavily through his nostrils as he smacked his lips.

Along with being short, Basso was also thin, having the metabolism of a small animal, burning calories faster than he could shovel them in his mouth. At forty-five years old he was still wiry, capable of living on a diet of wine, pasta, cheese, cured meats, and pastries and still managed to keep the weight off. He didn't work out. He didn't exercise. She hated him for it, and for the way he refused to chew with his mouth closed.

"Don't worry," he raised a finger, emphasizing the words, "*if you want,* you'll be out of that uniform soon." He suppressed a burp and crossed his legs, unfolding the newspaper. "I should be candid, Ali. It's not so clear cut as I make it out to be. You making inspector, I mean."

Her eyes questioned him.

"It's between you and Fabiano."

"Oh," she said. "I didn't know that." She tried to sound unconcerned, but something akin to outrage pinged inside her.

"Si." Basso flipped the page.

She stared into the distance. The wind had pushed the humidity and smog out of the air, leaving a perfect view of the rolling green patchwork of the Tuscan region to the south.

Ali was just as content staring out into the country as Basso was staring into the daily news, but this news about Fabiano had her reeling inside. Dimitri Fabiano was a second-year recruit, which meant he was four years greener than Ali. And the man was an ass, not in the semi-endearing way like Basso, but in the truest sense of the word. He'd gotten the job because his father was an influential businessman—something to do with olive oil exporting to Asian countries and making a boatload of money in the process. Not only that, but Fabiano's father was also a beloved city official. Beloved to other ass-like city officials, mind you, but that's how he was often portrayed.

Her mood darkened, the familiar feeling of losing an unwinnable, rigged game rising inside her.

"But you're the better candidate," Basso said, keeping his eyes on the newspaper. "Shit." He flicked the newspaper. "The government's going to fail again. They didn't last a year before Manzano took over the labor party and screwed everything up. You have dead bodies being pulled out of the ground in Como. Inter won. Come on, give me some good news." He turned the page.

She stared out at the landscape, her eyes glazed over in thought, the anger rising. Of course, they wanted Fabiano instead of her.

She looked over at Basso, still lost in his reading. Why was he traipsing around with her for the next five days if she didn't have a shot? Maybe he was telling the truth and she was a strong candidate. Still, she never kissed ass and wasn't going to start now to get promoted. She had played the game by doing a stand-up job for the last six years. If they couldn't see that, they could kiss *her* ass.

I want to be just like you someday, Papà.

She realized Basso was looking at her, snapping his fingers. "Falco!"

"What?"

"This dead girl they pulled from the ground?"

She shook her head. "What dead girl?"

"In Como."

"Oh." She remembered seeing something on the television the night before. "What about her?"

"I asked if you lived near Brunate? This little town overlooking the city?"

"No." There was a map of Como printed on the page. The lake was shaded with lines, an X marked where they had found the body. She pointed on the extreme northwestern corner of the little map. "I lived up there. Along the lake."

Basso shook his head, clucking his tongue. "One of the construction workers took photos with his cell phone and leaked them to the paper. And of course they printed it. Bastards."

Ali scanned the page, seeing a grainy picture that purposely blurred out the head of the body, leaving an arm and torso for readers to get a good look at. The bones were nothing gruesome to see, no more disturbing than a mummy at a museum.

Without warning, visions of Ali's mother—her sunken, pale face in a casket—flashed in her mind. She stood up and walked away, leaning against the rail.

"Ahh!" She yanked her hands away as the hot black metal singed the skin of her palms.

"You alright?" The newspaper rustled. "Ali?"

"Yeah." She looked down the steep slope in front of her, trying to push the sight of her mother out of her mind.

When she turned around Basso had pulled out a pack of Marlboro blacks. He fished one out with his mouth and held out the pack. "Want one?"

"You know I quit." But she stared at the pack, as he wasn't putting it away.

They had been patrol partners for two years, and he had learned to read her well. "Suit yourself," he said, setting the pack on the bench next to him while he flicked on his lighter.

She sat, took one, accepted Basso's flame, and sat back on the bench, inhaling the smoke, looking out again at the landscape.

Thoughts of her mother and father kept surfacing in her mind, like bubbles in a glass of Prosecco, and it seemed no matter how hard she tried, she couldn't put a stopper in the bottle.

The irony was, she had come south from Como, from the top of the boot that was Italy, landing here in Siena, the boot's shin, to escape the memories, only to find herself locked more deeply into the past. Every fold of this beautiful vista, every long, thin cypress swaying in the wind, every fragrant whiff of the ancient rosemary bushes next to her, were synonymous with another memory of a Falco summer vacation, when they used to live in Como and travel here to the Tuscan countryside to get away. She couldn't even navigate a promotion without getting tangled in thoughts of how life used to be.

They finished their cigarettes in silence, Ali's buzz morphing from a warm relaxed sensation to an uncomfortable queasiness within a few drags. She could hold her nicotine better with alcohol in her system, but they still had five hours until their shift was over and she could have a glass of red.

"Back to the grind," Basso said, standing up.

She rose, stretching her arms overhead, feeling lightheaded from the cigarette.

They walked back across the street, weaving between traffic, down along the city wall, and back through the Porta Romana, into the cool shadows filled with the fragrance of food and sound of music floating from shop doors.

"I have to visit the ufficio." Basso thumbed down the Via di Santo.

"Do all men defecate as much as you?"

"Only the good ones."

They walked quickly, paced by Basso's urgency, threading the streets towards the secret toilet she knew Basso frequented on this side of town, found at one of his friend's bars, Il Corallo. As far as Ali knew the man stopped here for only one reason.

"Speaking of good men, I hear you have a blind date tonight," Basso said, looking over his shoulder, bouncing his eyebrows.

Her stomach twisted. My God, was that tonight? She would have completely forgotten had he not mentioned it.

Basso smirked. "That excited, are you?"

She said nothing, brainstorming how she could get out of it.

Clarissa, her best friend who worked upstairs in the station, would be pissed if she blew off the date she'd fixed her up with.

"It will be good for you," Basso said, starting up with the unsolicited advice again. "When's the last time you've been out on a date?" He upped his pace as they rounded a corner and Il Corallo came into view.

She said nothing, hanging back, forcing Basso to slow if he wanted to keep the conversation going.

"Fine." He waved his hand. "I'll be a minute."

"I'll be out here."

"You want another cigarette while you wait?"

"Hell no."

He jogged to the bar and disappeared inside.

Ali stood shaking her head. Why the hell had she agreed to the date?

In a moment of terrible judgement, Ali had acquiesced, letting Clarissa set her up, half-expecting the comment to go nowhere. But, sure enough, two weeks later, here she was—she checked her watch—six and a half hours away from her first ever blind date.

Blind? Not really. Ali had already done a thorough background check on the man. Francesco Tartaglia was thirty-seven, a pediatric dentist, a divorced father of a seven-year-old girl. He paid child support, on time every time, his ex and child living down in Rome. No prior arrests, only one traffic ticket, and two parking tickets, which were promptly paid.

He was very nice, according to Clarissa, who took her children to his dental office. Good on paper, and good by word of mouth. Not blind, Clarissa had made that distinction a hundred times already.

And Francesco looked good on social media, too. She'd seen his photographs, many of them with his shirt off, displaying an Adonis body, gleaming smile, tanned skin, chiseled jaw. Tall. A perfect ten, as Clarissa had also told her a hundred times. And, apparently Francesco, according to Clarissa, was into Ali as well. Ali was not big on social media, but Clarissa had covert photos taken of Ali—or had taken them herself, she was still getting to the bottom of that one—and had shown them to Francesco.

Whatever, Ali thought, observing the people walking past. More tourists, this time Americans, recognizing the Dallas Cowboys t-shirt. Her mother used to like the Broncos.

An irregular motion in the crowd drew her eye.

She looked just in time to see a woman fall to the ground, landing on her backside. She was elderly and overweight, and rolled sideways, arms flailing.

What the hell?

A man near the downed woman pointed and ran a few steps. Ali followed his finger and saw the man she'd seen earlier casing the German tourists—White Sneakers—the very same would-be criminal who had caught her eye earlier. He was running full speed, with a purse clutched in his hand.

The man was angling towards her. She tensed, crouching, ready to tackle him, or trip him as he passed. What would she do? It didn't matter. She would take him down. She steeled herself, clenching and unclenching her fists.

But he darted sideways before he got to her, disappearing down a street.

"Shit." She glanced quickly at the bar, seeing no sign of Basso. The man was not fast in this department, and every second she stood thinking, the purse-snatcher was escaping further into the maze.

She took off running, jogging fast, then sprinting as she rounded the corner onto the street where the man disappeared.

He was already gone. People choked the street, but they all

seemed preoccupied, some of them stopped in their tracks, many of them looking down another side street to the right.

She followed the gazes, taking the turn, and immediately spied the man at least fifty meters in front of her, swerving between people.

He had slowed to a jog, half his attention on digging into the purse, half on watching where he was going, none of it on Ali following him.

She kept her pace fast, darting between people, gaining on him with each stride.

And then, as if sensing her, he looked over his shoulder and did a double take, his eyes widening. He pulled his hand from the bag and put his head down, doubling his speed, taking the next off-shoot alley to the left.

She slowed and rounded into the alley herself, seeing his image flitting in and out of sunlight as he cut across perpendicular streets slicing through foot traffic, people stumbling and staring, shocked at the out-of-control freight train.

Damn fool! He could kill someone running at that speed.

She slowed, crossing the same streets slower, keeping safely away from the passersby, many of them children.

He was making his way toward Piazza del Campo, which, on a Friday afternoon in July, would be packed with people, and probably an easy escape into obscurity.

Once past the traffic, she sped up again, sprinting down the alley, her athletic-soled shoes scratching on the ground, barely audible over the heaving of her lungs in her ears.

She had been jogging lately, at least three times per week, but all she felt was the one cigarette she had just had with Basso clawing at her lungs, like fire ants were biting the inside of her chest.

But she wasn't done yet, and as the young man turned the

next corner, she caught a glimpse of his profile, and saw he was huffing hard for air.

She gritted her teeth and continued the blistering pace, certain she could catch him.

One, then two minutes passed, and Ali gained at least twenty meters on the man. His steps, once quick and light, were now long and loping, more straight-lined with less swerving to avoid obstacles. He was getting reckless, almost barreling over a family with two small children, and she began wondering if this pursuit was worth it.

And then it happened. He collided hard with another family, slamming into the back of a woman, who fell sideways, smacking into the cobblestone, but not before sending her young boy careening sideways into a wall.

With shock and horror, Ali watched as the boy hit his head on the stucco wall of a shop, landing hard on his side, then rolling onto his back, arms flapping like a doll.

Ali slowed, the world around her disappearing, only the boy in her view.

He lay still. His eyes were open.

My God.

And then he blinked, finally telegraphing there was still life within him.

"Gino!" The mother crawled to her boy. "Gino!"

The father rushed to the boy, huddling over him. "Gino!"

Ali didn't remember coming to a stop, but soon she was standing, panting, looking down with them.

The boy's hand lifted, pressing to his head.

"Are you okay?" the woman asked again, petting her son.

The boy nodded at his mother's question, looking too stunned to even cry. But as the moments passed, his face twisted and he let out a deafening wail, smothered by his mother's hug.

The father turned and looked at Ali, his eyes raking up and down, taking in her uniform, rage flaring behind his eyes. “What the hell?” he asked under his breath, looking up the road toward the man she had been chasing.

White Sneakers stood a few meters away, still clutching the handbag prize in his hands, a dead expression on his sweaty face. He looked at Ali, gave an almost imperceptible shrug, and sprinted away, narrowly avoiding yet another group of people.

Ali ran as hard as she could, the strain in her lungs and legs becoming background noise she easily ignored.

She pumped her arms, back and forth, her legs, forward and back, keeping her face completely blank, her focus only on closing the distance between the man and herself.

And the distance closed fast. Within a block she had already gotten within a single arm’s length.

He swerved around people, looking back at her again and again, as if wondering if he should stop and fight and take his chances. She welcomed it, already planning the flurry of punches and kicks she would unleash on him, the knees to the crotch, if only he would stop running.

There were more people here, and they were less than a hundred meters from Piazza del Campo, but still a few narrow twists and turns remained, forcing their chase into a slower, zigzagging path.

She stumbled, but caught herself, giving him another three or four arm’s lengths as he rounded another corner.

She cursed, upping her pace to full sprint again, remembering the force of that little boy as he had collided into the wall. If she had to run until her legs seized, until her lungs gave out, so be it, but she was going to end this day putting this man behind bars.

Another corner came up, and her feet gripped true on the cobblestone as she slowed just enough to make sure she remained upright. Through another turn, she pumped her legs again to a full sprint.

In front of her the man was slowing down, unsure, because in front of him stood a cluster of Carabinieri, fully uniformed, standing in a clump and chatting with one another.

"Stop him!" she yelled.

Three Carabinieri turned toward her, taking in the scene within a moment, instantly recognizing what was going on. One was a big man, aggressive, and stepped out and tried to tackle the thief.

And then everything happened so fast, too fast for Ali to comprehend, but somebody came alongside her and smashed heavily into her side.

As she twirled in the air, she saw the man who had hit her was uniformed, and as she slammed hard onto the cobblestone she realized he must have been standing on the side of the road, joining the chase just as she was running past.

Her head hit the ground, the noise like an impossibly loud splat inside her brain. She rolled, pulling up her arms to cover her head as she skidded to a stop on her back.

For a moment everything was tunneled down to a circle of light, and then the circle expanded, a billion tinkling bells chiming in her ears, dots of light swimming in her peripheral vision.

"Stai bene?"

A man's concerned face loomed over her.

She blinked, trying to shake the swirling stars. Slowly, the sound of the street came out from behind the bells, and she heard hushed voices, orders being called out, and the man still hunched over her.

"Are you okay?" he repeated.

"I don't know."

She sat up.

"Careful now," one of them said.

She looked past the men, seeing the perpetrator was on the ground, too, a Carabinieri cuffing his hands behind him.

"He stole a woman's purse," she said, her voice sounding muffled in her head.

"Easy, you hit your head."

She got to her feet. "I'm okay." But she was lying. Her legs ached, barely able to move. Her hip hurt where she'd collided with the ground, her hand burned, and she saw she'd torn off some of the skin from her palm.

She eyed the carabiniere who had been near her, recognizing him, but not knowing his name. She recognized the others, too.

One of them, a man named Carrerra, Mattia Carrerra, was among them, glancing at her but not coming to her aid. She had once been a close acquaintance of Carrerra, conversing with him often over the years, until he'd asked her out on a date.

She walked to him, shattering the cold wall put up between them since she'd politely turned down his advance. "He stole a woman's purse, between Porta Romana and the stadium."

"We'll take it from here." Carrerra dismissed her, turning to pick up the purse from the ground.

Three entities controlled law enforcement within Italy—the Polizia di Stato, the Carabinieri, and Guardia di Finanza. The Guardia di Finanza dealt with financial crimes, drug smuggling, and border and maritime patrolling. The Carabinieri were as commonly seen policing the civilian population as the Polizia di Stato, the biggest difference between them being the Carabinieri was part of the military, and that in matters of investigation and law-breaking control, the Carabinieri often took jurisdiction. The Polizia also had responsibilities concerning passports, visas, licenses, registration, and other bureaucratic matters.

And so, here and now, the Carabinieri had jurisdiction. She had no control over the situation. Which was fine. She had come to terms with scenarios like these years ago. She just didn't like the way Carrerra was acting superior about the whole thing. The reason she'd liked him in the first place, was that he'd been a man above that kind of behavior. Or so she thought.

The carabiniere who had been standing over her with concern remained nearby, watching her closely. "Are you okay?"

She nodded. "Yes. Grazie."

"I'm sorry," he said. "I saw him running past with a purse in his hand. I just reacted. I didn't even know you were after him. And then suddenly, you just bounced off me." He shook his head.

She looked at him, noting he was at least a hundred and fifty pounds heavier than her. He looked perfectly clean, unfazed by the collision. "It's okay," she said. The numerous red-hot pokers of pain prodding her body told her otherwise.

The man she'd been chasing was standing now, another carabiniere holding his cuffed wrists from behind. Carrerra searched his pockets while the others fanned out to disperse the crowd.

Carrerra turned and looked at her again. "Carry on, Falco. You did your part. We've got it from here. Get that hand looked at."

Ali looked down and saw blood streaking down her middle finger. She searched the crowd, spotting the little boy's father front and center. The man stared at the cuffed captive, his fists clenched. A carabiniere walked over and told him to move away.

Ali turned to the man she'd chased, and saw he was looking at her, eyes glinting with amusement, mouth upturned with a brief smile, unnoticeable to anyone but her.

She thought again of the boy hitting the wall, how her heart had stopped when the boy rolled over and stared vacantly into the sky. And she surged.

"Falco, what are you doing?" Carrerra put a hand up to stop her.

She slapped it away, and reached up, grabbing the man's face, squeezing his cheeks, puckering his lips, feeling the greasy sweat-laden facial hair in her hand. She wanted to rip the smile off his head. "You like what you did back there?"

"Falco!" Carrerra grabbed her arm and pulled it away.

With her other hand she threw a powerful jab, aiming for the side of White Sneakers's jaw. She punched through his face, like they taught her in her Krav Maga classes, and his head whipped sideways, and when it recoiled, she could see his eyeballs rolled back.

The man buckled, slamming face-first into the ground at her feet with a sickly slap of flesh on cobblestone.

"Madonna, Falco!" Carrerra yelled, wrapping his arms around her.

She allowed herself to be manhandled away without resistance.

"Get your hands off her! Let go!"

Basso's voice materialized out of the commotion, then his flailing limbs came into view, pulling and slapping the carabiniere away, stepping in front of Ali.

"If you haven't noticed she just hit the perp!" Carrerra was heated, but aware of the eyes looking at them, keeping his voice hushed. "Relax, everyone. Relax."

"Ali?" Basso looked her over, his eyes pausing at her hand. "You're bleeding."

"I'm okay."

Basso turned and squared off with Carrerra. The carabiniere was a good fifteen centimeters taller, but that hadn't stopped

Basso before. She had once seen him jump-punch a man for snickering about his name.

"Easy, *Basso*." Carrerra emphasized the last name, treading on thin ice and not even knowing it.

"Come on," Ali said, pulling on Basso's shoulder.

Basso stared up at Carrerra, clearly contemplating retaliation.

"Rossini!" Carrerra snapped. "Go with these two and find the woman whose purse this is."

"Find her yourself," Basso said. "Andiamo, Ali." Basso turned and walked away, the direction they had come, piercing a wall of people that had gathered around, holding cell phones, recording the action like a swarm of paparazzi.

"You got him," a woman said, stepping forward. "That's my purse."

"Go speak to those men in uniform. They'll help you."

"Thank you," she said, reaching out to shake Ali's hand.

Ali held up her hand, showing it was bloodied, and nodded instead, stepping into the crowd, wanting to melt back into obscurity. She wanted no more attention. All she wanted was another cigarette.

She weaved her way through the people, only then noticing the cell phone cameras were swiveling, tracking her.

2

Ali ran her hand under the faucet, watching blood wash from her knuckles, swirling in the sink of the Siena police headquarters second floor bathroom. As she scrubbed the wounds clean, she viewed herself in the mirror, seeing a sweaty young woman looking back at her, dark eyes in a face far too tired looking for her thirty years.

You're beautiful, Ali Falco. The most beautiful principessa in all of Italy.

Her father's childhood words echoed in her mind. As always, it was followed by a quick image of him standing over her mother, fist clenched, spittle flying from his lips as he screamed, reminding her who the words came from.

She patted some water on her head, taming some black coils of hair that had escaped her braid during the chase, then put on her cap.

She paused, staring into her eyes, thinking about the cell phone footage that was already circulating on the internet.

You did nothing wrong, Ali. Do you believe it?

More words from her father from a lifetime ago. He was active today. He needed to shut up.

She dialed back the concern in her eyes a few notches, sucked in a breath, then left the bathroom.

Three officers sat at desks in the squad room —Rossi, Taglia, and Patucci—scribbling with pens, working through stacks of paperwork. The remaining five members of the headquarters roster, including Fabiano, were either home or out on patrol. At least that much was in her favor.

She hadn't known she was in competition with Fabiano, but the more she thought about it, the more she realized Fabiano had been acting more like an egotistical jerk than usual over the last couple of weeks. He must have known something. More evidence she was playing a game without knowing all the rules.

Basso was over by the espresso machine, talking at Rossi, something about Mt. Vesuvius exploding, taking out Naples, and the football team with it.

The room went silent as she entered.

"Caffe?" Basso asked.

She nodded and sat down at her desk along the back wall.

It was stifling hot, the afternoon sun slanting into the windows, the ceiling fan above her whirling ineffectually, the tower fan near the window humming and gyrating, swirling more heat with heat.

Suddenly a cacophony of sound filled the space, sounding like a cage full of birds had gone mad, and she realized Fabiano had walked into the squad room, holding his phone up, the sound of a crowd coming out of his tiny speakers.

Fabiano's mouth was drawn in an "O," his eyebrows arched high, his attention latched onto the screen in his hand.

"Here it is ... oh!" Fabiano turned the screen to Patucci. "Have you seen this? It's all over the web!"

To Patucci's credit, the man shook his head and looked down at his paperwork.

"The way he hit the ground. Remind me to never piss you off."

"You might want to put the phone away then," Ali said.

Fabiano pocketed his phone, then looked at her, glee on his face. "Woman...what did you do?"

"Isn't this your day off, Fabiano?" Basso asked, putting a small cup of foamy espresso, a packet of cane sugar, and a plastic stirrer on the desk in front of her. "Don't listen to this pissant." He looked Fabiano up and down. The young officer was in civilian dress, wearing a dark suit and tie worth more than a month's pay. "Off to see Papà, are we?"

Fabiano's eyes darkened. "You'd be smart to talk to me better than that, *Basso*."

Basso cocked his head, stepping toward Fabiano. "I don't like the way you just said my name."

Fabiano was ten centimeters taller than Basso, but he shrank back, swallowing.

"You touch me and you're through in this department."

Basso jerked, and Fabiano flinched. Cursing under his breath, he turned and left the room, heading down the steps.

"Ciao Fabiano!" Rossi called, chuckling with Taglia.

Ali looked at them, eyes flaring. "Is that how you act when I leave the room?"

The two men looked at each other, their smiles fading.

"Get back to work, you gorillas!" Basso said.

"And I don't need you fighting my fights," she said under her breath.

Basso put up one hand, his other bringing up the espresso to his mouth. He patted her shoulder and walked to his own desk, sitting with a sigh. "Damn, my ass. I haven't run that much in years."

"Running?" Patucci asked. "What's that?"

Thinking of her own backside, Ali threw the packet of sugar

in the trash and sipped the espresso black, feeling the caffeine taking effect, soothing her from the inside out.

She pulled a bandage from her pocket, checked her hand, saw it had stopped bleeding, and chucked the bandage in the trash, too.

She wiggled her computer mouse and clicked open her email. One of her new messages bore the subject line "Tonight's dinner." From Francesco.

Again, her stomach quickened. She still hadn't cancelled the date, and if she was going to, she needed to get on with it quick. Maybe Basso's earlier life-ism was right this time, though, and she should go. If anything, she could use the drink.

But she despised the game—sitting and making small talk, judging, being judged back—which was the reason she hadn't played it for years. It had been a dozen years, she reminded herself, since she'd really given a man a chance.

She stared at the unopened message, memories swimming past like streaking fish, she and Matteo holding hands, smoking cigarettes by the lake after school, their bodies intertwining on his musty sheets.

She blinked out of the reverie and clicked open the message.

Hello Ali. I hope you are doing well. I just wanted to let you know I'm looking forward to tonight. I'll meet you at the restaurant at 8:30, as per our prior communication. See you then!

"What are you doing?"

The female voice materialized behind her. Clarissa. Her best friend worked as one of the three administrators to the building up on the third floor near Ferrari's office, acting as the accountant in an official capacity, unofficially a de facto personal assistant to the Headquarters Chief.

Ali sighed, shutting down the email window. "Don't you have payroll to make or some other important bean counter task to do?"

"Talking to Francesco, eh?" Clarissa came into view and sat on the edge of her desk. "Here. Give me this." She took the mouse and clicked the keyboard, navigating to the Facebook website, and then to Francesco Tartaglia's profile page.

She clicked, and then again, bringing up some photographs.

Ali rolled her eyes. "I've seen these."

"Then you've seen this one?"

She clicked open a picture of her imminent date standing with his shirt off, dripping wet with sea water, a kite board surfing rig on the sand behind him, his tanned skin rippling with muscle. His slicked back dark hair, gleaming movie star smile, and brilliant blue eyes bejeweled a chiseled, stubbled face.

"Yeah, yeah. I've seen that one."

"You're nervous."

"You're annoying."

"You going to come sit over here next?" Patucci made a kissing sound.

"Ew," Clarissa said. "Ew."

"I love you, too."

She clicked the mouse again. "Don't worry. I know I've already said he's a good guy, but I'm telling you, he really is. Look what he posted this morning."

The next photo was a cartoon toothbrush with a mouth and eyes saying, "Remember to brush your teeth, kids!"

Clarissa's smile beamed.

"Maybe you should leave Leo and go out with Francesco yourself."

Clarissa paused a little too long at that suggestion, then said, "Oh, come on, Ali. Don't you get the least bit excited thinking about tonight?"

"What are you doing here?" Ali asked.

"Where are you guys going?" Clarissa asked, ignoring her question.

"I'm not sure I'm going to go."

Clarissa's mouth dropped open, utter disappointment in her eyes, like a little girl who'd learned her dog had died.

"I'm busy, Clarissa."

"Busy doing what?"

"Busy..." She gestured to her hand, and the wounds, "...not going on dates. Busy getting plastered all over the internet. Probably busy getting fired."

"I can't believe this. After all the talking up I did for you?"

Ali rubbed her temple. "Listen, I didn't ask for you to set me up. I didn't ask for you to talk me up to a random stranger."

"Maybe you should've asked."

Ali frowned. "Huh?"

Clarissa looked at her, her blue eyes unblinking, her mouth locked shut, clearly holding in words to avoid hurting Ali's feelings.

"Didn't you see what happened this morning?"

"That's why I'm down here. Ferrari wants to see you."

"What? Why didn't you say so in the first place?" She got up and walked out the back exit of the room.

Clarissa followed, the pair climbing the marble stairs to the upper floor. "Ali, listen. I know you don't want to go on this date, but that's exactly why you should do it."

Ali ignored her, concentrating on the steps, and then the entrance to the top floor offices.

Bruno and Alicia were standing near the window looking at a phone, and by the way they lowered it and looked at her she knew what they were watching.

"...and then there's a different outlet for you, Ali. A man like Frances—"

"Excuse me." Ali turned around, facing her with a lowered

voice. "I have to go see Ferrari—my boss—right now. Could you please shut up?"

The words bounced off Clarissa. "Call me tonight the second your date is over. I want to know everything."

Ali rolled her eyes. "Okay, fine. Then will you leave me alone?"

"No." Clarissa walked to her desk and sat. "The Chief is waiting to see you," she said using an official tone, pointing at the wall behind Ali.

She turned, facing the heavy wooden door, and knocked.

"Come!"

She twisted the worn brass knob and leaned inside. "You wanted to see me, sir?"

"Falco." Ferrari stood by the window, one hand poked out an open window, holding a smoldering cigarette. "Come in, close the door. Quickly."

Smoking indoors within Italy had been banned for twenty years, but that didn't stop the Chief of Siena police.

She shut the door behind her and stood at attention.

"Sit down, per favore." Ferrari had a baritone voice, and he was using the bottom of the register, which gave his words a hint of menace.

She sat on a creaking plastic chair in front of his desk.

Ferrari took a greedy drag and flicked the cigarette out the window, then sat down. Smoke shot out of his nostrils as he looked at her, his blue eyes drooping like a basset hound.

His desk phone sat on the corner of his desk, and below it, collated stacks of paper fanned down. The man was meticulous, keeping his office spotless, giving the overnight cleaners nothing to do when they stepped foot in this space, and she knew he would later go outside and pick up the cigarette butt he'd flicked into the headquarters courtyard just now. She'd seen him do it before.

Ferrari pulled his cell phone from his pocket and put it on the center of the desk, his fingers tapping on the wood next to it. "Tell me about it."

"About what?"

"Don't play coy with me. What happened?"

"I saw the suspect steal a woman's purse. I pursued on foot." She shrugged. "We happened upon the Carabinieri, who took it from there."

He stared at her. Outside a fifty-CC motorcycle sped down the narrow street, the grating noise bouncing off the tall walls and in through the double windows of the corner office.

"And he made you angry, so you punched his lights out."

"He knocked over a little boy, collided with a woman. He could have killed the boy. He hit his head on the stone. I was angry."

Ferrari said nothing for a long moment. "And now our man will walk, with good reason to bring litigation against this headquarters and the Carabinieri for his treatment."

She said nothing.

"Aren't you sorry?"

"I thought we already established that, sir."

Ferrari exhaled. "I would expect an inspector in this department to reign in their emotions during such an exchange."

"I'm not an inspector."

"No, you are not." Ferrari remained still, staring at her for what felt like a full minute. "Don't you care about your career advancement, Ali?"

"I care about doing a good job for this department, sir. For protecting this city."

"And you have not done a good job today." He got up from his chair, clasped his hands behind his back, and looked out the window.

She blew air from her nose.

You did nothing wrong.

She didn't feel so sure of her father's words now.

"You broke his jaw. He's in the hospital. You have three cell phone videos circulating around the internet, none of which show the actual pursuit, only the good part at the end where you drop him to the ground. We have some people calling for your immediate removal. One of them is a city official who happens to have a son in this department. A son who is also up for consideration to be promoted into the open inspector position."

He turned and looked at her.

"Do you think Officer Fabiano is a better candidate for inspector than yourself?"

So this was it? He expected her to plead for the job now, ticking off reasons why she was better than that low-life Fabiano, because he couldn't see it himself? That's all she needed to do, and she would be like Papà.

Suddenly the thought of patrolling the city on foot for the rest of her life didn't seem so bad. And if that got too boring? She could figure out another career path if she really wanted to.

"Do you think I should fire you for this?"

She shrugged. "I think you should do what you feel is best for the department."

He sat down, his face turning red. "That's all you're going to give me? No pleading? No begging for a second chance? After six years of service, now you can become part of the inspector team that will take you outside these city walls. And you shrug to me?"

She said nothing, trying her best not to blink.

Ferrari rolled his neck, landing a warm, sympathetic, eyebrow-arching gaze on her. "Listen. Why don't you take the weekend, and Monday and Tuesday off, too. Get out of that uniform, and try to keep off cell phone videos in that time, can you do that?"

She nodded.

He studied her, then shook his head. "What happened to you, Ali Falco?"

"Can I go now?"

Ferrari nodded. "Yes. You can go."

She got up and left, leaving the door swinging open behind her.

3

Ali stood at the edge of the Piazza del Campo, under a smoldering orange sky.

Foot traffic swirled around her, flowing in and out of the wide-open space stretched in front of her. She watched lovers hold hands, children eat gelato, teenaged boys wrestle while teenaged girls ignored them, all this life perfumed by the fragrant scents of cooking onions, basil, and tomatoes wafting down from the streets spoking off the piazza.

The Torre del Mangia bell chimed once, indicating it was half-past eight.

She spotted her date through the crowd, Francesco standing near the menu stand of the pizzeria, chatting easily with the host. He smiled and cracked a joke. A passing waiter said something, causing all three men to laugh.

A woman passed by, eyeing him up and down, and Francesco nodded.

He swiveled on his heel and looked around again, squinting as he turned towards Ali.

She ducked behind the wall out of sight, looking down at the sheer black dress draped across her body.

A man passed, smiling at her. "Ciao bella."

She ignored the man, pulling out a cigarette from her purse from the fresh pack she'd picked up after the meeting with Ferrari.

The man walked up with a lighter, flicking it on.

She dug for her own matches in her handbag, ignoring the offered flame, then relented and accepted it.

"You look incredible. He's a lucky man, whoever he is."

"There is no lucky man." She exhaled.

"Oh, really? Are you looking to grab a drink tonight? If so, I'd love to buy you one."

"No thanks. But thanks for the light."

The man saluted with a finger and walked away.

She snuck a peek around the corner and saw Francesco looking at his watch, politely nodding now as the host said something else to him.

She ducked back and took another drag, and the memory of Matteo leaving played fresh in her mind, as if she were standing right there a dozen years ago again, watching his slim frame walk away into the rain, out of her life forever. Heat rose within her, matching the anger that had flared inside her so hot that day, anger she had so mistakenly directed at the only love she'd ever had.

She sucked another drag, picturing how right now Matteo was probably in his beautiful apartment tucking into a nice dinner with that beautiful wife he'd gone on to marry, and their three beautiful children she'd seen pictures of on Instagram.

Her handbag buzzed and chimed, snapping her out of her thoughts. It was probably Francesco. She ignored it, puffing the cigarette, dismissing another glance from a passing man.

Come on, Ali. Are you going to do this or not?

She dropped the cigarette in a nearby sand-filled ashtray and pulled out her perfume, spritzing herself, inhaling the strong scent of lavender, hoping it overpowered the stink of tobacco smoke she knew many people couldn't stand. She'd been one of them before she'd allowed the disgusting habit to take hold of her this second time in her life.

She froze, her heart leaping as she recalled the incoming name she'd just seen displayed on the screen. It had not been Francesco. The name had read *Papà*.

The preview-message-on-lock-screen function was enabled on her phone, so she could read the first line.

I'm sorry.

She clicked open the full text and saw there was no more to it, only the two words.

A short, simple message. But it was anything but simple, wasn't it?

She lowered the phone and put it in her handbag, realizing she'd been holding her breath. She allowed air into her lungs, and suddenly felt dizzy, the nicotine doing its work, or the stagnant memories suddenly kicked up like mud in her mind.

"Ali?"

Francesco stood a few meters from her. "Ciao. I was just wondering if I might see you...I was going to call. It's a few minutes past 8:30, I was wondering if you were going to make it."

"Hi, Francesco. Sorry. I ..." She didn't know what to say.

"You look amazing," he said. "Wow."

I'm sorry.

For what? Which part? she thought.

"Ali, is everything okay?"

"No. It's not, Francesco. I'm sorry, but I'm not going to be able to have dinner with you..." She almost added the word *tonight* but left her sentence as it was.

She turned and walked away, ignoring the disappointment on his face.

"Join the club," she said under her breath, as she rounded the nearest corner.

4

Matteo's car skids to a stop outside the closed gate, and only then does Ali realize he's shut off the vehicle, cranked the handbrake and turned in his seat to stare at her before the vehicle even comes to a complete stop.

She laughs. "Idiota."

"I'm not an idiot. I'm mad."

"Oh, really?"

"Madly in love with you." He leans toward her, his beautiful lips leading first, his sapphire eyes expecting, wanting.

"Like I said. Idiota."

They kiss. At first, they barely touch lips, pecking each other, soft flesh to soft flesh, and then they both part their mouths.

She can taste the coffee and candy on his tongue from their trip to the café after school, the familiar flavor of his breath as he sighs.

She also sighs, and they begin to kiss harder. Hungrily. He reaches over and puts his hand on her leg, and she is electrified. She grabs his forearm, feeling the smooth skin, and caresses his arm. He rubs her thigh, higher, and then between her legs. She invites him, opening her legs and putting one foot on the seat next to the door, and for a time life is only Matteo's lips and his strong hands, and the shaking waves of pleasure coursing through her.

She pulls her lips away, pops open the car door, and twists out of the seat. She closes the door and leans in the open window.

Matteo is still frozen, leaning, pursed lips, confusion creasing his forehead.

She laughs heartily. "I have to go. I told you. And I am already late."

"You kill me, Ali Falco."

She smiles at him. He leans hard against the seat with a sigh. "Are we going out this weekend?"

"Yes. If you want."

"I want."

She leans in. They kiss again, this time only a peck. "I want, too."

"Then get back in the car."

"I also want my father to not kill you."

Matteo relents at that. "Tell your beautiful mother and...happy, loving, scary father hello for me."

She smiles. "He's not scary."

"He wears a gun all the time, and when you're not looking, I can tell he's wondering if he should use it on me."

"Maybe because you are always groping his daughter within plain view of the security cameras."

"You guys have security cameras?" He leans forward, searching out the windshield with wide eyes.

She laughs. "No. Ciao. I'll talk to you later."

She turns and punches the code into the keypad and the iron gate whirs to life.

Matteo's twenty-year-old Fiat Panda roars to life, a black plume of smoke ejecting from the tail pipe. The engine sounds like a blender full of rocks as he turns around and drives away, whistling a cat call out the window as he disappears around the corner.

Idiota, she thinks. He forgot to watch her make it inside without incident. Maybe he'll learn chivalry one of these days.

She walks through the gate and down the driveway, looking up at the trees lining the way, inhaling the magnolias' sensual scent.

Her mother's car is parked in front of the house, backed in, in her usual anal-retentive way. One of her doors is ajar, and so is the front entrance to the house. She's usually home earlier from working at the women's clinic. Perhaps she had a late patient, or an emergency.

Maybe she picked up pizza on the way home. Ali's mouth waters in anticipation. She had not eaten anything since lunch, not even a snack after school. She'd been too busy with Matteo. Her skin flushes at the fresh memory. They were getting so close, so intimate with each other's bodies.

She needs to pull it together. Thinking about the birth control talk she'd had with her mother last week brings her feet back to the ground with a sobering thud.

Ali stops, because there are loud shouts coming from the house. It is so startling, so out of character of her mother and father that she wonders if someone else is there with them. Perhaps some crazy person. Somebody who her father had put in jail perhaps? Is this the doomsday scenario her father has spoken about before coming to fruition?

And then her mother comes tumbling out of the entrance, landing hard on her hands and knees. Her handbag tumbles to the tiled porch.

"Mamma!" she yells, wanting to run to her, but freezes.

Her father appears in the doorway, stepping over her mother, grabbing the bag and throwing it towards the car. The bag bounces off the vehicle and lands on the pavement. Her father leans down, grunting in her mother's ear. There is hatred in his eyes, in his clenched jaw, in the spittle coming out of his mouth.

"Vai!" Go! *His voice echoes in the stillness. "Vai!"*

He stands with his hands on his hips and spots Ali. He blinks, as if coming to from a fever dream at the sight of her.

"What is this?" Ali's voice is high pitched, shrill.

Ali's mother, still on her hands and knees, sees Ali, too. She looks like she wants to say something.

When nothing comes out of her mouth, Ali fills the silence. "What the hell is going on?"

Her father turns back toward the house. Her mother gets up, her eyes lowered, picks up her bag and tosses it in the back seat.

Shutting the door, her mother rounds the car. Her face is streaked with tears as she gets in behind the wheel. The car revs to life and her mother drives past, a deeply disturbing look on her face as she rolls past, holding up her hand to Ali as if she knows she is saying goodbye for the last time.

I'm sorry.

Her father is standing in the doorway. His clean face is streaked with blood dripping down from his hairline. His mouth is moving as rivulets of red stream off his chin.

I'm sorry.

Ali opened her eyes, watching the strange vision of her father disappear like the afterimage flash of a camera.

Something was buzzing, like a jackhammer working on the floor above her. It had been happening all morning, and now that she was conscious, she remembered the noise had filtered into her sleep.

Her mouth was dry. Her tongue felt like cigarette-flavored sandpaper.

Water. Now.

She sat up, and a rock inside her skull slammed her brain, sending a nauseating wave of unease through her.

"Ahhh."

She still had her socks on. She was so hot. Why did she have her socks on? And her pajama pants, too. Normally she shed clothing and turned on the ceiling fan before bed, but now the fan sat idle, the air inside her apartment like the inside of a moist oven. Sun streaked in through the east-facing windows, the sun blazing so bright she had to put her hand up. She'd been too drunk to think of pulling the shutters closed last night. Probably a good thing. She might have fallen out of the third-story window if she had.

The noise stopped, and it was then she realized it was her phone on her nightstand that had been vibrating.

She stood, breathing through light-headedness, putting a hand on the wall, and clicked on the ceiling fan. She shuffled to the kitchen for a cup of water, passing the two empty bottles of wine sitting on the table.

My God.

She filled a glass of water and sucked it down. Then another.

She picked up one of the bottles of red off the kitchen table and saw it was half-full. She didn't need to pick up the other one to know it was empty. A bottle and a half, ingested. And now she was paying the price. Last week she had told herself she would never do this again, and here she was.

She sucked down another glass of water, realizing she hadn't eaten after returning home, just a handful of nuts and raisins from her cabinet.

She stared out the windows at the shadowed hills northeast of Siena. Any other day, she would have been awestruck at its beauty this early summer morning, but she just wanted to climb back in bed and close her eyes.

In her room, her phone buzzed again, its insistent staccato buzz pattern like a snare drum in her skull, and with a start she wondered if she had responded to her father last night after all.

And who the hell was calling? Was it him?

She remembered last night, typing in the words *Screw you* as a response to her father's text, then deleting it. Had she been so drunk later that she'd sent something?

No. She may have been inebriated, shitfaced even, but she remembered going to bed.

The phone stopped for a moment, then began buzzing again.

"Shut up." She walked to her nightstand and silenced it.

It had been Basso, the notification said, and below that there was another notification bubble telling her she'd missed sixteen calls.

The time read 7:25 am, and with another start she wondered if she'd missed her shift, and Basso was waiting for her out at a coffee shop, wondering where she was.

No. It was Saturday. Her day off. And on top of that, she'd been told by Ferrari to stay away until Wednesday. What the hell was going on? Every time she decided to drink there was always something that came and bit her in the ass the next day. It was a law of the universe, she decided.

Her phone buzzed in her hand. Basso again. She pushed the button.

"What?"

"Ali."

"What?"

"It's me, Basso."

"I know. What?"

"We have been trying to get hold of you. I've been buzzing your apartment."

She frowned, looking at the phone hanging on her wall that served as the buzzer from the front gate. She hadn't heard it ring. But she'd been pretty out of it.

"It's my day off. I'm not covering somebody's shift, if that's what you're—"

"I'm downstairs. Let me up. I'm going to the gate again."

"Why?"

The line clicked.

"Shit." She went into the bathroom and looked in the mirror, finding a face smeared with makeup staring back at her, dark circles around her eyes, twin mascara streaks down both cheeks.

She turned on the water and heard the buzz of her apartment phone. She walked to it and poked the button.

"Yeah?"

"It's me."

She pushed the gate open button, unlocked her apartment door, and went back into the bathroom.

After a few minutes she'd scrubbed her face clean, brushed her teeth, scooped her curls into a ponytail, and came out into the apartment.

She expected to see Basso in the kitchen preparing an espresso, but he stood leaning up against the counter.

If the splash of water had woken her up a little, the somber expression on his face slapped her awake.

"What's going on?"

Basso was dressed in jeans and a button up short sleeved shirt, his weekend attire. He didn't answer her, just kept staring down at the table in front of him.

She picked up the bottles of wine, poured the half empty one out in the sink, and dropped them in the recycling.

Basso picked up the empty pack of Marlboro Blacks and put it in the trash. He straightened the chairs.

She looked around, saw her dress on the floor in the living room section of her studio apartment, her underwear lying next to it.

She walked over and kicked them toward the bed, out of sight around the corner.

“Speak, Basso! It’s Saturday morning. My day off. Your day off. Why aren’t you out playing in the piazza with your children?”

“Your father is dead, Ali.”

She looked at him.

“How?” But as she asked, the text message he’d sent last night gave her the answer.

5

Ali opened her eyes from a dreamless sleep. She sat up, wrestling with a seatbelt as it raked across her face.

"Ali."

She looked over and saw Basso with both hands on the wheel.

"How are you doing?" he asked.

She raised the seat and sat upright, wiping sweat off her forehead.

The engine of her two-door Citroen screamed underneath her. Warm air flowed from the vents even though the air conditioner was set on its coldest setting. She still needed to take that in to get fixed.

"Are you feeling better?"

"Yes. Thank you."

She was thirsty, her mouth dry. She looked out the window and saw the land alongside the A1 was flat as a board, carpeted with green grass and corn fields. In the distance a faint forest of buildings emerged from the heavy, smog-laden air.

"We're almost to Milan," Basso said.

The dash clock read 3:14. They had been driving for three

and a half hours and for three of them she'd been asleep. Since it was a Sunday, traffic was light.

"How's the car holding up?" she asked.

"Not bad. Not exactly a Ferrari through the Apennine but doing just fine here." Basso patted the wheel.

"Thanks for driving," she said.

"Enough." Basso waved his hand.

Basso had come up with the plan—drive Ali up to Como in her own car, allowing her to rest. Then he would take a train back down if she felt comfortable taking care of things in Como on her own.

Chiara, her best friend from school, had a short-term rental apartment that Ali would stay in. And Ali had every intention of sending Basso home as soon as she was situated in the apartment.

She stifled a yawn, wondering how much more sleep she was going to need to get rid of her two-day hangover and start to feel normal again.

Your father's dead. Your mother's dead. You're an orphan now.

Her lack of energy probably had something to do with the incessant depressing thoughts cycling through her head. After learning the news from Basso the morning before, she'd spent the rest of her Saturday on the phone, having difficult conversations while fighting a pounding headache, chatting with the Como coroner, their recommended funeral home, her father's old colleague at the Carabinieri who had been at the scene firsthand, lining up lodging. The list went on. Her mind felt like it had run a marathon, a mind that had been woefully out of shape to begin with.

Her thoughts came back to her father, and their destination—Como. She had been born and raised in the city on the lake at the foot of the Italian Alps. She had a good childhood, living in an apartment inside the city for the first five years of her life, and then along the lake north of the city in a villa her father had inherited from his father.

The villa was not exactly matching the opulence or size of some of the celebrities that had sprawling properties along the lake to their north, but the place was beautiful, nonetheless. Her grandfather had done well creating a medium-sized concrete manufacturing company, amassing a modest fortune, and building the home on a small piece of land where aristocracy from around Europe had visited for thousands of years, but he had died of a heart attack in his late fifties. After her grandfather's untimely death, she had moved into the place with her mother and father, keeping her grandmother company in the empty home.

Her grandmother had died close on the heels of her grandfather, suffering complications of a heart attack of her own, leaving Ali and her parents to take care of the villa.

Ali loved the place, the old atmosphere of the stone structure, her big bedroom, the large, lush trees, and the lawn that stretched to the lapping cool waters of the lake. She lived there until she was nineteen years old, until the good turned bad, and her mother died in a car accident. Until it became clear the place must have been cursed, and she wanted nothing to do with it anymore.

Ali was thirty years old now, and except for passing through once five years ago on the way to Switzerland, she hadn't returned to Como in eleven years. After her mother's death, the idea of staying in Como had been abhorrent, so she had entered the academy in Ancona and never returned, working a stint at the academy itself after graduation before transferring to Siena.

On her way out of town she had had the blowout with her father. Her father had waited a year to reach out to her the first time, sending her an email that detailed his decision to quit the Carabinieri in Como, to take a job with the Guardia di Finanza down in Rome, and that he was proud she had done so well in the academy. She hadn't responded to that email, and he had never made a second attempt to reach out to her.

Since that message she assumed her father was still in Rome, working for the Guardia. In that email he had made it clear he didn't want to stay in Como either, that he was haunted by memories and regrets, and she had assumed he had sold his father's cursed place and moved on.

But he hadn't. He had kept it. And he had come back to commit suicide, shooting himself once in the side of the head, but not before texting his daughter first.

I'm sorry.

And this sick, twisted final act by her father raised a whole new line of questions in her mind: Why not just do the deed in Rome? He would have known she would be deeply disturbed by the news, and his choice of where he'd offed himself. And why hadn't he reached out to her again?

Why hadn't she responded back then? Why hadn't she broken the stubborn silence between them and reached out herself? Clearly if she had, things would be different.

A fist tightened around her heart. And here her mind was again going round and round.

Basso's phone buzzed and he picked it out of the center console. "Ferrari." He pressed the button. "Si?...bene, bene. Grazie." He eyed her. "Si. Bene. Arrivederci." He hung up. "Ferrari says the coroner has been notified we're arriving and will be waiting for us."

Ali nodded and stared out the window, trying to keep her mind off the prospect of seeing her father's dead body.

A Falco never gives up! Another thing her father had once declared. She could still picture his stiff spine, his deep, bellowing voice as he said it.

She blew air from her lips at the irony of those words. Her mother had given up, and now him. What a crock of shit.

"What is it?" Basso asked, looking at her.

"Nothing." She turned up the radio.

Traffic gradually became more congested as the autostrada wove north past Milan. It was a clear day, rare for this northern region, where the flat Po River plain meets the jagged Alps. Mont Blanc, the tallest peak in western Europe, was visible through the light haze, its glaciers gleaming white.

The highway climbed, weaving into the Alpine foothills, and they exited the autostrada and got onto the tangential highway leading to Como, joining a Sunday-afternoon train of cars snaking its way toward the lake. Since it was sunny weather, and the weekend, the Milanese swarmed the towns crowding the edges of the deepest lake in Italy, creating hordes of civilians hungry for a gelato, pizza, and a walk by the lake.

The buildings, too, crammed closer and closer, a veritable stormy sea of clay roofs. They had yet to catch a glimpse of the lake, and she knew that they wouldn't until after the trip to the coroner's office, since the coroner was on the outer edge of town.

Basso drove with more patience than she had ever seen from the man, keeping his muttered curses to a minimum, as if constantly reminding himself of the dire nature of their trip.

She was touched by his selflessness—first after the chase through the streets of Siena, and now this. He'd probably been awakened from a dead sleep at home by the disturbing phone call. He had taken the responsibility to come to her apartment and break the news to her, and now here he was driving her five hours, ending the journey in the worst traffic Italy can produce. He didn't need to do any of it.

She watched him. He was clearly driven by a set of strong beliefs, ones that drove him to do the right thing in every scenario. She decided it would do her well to try to be like Basso on this trip—strong willed, calm under fire, taking what needs to be done and doing it with a stiff upper lip.

"Piece of shit!" Basso jammed the brakes and pushed the horn. "Bastard cut right in front of me."

"Keep straight here," she said. "We'll get off the main road and take the back streets to the office."

"I haven't seen this much traffic in years."

"Makes you appreciate Tuscany even more, doesn't it?"

The tension in his face melted. "Sorry. Where's the lake?"

"We probably won't see it until after the coroner's office."

They drove another ten minutes, Ali navigating with the app on her phone. The coroner's office was a boxy, two-story structure once painted a bright lemon color, now stained with decades of soot and exhaust.

They parked in a nearby parking lot and got out. "Humid," Basso said. "Hot."

She grabbed her jacket, then dropped it back on the seat.

"You'll want that." Basso slipped on his own jacket. "It will be cold in there. Unfortunately, I know from experience. Another perk of the inspector's job."

She grabbed it and shut the door, slipping it on.

They walked in silence down the sidewalk on the remote side-street in the heart of Como.

Although she'd never been to this particular place, it felt like Como in every way, with the tall foliage-choked mountains looming to the east and west, the sounds of traffic echoing through the buildings, hundreds of cars beeping and revving, coming together to make a thrumming sound that filled the valley, the scent of the lake saturating the air, the humidity making her sweat beneath her jacket.

They walked up the metal stairs and Basso opened the door.

Entering a cramped reception area, the air was just as

boiling hot as outside, this time scented with body odor, presumably from the man sitting behind the desk.

"Falco and Basso to see doctor..." Basso patted his leg, pulling out his phone, muttering under his breath.

"Doctor Vespucci?" the man asked.

"Yes."

"Please have a seat. He's expecting you."

They sat on plastic chairs along the wall, feeling the hot breath of the ceiling fan waft down.

The interior door opened with a clack and a man in a white lab coat stepped out.

"Ali Falco?" the man asked.

They stood and shook hands.

"I'm Doctor Leonardo Vespucci. I'm sorry to be meeting you like this."

She nodded, noting how well-practiced the man was at this routine.

"Follow me, please."

Ali and Basso walked behind him into a hallway, and into a sea of frozen air. A chill shivered through her body as she pulled her jacket tight around her.

They snaked through some corridors, past darkened offices and darkened hallways.

"Thank you for meeting us on a Sunday," she said.

"It's no problem."

He led them down a stairway, and into even colder air. The scent of embalming chemicals hung heavy in the cramped hallways of the lower level.

"In here." Vespucci led them into an office and sat behind his desk, motioning to two chairs. "Please, sit."

Ali remained standing. "If you don't mind, I'd like to see him. And...I'd like to get it over with as soon as possible."

Vespucci stared for a beat, then nodded, standing. "Of

course. But you know we've already officially identified his body. Two men he used to work with were on scene."

"I know. I just..." she shrugged.

"This way."

She followed Vespucci through another door, and into the morgue.

The doctor walked to a body locker door, clicked it open, and pulled out a tray on silent rails. Her father's outline lay motionless underneath a white sheet as the shelf fully extended.

The coroner looked down at her father's form for a moment, then walked around to the other side and lifted the sheet.

The first thing she saw was his gray, nearly white hair, which shocked her. She'd remembered it as jet-black. Of course, he had colored it. Another thing her father must have given up on.

Vespucci hesitantly opened the sheet further, until his face came into view.

She stared down, the room seeming to close around her to a point that contained only her father's face. He looked so much older than she remembered, with deeply wrinkled skin and bushy gray eyebrows. His mouth sagged down unnaturally, and one cheek was sunken, giving him a grotesque, misshapen appearance that looked nothing like the vibrant man she'd left twelve years ago.

There was a hole in his head, a dark red circle on his right temple. It had been cleaned, turning some of his hair pink around the wound.

Vespucci was clearly shielding her from the worst part, the hole that would have blown out the other side of his head, given that he most likely used his service .45 caliber Beretta PX4 Storm to take the shot.

She nodded and turned away.

Vespucci tucked her father away back into the locker and shut the door, then led them out of the morgue to the office again.

"Thank you," she said, sitting down.

Vespucci nodded somberly. "I believe you spoke to my assistant on the phone yesterday."

He pushed a piece of paper across the desk. "This is a release form for your father's remains to be transferred to this funeral home," he said, pointing. "The owners are very kind, and they will help you through every step of the process. Their phone number is here. This is their address."

She signed the sheet, and then another.

Basso sat stolidly, watching her.

And then they left.

Once back up on the ground level and outside, she unbuttoned her jacket and let it fall open, welcoming the warmth. She stood on the sidewalk, closing her eyes and sucking in a deep breath.

Basso stood next to her, watching. When she opened her eyes he asked, "Still okay?"

"Yes."

She took off her jacket, smiling at Basso. She hugged him, then kissed him gently on the cheek.

"What was that for?"

"For everything. For driving me up here. For," she gestured to the building, "that."

Basso nodded. "Don't mention it. It's what inspectors do for each other."

She scoffed. "I'm not inspector yet."

"But you will be."

She held out her hand. "Give me the keys."

Basso dropped them in her palm. "Where are we going? The apartment you're staying at?"

She nodded. “And then to the train station for you.”

“Are you sure? I can stay the night.”

“If you stay, you’ll have to get a hotel. They’re expensive up here.”

Basso looked at his watch. “There are a few more trains to catch before the end of the day.”

“It’s Sunday. There is one. And it leaves in an hour and a half.”

“Are you sure?”

“Enough,” she said, waving her hand.

6

"Please, take a seat, Signore Falco." The school principal's eyes widened, latching onto the Beretta holstered on her father's hip.

"Inspector Falco," her father says, watching Bianco's eyes. "I work for the Carabinieri."

Bianco exhaled, the tension visibly draining from his body. Her father is one of the few Carabinieri who wear plain clothing to work, his badge hiding away in his wallet. "Please, Inspector Falco. Have a seat."

Her father sits in the chair next to Ali. "What happened? I got a call from my wife. She couldn't make it."

Bianco bridges his fingers, putting his elbows on the desk, examining her father like he does all his students—with superiority and condescension. "Your daughter was involved in an altercation with another student – a boy -- in the hallway this morning."

"Altercation?"

"A fistfight."

"And?"

"And...your daughter punched this young boy."

"I'm sure she had good reason."

"I assure you, Signore Falco—"

"Inspector."

"Right, sorry. Inspector. There is never good reason to hit. In fact, it is written in our school bylaws."

"But my daughter doesn't just hit, unprovoked. Like I said, I'm sure she had a good reason."

Ali does in fact have a good reason, but she still has not been afforded the chance to tell her side of the story to the preside. He hasn't asked.

"That's not what the boy is saying," Bianco says.

"And this boy is a piece of shit liar."

Bianco smiles, blinking rapidly, a tittering nervous laugh bouncing his Adam's apple. "This boy's father is a very prominent man in the mayor's office."

"No coincidence there. The mayor's a piece of shit, too."

Bianco swallows, looking like his face is offline for an instant, eyelids locking closed as his eyebrows raise ever higher.

"What happened, principessa?"

The nickname her father uses usually makes her face red, but the tone of his voice is no-nonsense.

"He pulled the books from my hand," she says. "Kicked my test." She gestures to the desk, and the neat stack of ripped and haphazardly folded papers, some of them with footprints on them.

"Mario says he accidentally stepped on them in the altercation. That she rammed into him, dropping her schoolwork, and attacked him."

Her father turns slowly to the principal his face a cold mask. "We're talking about Mario Emilio? Son of Pino Emilio in the regional minister's office?"

Bianco looks like he's said too much, nodding reluctantly.

"You don't believe for a second that my daughter did that, do you, Principal Bianco? Nor do you believe that a delinquent like that is telling the truth about this?"

Bianco shows his palms. "Whatever happened, she was the one who broke Mario's nose, and punched him a dozen more times, refusing to stop even as a teacher arrived to break up the fight."

Her father looks at her.

She looks back, then slides her gaze to the floor.

"What's it going to be?" her father asks. "Detention? Suspension?"

Bianco swallows, shaking his head. "I'm sorry, signore. The bylaws are very clear. There is a strict no-fighting code. She is officially expelled from Dario Verello Primary and Secondary School."

Ali's eyes immediately well up and tears stream down her cheeks. She holds her breath, not wanting to gasp, to show any weakness, but she wipes her face.

Her father looks at her, seeing her cry. He speaks in a harsh whisper. "Look what you've done, Preside. You have my daughter crying tears of joy."

Bianco sits motionless.

Her father scoots forward and slams his hand on the desk. The booming sound in the small office makes Ali and the preside jolt in their seats.

Her father jumps to his feet. "I want to thank you for finally giving us good reason to leave this third-rate school, and the sniveling asshole who runs it. Come, Ali."

He turns on his heel and holds out a hand to his daughter.

She looks up, more scared of her father than she's ever felt in her life, and sees his face is a mask of complete relaxation, his lip upturned in a half smile, an amused glint in his eye. His fingers wiggle.

She takes his hand and stands, glancing at Principal Bianco, who sits with closed eyes, sucking in a breath through his flared nostrils.

They walk out at a brisk pace, her father keeping a gentle hold of her hand as he marches through the receptionist's office, and out into the hallway.

They go outside, and into the warm spring day, and they continue to walk.

Her father never lets go of her hand while walking at an uncomfortably fast pace for Ali's short legs.

"I'm sorry, Papà," she says.

Her father ignores her as they pass the chain link fence, and the yard filled with students at recess. He marches her into the parking lot, beyond the trees, out of sight of the school grounds, where they round his Carabinieri cruiser and finally stop.

He turns to face her and kneels so he's looking up at her.

"It's okay, principessa. You did nothing wrong. Nothing wrong. Do you believe me?"

He wipes her cheeks.

She says nothing.

"Tell me you know you did nothing wrong."

"I did nothing wrong."

"Do you believe it? Because I do." He smiles. Again, he wipes the tears from her cheeks and brushes the tendril of her hair caught on the wind behind her ear. He places both hands on either side of her face. "I love you, Ali. So much."

"I love you too, Papà."

She blocks both his arms aside, stepping in close, hugging her father, her arms vibrating with exertion as the last two hours of pent-up anguish leave her body.

Her father laughs, returning the hug, and then kisses the top of her head.

"Okay. So, let's get out of here. We have a lot to do today."

"What are we doing?"

"What are we doing? It's sunny. But it's windy, so we shouldn't go to Boca Boca for gelato. Too much wind coming off the lake. We'll need to go to the piazza."

Ali breaks down in tears, looking at the ground.

"I'm sorry," she says. "I got expelled from school."

"Don't be sorry, Ali. You did what you had to do."

"But now I can't go to that school anymore. I have to leave my friends."

"I know, principessa." He tilts her head up with his finger under her chin. "I know. It's difficult, Ali. You'll have to leave your friends. We'll have to start somewhere new. But I promise we'll find you an even better school."

"What if I don't make any friends?" Ali asks.

"You will."

"But what if I don't?"

"Ali." He looks at her with kind, gentle eyes, putting both hands on her shoulders. "If you want to have friends, you will have friends. That's how it works with the Falcos. You can't stop a Falco."

She rolls her eyes. Her father always gets on these rants, speaking about their family in the third person, like they are a clan of mystical beings from an ancient mythology.

"A Falco is strong, fast, and free, just like the falcon. It's how we got our name. When a falcon sees what it wants it takes it, swooping in and grabbing it with its strong claws. And if you want friends, you will swoop in and you will have friends!"

He put his hands on his hips and puffs his chest, and Ali laughs through her tears.

His face goes serious, and he kneels back down. "Listen to me, Ali. You can't let your future be dictated by men like that Principal Bianco in there, with his important friends in high places. Your fate is not determined by people like that. Or anybody else. You have to make your own fate, Ali."

She nods, wiping the last of her tears.

"Now let's go. Before all the gelato in Como melts, because my fate is a scoop of pistachio and a scoop of cherry."

They climb into the car, Ali in the front seat, her father slipping off his holster and putting it in the pocket of his door, as he always does before he puts on his seatbelt.

He turns and smiles, tilting his head at her serious expression. "What is it, principessa?"

"I want to be just like you someday, Papà."

Her father reaches over and pats her leg, his face beaming with what looks like pride to Ali.

And then he points two fingers to his head, right at the temple, and in a blur his head jerks sideways.

Ali snorted awake, sitting up.

Breathless, her heart hammering in her chest, she sat staring upwards at the fan twirling on her ceiling.

Not *her* fan. *A* fan. This ceiling was not hers.

She pushed aside the light blanket that draped across her fully clothed body and slid her legs off the bed.

The windows on the other side of the room framed glass fading of color, the sky outside losing the red of sunset, cut by the silhouette of mountains.

A woman's shadow moved, a plume of smoke jetting out of her mouth as she stood at the balcony railing outside.

Ali picked up her phone and read the screen, which told her it was still Sunday evening, just before nine o'clock pm.

She felt a thousand times better physically than the last time she'd awakened, but the final image of her dream still hadn't faded, leaving her stunned.

She shook her head, stood up, and went to the kitchen, her bare feet landing on cool tile. There was a box of pizza on the table giving off a mouthwatering aroma, an open bottle of red wine and a clean, empty glass.

She stretched her arms overhead and looked around the place.

The decor was sparse: a framed landscape photograph of green Tuscan hills, another featuring the hills after the harvest, a patchwork of combed brown soil.

Back in school, secondary and upper secondary, Chiara's walls would have been hung with pictures of scantily clad male singers. As this was a short-term rental, a legitimate source of income, shirtless Antonino pics were probably not conducive to five-star ratings.

The kitchen clock read 8:47. She couldn't remember falling asleep. After dropping Basso at the train station, she had gone to her friend's apartment, let in by the building manager. Chiara had told her she would come over to visit and bring dinner, when Ali had laid down on the bed and closed her eyes. Chiara had obviously slipped in quietly, allowing her to rest.

The wine glass perched on the table called to her, but she ignored it, slid open the door, and joined her friend on the balcony.

The air was humid and hot, the smells of cooking food rising from the streets below, laced with the cigarette Chiara was pushing into the ashtray, and her friend's floral fragrance.

Ali paused, seeing her friend in a black dress, necklace, and earrings. A pair of pumps sat next to the chair.

Chiara faced her with a sad expression, and Ali embraced her old friend. They stood in each other's arms for a time, Chiara rubbing her back and petting the back of her head.

"I'm so sorry," Chiara said.

Ali pulled away and gestured to her outfit. "Look at you. You look stunning."

Chiara waved her off.

Ali gestured to the pack of cigarettes on the table. "Can I have one?"

"I thought you quit."

"I did." Ali took one and lit it, sitting down on one of the chairs.

Chiara grabbed her own and sat next to her.

Ali watched the blonde curls tickling the center of Chiara's back as she sat. Her skin was smooth and tanned, her figure slender as ever. Chiara had always turned the boys' heads back then, and she'd grown even more beautiful as she entered her third decade of life.

"What?" Chiara asked.

"You look good."

"Thank you. You do too. I mean, under the circumstances."

"It's been so long. And why the hell are you wearing that?"

"I...it was just a function. And yes, it has been a long time."

At least five years by Ali's calculations. They usually spoke on the phone, only seeing one another if Chiara made an effort to see her down in Siena, or some other mutually agreed upon place that was never Como. And yet it always felt like they had never left each other. Ever since secondary school, the one she'd relocated to in the south of town, Chiara had been her best friend.

"How's Alessandro?" Ali asked.

"He's good. He sends his condolences."

"Tell him, thank you."

They sat in easy silence, smoking, listening to the Como thrum.

The apartment was on the fifth floor, and there was a portion of the lake in view through the surrounding buildings. A float plane throttled up, engine echoing through the city as it lifted off, dripping water from its skids, its strobe lights receding into the distance.

"This really is a beautiful place, Chiara. Listen, I want to pay you—"

Chiara waved her hands. "You'll stay here as long as you

need to, and it will cost you nothing. Now please don't mention it again."

Ali took a drag. "Thank you, Chiara."

Chiara snubbed out her cigarette and lifted her empty wine glass. "Do you want one?"

She probably shouldn't. This was the first time she'd felt completely sober in two days. "Sure."

Chiara returned with a glass of red, and they again sat in silence, sipping wine.

"How long are you staying?" Chiara asked.

"Good question."

"When will you have the funeral?"

"I haven't even begun to think of that."

"Then let's not think of it. Tell me about boys."

Ali rolled her eyes. With an exasperated smile she shook her head.

"What?"

"I stood up a blind date the other night."

"Why?"

Ali's smile dropped. She sipped her wine, thinking of Matteo. Again. She had dreamed of him the other night, and it was not a rare occurrence. Not a week went past without another vivid image of Matteo making an appearance in her sleep, or some strange avatar of a human being that was supposed to be him.

Again, she thought of his turned back, walking into the rain without an umbrella, his shoulders slumped from a broken heart.

"I'm sorry, Matteo. I need to leave here. I can't live in that house for another second. Not with my father. Not with the ghost of my mother constantly with me."

"We can move in together."

"It is not just my home. It's this city. I have to go somewhere else. I'm going somewhere else."

"But...I can't leave my mother."

"And I don't expect you to. Arrivederci, Matteo."

Ali could still hear her heartless tone and it still made her cringe inside every time she thought about it.

"I'm sorry," Chiara said, reading her face well. "He moved to Torino with his family, just so you know."

The thought of running into Matteo had added to the anxiety of her current situation. Seeing him happy, with three loving children, was hard enough to look at on social media. In person it would have been too much. With that news she felt a weight lift off her.

She shook her head. "It's pathetic. I swear I've moved on. It was just...I don't know."

Chiara put a hand on her forearm. "It was complicated. And you don't have to explain things to me."

Ali smiled, thankful for the compassion.

Chiara eyed her watch, then pulled out her phone and checked the screen. "I have to text Alessandro."

Ali stood up and went inside, grabbing a glass of water. When she came out, she glanced at Chiara's lit screen, seeing she had typed: *It will be a little later than I thought. Just go without me. I'll see you tomorrow.*

"Go without me?" Ali asked.

Chiara flipped her phone face down. "What?"

"You just texted for Alessandro to go without you. Go where?"

"Oh. It's nothing. Just...a show that's in town."

She eyed Chiara's outfit in a new light. She hadn't been coming from some place, she was on her way there. Ali had been asleep, and Chiara had let her rest, sacrificing her plans for her.

"What kind of show?"

"A play."

"Chiara." Her friend had always been involved in theater, acting and singing on stages across the city. It was a wonder she wasn't starring in movies by now. She loved the theater, and would have been looking forward to the occasion, undoubtedly. "What play?"

"It was my friend's debut performance at the opera house."

"Was? But you told Alessandro to go without you."

"It's going on right now. I was talking about the after party. Listen, Ali, I don't care. I care about you first and foremost, not some play."

Ali shook her head. "Go. I forbid you to sit here anymore. In fact, I think I'm going to go out for a walk. I've been sitting all day in the car, and now sleeping on the bed. I have to move."

"I'll go with you."

"In those pumps?"

"Yes."

"Chiara. I don't want you with me. I want to walk and think. Or...not think. Clear my head, you know?"

Chiara looked at her. "Are you sure?"

"Go."

"But..." Chiara looked at her.

"But what?"

"I'm just worried about you."

Ali squinted. "Why?"

Chiara said nothing. Her face went red. "It's just...first your mother. And now your father?"

Ali read her friend's face, realizing she was concerned for more than just her feelings. "You think I'm going to hurt myself? Is that what you think?"

Chiara's eyes teared up.

"You think I'm going to take my Beretta and put it to my

head and pull the trigger? Let my friends come over and find me dead?" She stood up and walked back inside. "Like I'm going to do something that fucked up."

She went to the kitchen and poured the glass of wine into the sink. Some of it splashed out of the basin onto the white countertop, looking like blood spatter. She stared at it, her own eyes watering now.

"Ali. I'm sorry."

Blinking the tears away, wiping with her hand, she turned back to Chiara. "Thank you for being concerned. I appreciate it. But I'm not going to do anything crazy if that's what you're worried about."

She smiled, kissed Chiara on the cheek, and stepped back, giving her a path to the front door.

Chiara took the visual cues and stood frozen for a moment, then put on her shoes and walked to the door. "I'll call you tomorrow morning."

"Okay."

"We can get coffee. I'm free after eleven."

"Okay."

Chiara looked at her, her eyes shimmering again.

"Stop crying, your makeup's going to run." Ali hugged her, and Chiara gripped her tightly back.

"I want you to be strong, Ali Falco," Chiara said. "I want you to fight. You got that?"

Ali released her, nodding. "I won't give up," she said. A little joke for her father's ears only.

"Exactly." Chiara turned, twisted the knob, and went out the door.

Ali clicked it shut behind her, locking the deadlock and sat in a chair at the kitchen table.

As she opened the pizza box, she thought of a casket door leaning open. She pictured her mother lying inside, a lifeless sunken face covered in makeup, so clearly caked on to cover the numerous injuries, a dead vessel that was not the woman she had known. She thought of her father's face, misshapen and pale.

"Shit." She stood up.

She thought she was haunted in Siena? This place was wearing her to the bone. She really did need that walk.

She went to the bed and unzipped her luggage, overturning the duffel bag and spilling its contents onto the mattress.

Her Beretta, tucked into its leather holster, poked out from under her clothing. She put it aside.

She pictured taking the gun out of the holster, flicking off the safety catch, putting the barrel to her head, threading her finger through the trigger guard, and pulling the trigger.

She didn't flinch in the least thinking about it. Did that make her sick? Probably just as sick as her mother and father combined.

She went to the kitchen sink again and sucked down another glass of water.

And then as she looked down again at the wine stain, just as sudden as the muzzle blast of a gun, a thought came to her. And this time she did flinch, standing straighter.

As if hypnotized, she walked back to the bed and looked down at the gun. Staring at it, she pictured the hole in her father's head where a bullet had entered, and the other side where it had exited, undoubtedly spattering the furniture, or the wall, or the floor, or whatever had been next to him.

She needed to see exactly where her father had killed himself, she thought. She slipped on her shoes, grabbing her keys off the nightstand.

7

Ali's vehicle swerved side to side as she took the familiar turns of the Via Regina—the narrow road snaking along the western edge of the lake. As if she were running a hand over her arm, noting the freckles, imperfections, and tiny hair patterns, she watched the familiar pothole spots come and go in her headlights, the scrapes and dings on the railing of the small bridge spanning a creek that flowed off the mountain into the lake, the rock walls with faded arrow signs screwed to them. All of it was as it had been eleven years ago, back when she was nineteen. It was amazing how her muscles steered the vehicle as if she hadn't left.

The lake had an oily stillness to it, reflecting the mirror image of the lights on the other side with perfect symmetry. The radio was off, only the sound of the car revving.

As she entered a copse of trees choking the edge of the lake, she steeled herself for the sight that would lay ahead.

The road turned left into a clearing, where an inlet of the lake opened. On the other side of the long, sweeping curve, the villa grounds sat sleeping, waiting for her homecoming.

Her heart pounded in her chest. She saw lights on, dotting

the property, illuminating the trees within. One of the poles where she remembered a powerful flood light, which used to shine towards her as she drove this stretch, was now much dimmer, setting aglow an encroaching tree branch.

Back then, she would have seen most of the rear of the villa poking up over the rock wall, but now only a small, dimly lit, portion of the yellow-stucco façade shone in the otherwise dark mass of trees.

She pulled the Citroen around the inlet, then up to the rock wall that surrounded the property, which spanned from the lakes edge, then up along the road for fifty or so meters, and back to the lake, apportioning off the Falco's slice of lakefront property. Once a charming rock wall with carefully manicured vines and shrubs playfully clinging to it, now it was choked with clumps of unruly foliage, dead vines protruding everywhere from the green wall.

She slowed at the electric gate, noting the vines and shrubs had been cut away to keep the entrance open.

Shutting off the engine, she got out into still, humid air smelling richly of leaves, wet earth, and lake water. It smelled like childhood.

Her legs swished through long grass as she went to the gate. There was a heavy iron door the width of two vehicles that rolled sideways on a track, powered electronically. Next to it was a jail-cell barred gate for pedestrians that opened by use of a key. A piece of crime scene tape was strewn across both.

She walked up and pressed the old code on the keypad for the car gate, wondering if it still worked.

Nothing happened. The light atop the pole remained dark, and the gate didn't move.

She put her key in the pedestrian gate lock, twisted, and the familiar click told her the gate was open. She pushed, and the familiar shriek of the hinges howled into the still night.

She stepped inside the grounds, into more familiar scents, this time of decaying magnolia petals and cypress pines.

The long driveway extended ahead, bending slightly to the right, lined on both sides with the tall conical cypress that reached up into the dark sky like giants. Two dim yellow lights shone in the distance, the porch lights still on for her after all these years, illuminating a vehicle parked in front.

She stared at the car. A BMW. Her father's BMW. The same one he'd had more than a decade ago.

Beyond the house to the left she saw the lake shimmering like black ink, the dock jutting out into the water, her father's Riva boat conspicuously missing, sold after her mother's death.

She looked back at her car, the headlights casting long shadows into the grounds through the gate.

With an exploratory push of her hand, the car gate moved sideways on the tracks, rolling sluggishly. She leaned into it and pushed harder, getting it open enough to drive through, then got back into the car and started the engine.

She rolled down the driveway with her high beams on, marveling at how tall and thick the cypress had become, keeping a wary eye in the shadows, seeing nothing out of the ordinary, minus her father's car and the unshakeable feeling he was watching her right now.

Parking next to her father's vehicle, she got out and shut the door, standing once again in the silence. Como set the night sky aglow kilometers to the south, beyond the villa, but only the faintest sounds of the city skated up the valley.

She tried the passenger door of her father's vehicle. Finding it locked, she went to the driver's side and found it unlocked. She popped it open and stood frozen, taking in the familiar scent of his cologne and the leather interior as it flowed out of the cab.

She ducked in and looked around, kneeling on the driver's

seat, only seeing a copy of the *Corriere Della Sera* folded on the passenger seat. Otherwise, the vehicle was spotless, just as she always remembered it.

She checked the glove compartment, the center console.

Finding nothing out of the ordinary, no note of explanation why he'd shot himself tucked under the registration, she climbed out and shut the door.

If he had killed himself. Something was very off, and she needed to get inside to see if she was right or if she was going crazy.

Taking a breath, she eyed the carved wooden front door and walked toward it, her feet scratching on the stone walkway, then up the single step to the covered tile porch.

She pulled her keychain from her pocket, trying the familiar brass handle first. It turned in her hands, and the door squeaked as she pushed, swinging open.

She paused on the threshold, staring into the darkness inside. It had been so many years, and never once had she seen the place so devoid of light. Or life.

The scent coming out revolted her, smelling of burnt food, and something she dared not put a name to.

Decidedly not like childhood.

She cleared her throat loudly, kicking herself into gear, piercing the silence with her presence, and reached in and flicked on the light switch.

She started at the sight of her own reflection staring back at her on the opposite wall, the familiar imperfection in the mirror elongating the middle of her body.

She moved inward, into the large anteroom that angled left. She began to push the door closed, but left it cracked open.

The stairway coiled along the left wall, up to a darkened second level. Deciding to start with the lower floor she walked into the hallway toward the kitchen, and the living room beyond it.

With soft, silent steps, she walked into the kitchen, freezing as she saw an irregularity in her peripheral vision, a darkness along the wall inside the family room.

Without moving her eyes, she noted the height of the dark smudge and knew then where her father had killed himself.

She focused her attention on the kitchen for now, contemplating a pan of sauce sitting cold and congealed on the burner, a half-cut onion on a cutting board, a knife lying next to it, some oregano, a pot of water gone cold, an unopened box of spaghetti perching next to an open bottle of wine.

She looked at the parts of the scene in turn, taking none of it in, still thinking of the discoloration on the wall a few meters from her.

Without further deliberation she turned and saw the wall was spattered with blood and other particulates, which she knew to be bits of skull and brain. She didn't see the photographs of her as a child in a bathing suit, or her mother and father skiing in the Dolomites, just the dark-maroon mess spraying all of it.

She went to the threshold of the living room and flicked on the light, illuminating the space fully.

She looked down, studying the pool of dried red on the tile floor next to the end of the leather couch where he always sat. Then she looked at the couch, where there were more red splashes, splotches that dripped and smeared the leather, an inkblot test made of her father's blood.

The television in the far corner of the room had a hole in it, the glass display shattered.

She shook her head, staring, separating the whole scene into pieces—the gunshot into the television, where her father's head lay after the shot to his head, the way he had leaned out to the left, bleeding onto the floor.

Everything was on the left side—the spatter, the way he slumped. Everything but the hole in his head, which had been on the right side. There was only one problem with that, and it was a very big one. He had shot with his left hand. He had been ambidextrous with many things, the way the knife lay next to the right side of the cutting board was testament to that, the way he used to throw with his right hand, the way he wrote with his left. But he had shot with his left. That she was dead sure of.

Her eyes instantly welled up and she began crying. "Oh, Papà," she whispered. "What happened to you?"

8

Corporal Inspector Marco Vinci of the Como Carabinieri regional division headquarters paused his progress filling out the Monday morning paperwork and checked his watch again. He still had five minutes before the meeting. Should he go in early?

He pictured the coming scenario...private conversation among the high-ranking Carabinieri, the mayor of Como present himself. Inspector Vinci enters the office as they descend into uncomfortable silence—staring at him as he slides along the wall trying to become invisible.

He decided 8:30 meant 8:30, anything else might have been presumptuous. Everyone was already on edge around here. He didn't want to ruffle any feathers, so he went back to studying his notes, looking at photographs of the dead body they'd pulled from the ground up on the mountain, preparing for the meeting. The images of the woman's broken corpse, twisted, jutting from the ground, had been seared into his brain by now. Looking at them again from different angles gave him no further insight.

Salvaggio came into the squad room and spotted him. Not

bothering to drop his bag at his desk, he walked straight to Marco.

"You see that last night?" The corporal sipped a plastic cup of espresso, his bushy eyebrow cocked.

Marco pressed the pen to paper again. “I assume you’re speaking about the game?”

“Hell yes I’m talking about the game. What else would I be talking about?”

“Yes, I did see the game,” Marco said. “He’s a has-been. He'll be fired within the month.” He cocked an eyebrow, looking at Salvaggio.

Salvaggio shook his head. “That wasn’t his fault. It was the midfielder’s job to cut off that pass before it got there. The shot was a miracle. Nobody could have saved it.”

“I agree. Not with those reaction times.” Marco suppressed a smile, flipping to another page.

“That’s not what they’re saying, you know that, right? You think your time spent on the junior team gives you insights none of the FIFA analysts have?”

Marco sighed, putting down his pen. “Is that what they’re saying? Did you listen to them this morning?”

Salvaggio’s confident smile cracked, but the arrogance shone through again. “The haters say the same thing every morning.”

Marco used a patient tone, like he was speaking to a schoolboy, which he knew infuriated the young soldier. “With qualifiers coming in two months, they'll need to grow Manasco in time. Which means your favorite goalkeeper will be gone by the end of the month."

"*Madonna*. You are crazy, you know that?"

Marco set down his pen and bridged his fingers. “Ten euro? Lapida will be out by the end of the week. Manasco will be in.”

Salvaggio blinked rapidly, considering the bet, the first sign he was suspecting Marco might know something he didn't.

Inspector Tedesco came over, slapping Salvaggio on the shoulder. "What's going on here?"

Salvaggio eyed Tedesco, brushing the shoulder of his uniform, brushing the spot where the big inspector had touched him. "We're just discussing a wager. Vinci thinks Lapida's days are numbered."

Tedesco frowned, looking between the two of them. "But didn't you hear—"

"He thinks that Lapida has a chance to stay on the team," Marco said, cutting him off.

"Yeah, Vinci. He gets the bet," Salvaggio said.

"Salvaggio." Tedesco folded his arms. "When's the last time you've won a wager with this man?"

"More times than you know, Inspector Tedesco. How about you mind your own business?"

Tedesco put up his hands, taking a step back.

"Okay, fine," Salvaggio said. "Ten euro."

Salvaggio jutted his hand out to Marco. He took it and shook.

"Easy money," Salvaggio said, walking away.

Tedesco watched the young soldier leave, then turned back to Marco. "You know they announced they were trading him this morning, right?"

Marco frowned in mock confusion. "They did?"

Tedesco shook his head. "That kid needs to start listening to the radio."

Marco eyed the clock. 8:27 am. He stood up.

"The meeting with the brass?" Tedesco asked.

Marco nodded.

"Did you meet the captain?"

"Not yet."

"You should have seen him strut in here, handing off his bag to me like I'm some kind of butler."

Tedesco waited for him to say more, but he didn't. Marco knew part of the reason he himself had worked his way up the ranks was because when it came to speaking of others, he kept his judgments to a minimum, and always kept them to himself.

Tedesco cleared his throat. "Well, I'll be out here waiting for you, okay?"

"You and Vincenza head back up to the mountain. I'll be up there after the meeting."

"Yes, sir." Tedesco walked away.

Marco's desk phone rang and he picked it up. "Carabinieri Inspection Division. Marco Vinci."

"Why aren't you answering your cell phone?"

He sighed inwardly. "I'm sorry, honey. I have it on silent. I'm going to be in an important meeting soon. In fact—"

"—Why did two more packages from Guido's just arrive?"

Marco rubbed his forehead with his fingers.

"Well?" she asked. "Why are there two more packages?"

"Maybe because the remainder of the place settings order is inside those boxes? I don't know."

"Place settings? Guido's is invitations. Remember?"

"Oh. Yeah."

"So why are there two boxes of invitations sitting out here?" She all but screamed the question. "Did you check the two boxes we got from them last week?"

"I did not." He felt a cranium cramp coming on.

"You were supposed to check before you gave them to Marta for calligraphy. Marco, I cannot believe you."

The office door opened down the hallway. Dante leaned out and waved at Marco to come in. "Listen, I have to go."

"You have to wait till I open this box. If this isn't the right box, then it means those other two, the ones that you were supposed to check and count, that you didn't, for reasons I don't understand, don't have the correct invitations inside of them and Maria, the person I would not trust with a toilet brush to...Well. Okay. Wait. These are somebody else's invitations. Why did they send them to us?

"Honey, I have to hang up."

"Still, I have to check with Maria to see if those were the correct invitations. We're coming down to the wire here and I gave you one thing. I didn't check, because I told you to check, Marco. I told you."

"Bye, Valentina."

"Call me at lunch," she said as he hung up. He straightened his shirt, making sure it was properly tucked in, and walked to Second lieutenant Colombo's office.

The door was still cracked open, Dante already back inside.

Marco stepped inside, always feeling like he'd walked through a portal into another dimension when he came here, one filled with leather and dark wood, wainscoting, and paintings on the walls. Colombo's office was a mere few meters beyond Dante's, but it may as well have been in a different building with how inaccessible the man was to a common inspector like Vinci.

The Capitan, Second Lieutenant Colombo, Marshal Dante, and the mayor of Como stood near a side table, looking down at an array of photographs Marco recognized well from the last few days.

Dr. Vespucci, the head regional coroner and forensic specialist, stood nearby, nodding at Marco as he entered. The other men let Marco's entrance go unnoticed.

Marco took up an inconspicuous position along the back wall and stood at attention.

Captain Carlotta, the so-called asshole Salvaggio had been speaking of earlier, grunted to the men next to him. Vinci did not know him personally, nor would he have expected to meet someone so high up the ladder, at least a full rung above the Second lieutenant himself. But Marco would have liked to. The captain was indeed a very important man in the military and presiding in Rome, which was exactly where Marco, and his loving and pushy fiancée, hoped to move one day.

This wasn't the time, though. As Marco leaned against the back wall he reached into his pocket, making sure his phone was silenced.

"How are you, Vinci?" Dr. Vespucci asked.

Marco nodded.

The mayor, noticing somebody new had entered, turned around. "Ah, Inspector Vinci, isn't it?"

"Yes, sir."

"How are you?"

"I'm fine, sir, thank you. And yourself?"

"Si, si. Did you see that game last night?"

"Yes, sir."

"It was a disgrace. They traded Lapida, you know. This morning."

"I had heard something about that, yes."

"And I bet you would have done better at forward than that Claudio character we're paying way too much for."

Marco smiled politely. The mayor knew about his junior career with the Inter squad and made a point to mention it the last two times they'd met. The man was charismatic, making an effort to know those around him. No wonder he was mayor.

"Maybe in my next life," Marco said.

The mayor's eyes flicked downward, his smile sympathetic. "With a better knee."

"That's right, sir."

The mayor tapped the captain's shoulder. "Sir, this is Inspector Marco Vinci. He's one of Colombo's finest inspectors.

He used to play for the Inter Junior team. He got injured right before his chance at the big show."

Marco's face blushed as Captain Carlotta turned, eyed him, nodded, then looked back at the pictures.

"Let's get started, shall we?" Dante directed the men away from the table.

Dante sat along the wall in an antique wooden chair while the captain and mayor took the two chairs immediately in front of Colombo's desk.

Dr. Vespucci and Marco remained standing, as there were no other chairs.

Colombo walked to his desk and sat. The second lieutenant's eyes had dark rings under them, the sclera red. Marco had not gone to the scene of the former carabinieri inspector's suicide yesterday morning, but he'd heard plenty about it. The rumor was Colombo, Dante, and the deceased man known as Falco were once close. Adding this high-profile case of the girl's body pulled from the ground, and Colombo looked like he needed a few weeks on a Sardinian beach.

The captain cleared his throat. "Well, I know we've already talked about this, but I just want to open this meeting with my condolences to you two. It is such a shame about your colleague. The mayor told me about it this morning."

Colombo nodded solemnly, looked at the wall next to Marco, then lowered his eyes.

Marco snuck a glance and saw a faded color photograph hanging next to him, the image showing Colombo as a much younger man, with less weight on his shoulders, more humor in his eyes. He stood next to another man of about the same height with chiseled features, tanned and handsome—both dressed in their academy uniforms, their graduate diplomas in their hands.

Dino Falco, he presumed.

The room descended into silence, the sounds of the street traffic four floors below seeping through the window behind Colombo.

The mayor cleared his throat and nodded to Dr. Vespucci. "What about this watch I'm hearing about?"

"Inspector Vinci and his team were up at the site and pulled it from the mud a meter or so from where we found the body," Vespucci said.

"I didn't see any pictures of it over there."

"No sir. I haven't fully processed it yet," Vespucci said. "It's very dirty, covered in rust. It will take some doing to clean it up. My team is trying to be very careful. It's unlikely there'll be any forensic evidence on the timepiece, given the time the girl has been underground. If there is, we'll find it."

"So, we're talking Il Duomo," the mayor said with a chuckle, referring to Il Duomo di Milano. Construction of the cathedral had begun in 1386, the final details applied over six-hundred years later in 1965.

The room's mood lifted slightly.

"I'll be thorough, but I plan on having it properly cleaned in the next few days. If there is organic material on it, then we'll have it tested."

"And if there is forensic material, we'll expedite tests, right?" The captain said, looking at Colombo.

"Yes. Of course."

"Those cell phone pictures are all over the internet," the captain said. "I know you've confiscated the photographs, reprimanded the individuals, but the damage has already been done."

Marco felt a stab of guilt, exchanging a glance with Dante. Dante shook his head slightly, indicating it was not Marco's fault, nor did the captain think it was. At least, Marco hoped that's what the look meant.

Marco and his team had been the first on scene to the young woman's body after the local Polizia. He had point-blank asked the construction crew that had dug up the body if they took cell phone photographs, and they had all denied doing so. They had been lying, and those photos were forever circulating on the internet now.

"Understood, Captain," Dante said. "We'll work with the utmost speed," he gestured to Vespucci, "while maintaining accuracy, of course. Dr. Vespucci, can you please summarize for everyone here what we have so far on the case?"

Dr. Vespucci gestured to Marco. "We may as well start from the beginning. Inspector Vinci was the first inspector on scene. Vinci, why don't you tell us how you found it."

Marco nodded, feeling his temperature rise as the men looked at him.

"Yes, sir. As you probably know, Cellulario Interna are putting up a series of new cell towers around the lake. They were clearing out some trees near the top of Monte Boletto when one of their diggers uncovered the body.

"The digger operator stopped before he'd done too much damage, but he did cut into the torso of the corpse as he pulled it out of the earth." Marco wasn't sure if he was going into too much gory detail or not, but he continued.

"We received a call from the Polizia di Stato, who had been first on scene. They contacted us, and my team and I arrived, taking over shortly thereafter. On that note, sir," he looked at the captain. "I take full responsibility for the pictures leaking. We thought we had covered that contingency, but clearly we hadn't."

The captain nodded, looking unimpressed, motioning impatiently for him to continue.

"We ascertained the body was clearly that of a girl or a young woman. Long dark hair, as you can see in those photographs. Her clothing was faded, very much damaged, but it was still easy to tell she wore a pink jacket with patches sewn onto the denim, and denim jeans. Young clothing, we thought."

"As you can see, her body was badly deteriorated. The time in the ground, the wet climate, and the insects in the acidic soil had made sure of that. We did notice there was a hole in her skull, but I wasn't sure if it had been made by the teeth of the mechanical digger upon excavation, or if it had been related to the victim's death." Marco gestured to Vespucci, realizing he was dipping into the forensic specialist's territory.

Vespucci nodded, taking the cue. "That's correct, there is the hole, caused by a blunt instrument struck with a lot of force, and then there was the scarf we found on her. Both of these things of great interest when I performed my autopsy."

"What about the scarf?" the mayor asked.

"It was wrapped multiple times, extremely tight. I found blood residue on the fibers of the scarf, and she had a cracked vertebra. The amount of force used would have been substantial."

"My goodness," the mayor said.

"Which is to say we suspect a man killed her," Vespucci said. "And we've identified her."

All heads rose, including Marco's. He'd gone to sleep last night wondering if there was a family out there waiting for answers, wondering how anybody who had known this young woman, searching for her, could be silent after so much attention from the media. The only answer he could come up with was nobody was looking for her. And that the only person who knew she was dead was her killer.

"Who is it?" the captain asked.

"A woman named Elisabetta Sottocornola, according to dental records."

"Elisabetta Sottocornola?" Marco asked, too interested to

ignore his rule to shut up in front of these men. "She never showed up in our missing persons database." Marco knew the few names by heart, and hers had not been on any of the lists.

"You didn't know that?" the mayor asked.

"No, sir," Marco said.

"This is the first we're hearing about her identity," Dante said.

"I got a definitive match this morning," Vespucci said. "A dentist over in Lecco."

"So, she's from Lecco," the captain said.

Lake Como was shaped like an upside-down Y on the map, with Como sitting on the lower left arm of the Y, and Lecco on the right arm, thirty kilometers away.

"Perhaps." Vespucci shrugged. "Perhaps she moved to Como. I spoke to the dentist, who told me the last time he'd seen her was when she was eleven years old, still with the primary second molars in her mouth, as found on the dental records. At the time of her death she was five to ten years older, with a full set of adult teeth."

They sat in silence a beat.

"Nobody reported her missing over in Lecco?" The mayor asked.

Marco shook his head. "That name did not show up on any of our databases."

"So, she has no next of kin? No family looking for her?"

"Or," Marco said, "Next of kin and killer may be one in the same."

"That's a good point." The mayor pointed a bobbing finger at him.

Colombo's gaze locked onto Marco. "Put that on the agenda for today—finding next of kin. And if you do that, figure out their reason for keeping their mouths shut for a decade."

Marco nodded. "Yes, sir."

"A decade?" the captain asked. "Can you tell that's how long it's been?"

Dr. Vespucci shook his head. "I'm afraid it's not—"

There were two knocks at the door, followed by another three, more insistent knocks.

The captain sat back hard in his chair, annoyed.

"Si!" Colombo's voice boomed.

Marco realized it was probably his duty to go to the door, so he darted into action. But before he could get there, Regina, the fourth-floor receptionist, poked her head in.

"What is it?" Marco whispered.

"I'm sorry." Regina looked harried. There was a woman very close behind her, looking ready to barge past.

Marco frowned, stepping closer, appraising the woman. Dressed in jeans and a blouse, she was good-looking, with dark eyes and hair, her expression hard and demanding. What was this? A reporter? He didn't recognize her.

"What is this, Regina?" he asked.

Then the woman thrust an arm past Regina, pushing open the door, crashing it against the wall. She ducked under Regina's arm and appeared in front of Marco, moving with lightning speed.

"Hey, what are you doing?" Marco put his hands up.

With another fast move he more felt than saw, she grabbed both his arms, somehow manipulating his weight to stumble aside, giving her a straight lane past him, which she took.

Shit.

He felt like he'd blown a defensive play, leaving the goal open for a shot.

Without hesitation, he righted himself and caught her by the arm, clamping hard on her biceps.

"Ah!" She turned to him with fire in her eyes.

She lurched, trying to twist out of his grip, but he kept his hand clenched.

"Marco, let her go!" Colombo's voice commanded.

He hesitated, then let go and stood back, straightening his shirt, catching his breath.

"What is this?" The mayor was standing now.

"I'm sorry, sirs," Regina said. "I tried to stop her. I told her you were in a meeting, but she pushed past me."

Salvaggio rushed in through the door, followed by another soldier.

"Everyone calm down." Colombo walked from behind his desk with his hands up. "Thank you, all. Regina, you can leave us. Please close the door behind you."

They all watched, including the woman, as Salvaggio, Regina, and the other soldier left. The door clicked shut, and they stood looking at the newcomer.

"I need to speak to you," she said to Colombo, as if she knew him, as if they were intimately familiar. She eyed Dante next. Dante remained in his seat, calmly staring back at her.

"I demand to know what is going on." The captain sat rigid.

"Everyone, this is Ali Falco. Dino Falco's daughter." Colombo emphasized the name, clearly hoping the point hammered home that they were in the presence of the daughter of the man who had committed suicide that weekend.

Slow realization softened the captain's and the mayor's faces.

"Oh." The mayor shook his head. "I'm very sorry to hear about your father."

Her gaze darted around the room, briefly landing on Marco before moving to the table containing the corpse photographs. She seemed struck by the sight of death strewn across the tabletop, pausing a beat to look at the pictures.

"Please," the mayor said, still standing. "Take my seat."

Marco was ready to reach out and grasp her even though there was clearly no need.

“I’m sorry,” she said, turning back to Marco. “I hope I didn’t hurt you.”

Marco realized he was still tense. He released his jaw, standing straighter.

“He’s fine,” the mayor said with a chuckle. “Please, Ms. Falco. Sit.”

“I was hoping to speak to you and Dante,” she said to Colombo. “Alone.”

Marco studied the woman named Ali Falco. Her eyes were dark brown, as if they were all pupil, glistening with intensity and zero self-consciousness. She wore a white blouse and jeans, a plain outfit he decided looked very good on her athletic frame.

"Vinci!" Dante snapped his fingers.

With a shock he realized everyone was now staring at him.

"Yes, sir?"

"I said could you please get Ms. Falco here an espresso?"

“Yes, sir.”

"No, thank you," she said. "I don't need another one. I've already had enough this morning.”

Marco looked at Dante. Dante nodded imperceptibly.

Then Ali Falco walked straight toward Marco, stopping centimeters from him, bathing him in her floral scent as she wrestled a picture off the wall next to him—the picture he’d noticed before, with Colombo and a man at the graduation from the academy.

“Look at this,” she said, putting the picture on Colombo’s desk. “Look at my father’s holster.”

Colombo didn't look at the photograph. Instead, he looked at the captain and mayor. “I’m sorry, gentlemen.”

“Listen,” the mayor said. “I am headed up to the mountains now with Gloria. Clearly you are on track here with your investigation, you don't need me to tell you that. I'll leave you to discuss this matter, and I'll be in touch when I get back for an update."

The mayor walked out, but not before putting a hand on Ali's shoulder, a sympathetic look creasing his face.

"Uh, me, too," Captain Carlotta stood. "I have a coffee meeting later this morning anyway. We can resume this meeting later today."

Marco walked them to the door and let them out, then looked to Dante again. Again, Dante nodded imperceptibly.

Marco shut the door and took up his place along the wall again.

"This is Dr. Vespucci, Ali," Colombo said. "He's the regional coroner, and head of our forensics department."

"I know him. I met him yesterday when I saw my father."

"And this is inspector Marco Vinci."

She nodded, only skirting her gaze on Marco before looking at Vespucci. "Did you test for gunshot residue on my father's hands?"

Vespucci nodded. "Of course."

"And?"

"And we found gunshot residue."

"On which hand?"

"His right."

"Your father..." Colombo held the picture at arm's length, staring at it with a confused expression "...shot with his left hand."

She turned to the second lieutenant with excitement that hardened her eyes. "Yes. Exactly!"

The room went silent. Colombo slowly set down the picture, his face telegraphing his racing thoughts.

Marco flicked his eyes to Dante, who had a similar, revelatory look on his face.

"The blood spatter was on the left wall." The woman—Ali, Marco reminded himself—spoke quickly. "He was sitting on the couch, the gun was in his right hand. The hole in his head, also in the right side. But he was left-handed!"

"He used the standard magazine release on his gun, even though he was lefty." Colombo's eyes were unblinking. "I used to make fun of him, telling him to switch the damn thing over to the other side. But he liked using his finger."

Colombo suddenly stood up, turning to the window.

More silence ensued as they watched Colombo think. When the second lieutenant turned around, his face had taken an ashen hue. "I can't believe I didn't notice." He looked at Dante, almost accusingly. "How did we not notice?"

Ali sat down.

Dante shook his head. "I..." He was clearly at a loss for words. His face went red. He stood for a moment longer, then sat in the chair next to Ali, placing a hand on her back.

Marco crept his way closer to the desk, keeping his distance. Vespucci was no longer leaning against the wall, a riveted expression frozen on his face.

"He shoots with his left hand," she said quietly. "Not his right. That means he was killed. He left a half-cut onion on the counter. He was in the middle of making dinner. There was sauce in the pan. Pasta on the counter. It's not natural, especially for my father, to stop the process of preparing food to do anything.

"And then there're the two shots. Why would he shoot the television and then himself? Clearly somebody shot him, then placed the gun in his hand to put the GSR there." She turned and looked at Vespucci. "Is there a way to prove if he shot once or twice with his hand? If somebody had placed the gun in his hand and only shot once?"

Vespucci blinked out of his shock. "No. There would be no

way to ascertain that much information from a GSR test. I'm sorry."

"Did you check his cell phone records?" She turned to Dante.

"We got into his phone. Which led us to see his outgoing text messages."

Marco cocked his head at the way Dante said the words.

"He texted you, though." Dante spoke haltingly. "Didn't he?"

What text? Marco thought. He exchanged another glance with Vespucci, who was obviously thinking the same thing.

Dante answered their silent question. "He sent you a message Friday night, right about the same time we...Dr. Vespucci...calculated to be the time of death."

"He did." She nodded, all but ignoring the point. "The stove was turned off, right? Otherwise, that sauce would have been burned to a crisp. So, if he killed himself, he was in the middle of making food. And he stops. Turns off everything. Sits down on the couch. Texts me. Then he shoots the television, with his off hand, and shoots himself with his off hand." She scoffed, sitting back in her chair. "That's what we're going to believe happened here?"

Dante put up his hands, defensively, like he was warding off an attacking lion. "Ali. If I may play devil's advocate for a moment."

"Okay. What?"

"I didn't know your father all that well. I was a little later to the force, as you know. But now that I think about it, your father was an ambidextrous man, wasn't he?"

"He threw and kicked with his right side," Colombo said, turning back toward them. His voice was wistful, his gaze distant. "He wrote with his left hand. He shot with his left hand. He used to play guitar—both his hands flying on the fretboard. He was a freak of nature the way he could use both sides for things."

"Could he have," Dante shook his head, "I don't know, had the gun sitting next to his right hand. Say he saw something that angered him on the television, and he fired at the screen?"

Ali shook her head.

Dante's hands were still held up. "I'm just trying to..." His sentence trailed off.

"You're trying to what? Argue my father killed himself?"

Dante lowered his hands, his voice rising. "I'm trying to not instill false hope in a situation where we're dealing with a small amount of evidence."

She sat back, folding her arms on her chest.

Colombo held up a hand to Dante. "It is suspicious, Ali," he said.

Ali spoke again, this time her voice low. "To me it seems he was killed. He was made to sit on the couch, forced to sit in the middle of making his meal, and then he was shot in the head. Then the person placed the gun in his right hand and shot the television to put the residue on his hand. And then, to add even more credibility to the suicide, they took his phone and texted me. Did he have a security pin number to unlock his phone?"

Dante nodded, turning to Vespucci.

Vespucci cleared his throat. "Yes. I cracked it using a software we have."

"So he was forced to unlock his phone at gunpoint. The killer texted, and then shot him." Ali sat back, arms still crossed, looking satisfied with the explanation.

Nobody spoke.

"When was the last time you've spoken to your father?" Colombo asked.

She shot him an accusing look, softening her expression as she took a deep breath. "I don't know."

"Since you left?" Dante asked.

"About that long, yeah. Why?"

"Did you do a fingerprint check on the phone?" Colombo asked Vespucci, changing the subject.

"No, sir. But we did a thorough check on the gun and all its parts, the cartridges."

"And?"

"His own prints were everywhere."

"It's the service weapon he's always had," Ali said. "Of course it would have his prints on it. Any smart killer would wear gloves."

The anguish in her voice cut Marco deeply. During the last bout of silence, he had found himself thinking of his own father. His dad was the reason he sacrificed so much to rise to his position as capo inspector at such a young age—to see pride on his father's face again when he spoke about his son, like he used to when Marco played soccer.

"Your father worked for the Guardia di Finanza?" Marco asked, knowing he was starting down a delicate path, one that could, as Dante had put it, could instill false hope into the situation. One that might get him in big trouble with Dante and Colombo.

She looked at him with weary eyes. "Yes. Down in Rome."

"What kind of work was he doing?"

Ali shook her head. "I can't say. Like I said, I haven't talked to him."

Marco narrowed his eyes.

"What are you getting at, inspector?" Dante asked, his voice edged with warning.

"Well, since I'm not sure what he was involved in, I can't really say."

"Well say it anyway." She lashed him with her words.

Colombo gestured for him to continue speaking.

"The Guardia works with smuggling, corruption, mafia and Camorra-run criminal operations, keeping tabs on a lot of shady individuals and organizations throughout the world. It would not be the first fake suicide we've seen over the last few decades, or even the last year. Think of the Swiss financier, what was his name?"

"Phillipe Blanc," Dante said.

Marco nodded.

Ali's eyes narrowed. She turned to Colombo.

Colombo's chest rose and fell. "If that theory is correct, if somebody has faked your father's suicide because of his work involving the mafia or the Camorra or any number of extremely dangerous organizations out there, they have task forces for this, well-trained individuals without families. Individuals who don't just believe they may die in their line of work, they expect it."

"Then we tell them our theory," she said.

Colombo put his hands on the desk. "That's all we have, Ali. A theory. You know how this works. We need evidence."

"Then find it!" She picked up the photograph off Colombo's desk and threw it on the floor.

Marco took a step forward, watching as the glass inside the frame shattered and spread across the rug.

She bent over, brushed the glass aside, plucked out the photo, crumpled it, and put it in the trash.

"You don't deserve to hang this on your wall."

She stormed to the door, opened it, and marched out.

Marco stood stunned, watching Colombo and Dante, who both sat motionless. Vespucci's eyebrows arched to his hairline.

"Stop her." Colombo looked up at him.

"Excuse me?"

"Stop her!"

9

Ali ran down the stairwell, her feet slapping on the terrazzo stairs.

She felt a slip of liquid on her index finger. It was bleeding, leaving a trail of blood droplets behind her.

She reached the ground floor and punched her hip into the door, popping it open.

Back out in the parking lot, she sucked on her finger, spit out the blood, seeing the spatter on the wall next to her father as it splashed onto the asphalt.

The Carabinieri headquarters was on a rise north and west of town, the trees thick enough they blocked out the view of the lake, but not so dense to stop a breeze flowing down from the Alps. The breeze dried the sweat from her forehead, burrowing into her shirt and cooling her overheated body.

Forget them. She could do some investigating on her own.

How, though? The question slowed her down as she walked. Damn it. The rage was wearing off, and she felt stupid for the way she'd left the office. She'd come for support from her father's former colleagues, and she'd gotten the reaction she had hoped for.

Why had she stormed out of there? What had she expected? For them to agree without playing devil's advocate? They had reacted like the two world-class inspectors she'd always known them to be.

She continued walking, pulling out her keys and pressing the unlock button, swerving toward the chirp of her Citroen, wondering if she should turn around and go back up. Because the truth was, she had nowhere else to go. There was no going back to Siena. At least not now. Not if her father had truly been murdered.

"Ms. Falco!"

She turned and was surprised to see the good-looking young inspector running out the door. He waved his hand overhead, jogging toward her.

What was his name? She'd been too worked up to pay attention.

She stopped and waited, watching the man relax, slowing from a jog to a walk. He moved with the grace of an athlete, slightly favoring one leg. He was taller than average, his body fit beneath a dark modern suit.

"Ms. Falco," he said as he slowed. He had short, spiky, dark hair and tanned skin, with blue-green eyes the color of a Mediterranean grotto. One of the dangerous types of men.

He stopped a few meters away. "Ms. Falco, I'm sorry. Colombo sent me to stop you."

She shrugged, hiding her relief with indifference. "And now you've stopped me."

"He wants you to come back inside."

"Why?"

"I'm not sure."

She eyed the man. "What's your name again?"

"Inspector Vinci. Marco Vinci."

"I'm Ali."

Marco nodded.

"So, what, are you the lead investigator or something?"

"I'm on the team of investigators. Marshal Dante leads everything."

"Right."

Marco stood patiently, watching her. The wind whipped past them, bringing a scent of his cologne to her nose. Masculine, but not overbearing.

"What do you think?" she asked.

"What do I think?" He shrugged. "I wasn't at the scene, mind you. But I think your ideas have some merit. If your father didn't shoot with his right hand, I think it would be strange for him to use it while shooting himself. I mean, it wouldn't feel natural for him. The habit would be to use his left hand, so he would use his subconscious mind to pick up the gun and shoot with that hand. His conscious mind would be too preoccupied with the decision of whether to kill himself. Maybe. I mean, I'm no psychologist."

She looked at him, feeling more conviction than ever with his explanation. "Thank you," she said.

"For what?"

"Ali!" Colombo came out of the building's side exit, waving his hand over his head. "Wait!"

Marco stepped aside as they waited for the second lieutenant to reach them.

This was the first time Ali had gotten a good look at Stefano Colombo in almost ten years. She had spent her childhood with the man. He used to come to their home to visit at least once per week.

He'd always been a big individual, at least a few kilos overweight when she'd known him, but his gait now was slower, wobblier than she remembered, telling of too many brioches with his coffee, too many desserts with his grappa, too little exercise in his days.

"Thank you, Marco." Colombo arrived, out of breath. "Please give us a moment."

"Yes, sir." Marco nodded to Ali and walked toward the building.

Dante came outside, keeping his distance, and stood with Inspector Vinci.

"Ali." Colombo looked at her.

She lifted her chin, waiting.

He looked past her with glistening eyes, staring into the woods off the edge of the parking lot. "I was home when I heard the news about your father. All I could think about was you. And how difficult this..." He looked at her, his eyes shimmering with building tears, lip quivering. "You've lived with so much pain since your mother's death."

She looked off into the trees as well.

"I'm just so worried about you, Ali. I'm so sorry for not noticing your father's shooting hand. I can't believe I didn't see it earlier. I'd like to think...shit, maybe once this other godforsaken case cleared up...I'd like to think I would have noticed it, too. I'm just worried, is all. About giving you hope if there is none to be had." Colombo shook his head. "I guess because I have seen your father numerous times over the years. And he was also in a lot of pain. Just as much as you. In pain for losing his wife, and then for losing you."

"But enough to kill himself?"

They stood in silence for a beat.

"If he killed himself then he killed himself. But if he didn't? Then we have to know. I have to know, Stefano."

Colombo nodded. "So do I, Ali. So do I. And I'm glad you came to us."

He sighed and took out a pack of Monte Carlo cigarettes and

put one in his mouth. He saw she was looking and tipped the pack toward her.

She shook her head.

He lit the cigarette and took a drag. "The question is, what are we going to do about it?"

"We talk to the people he was working with in Rome. We figure out what he was up to."

"And if it's connected with the mafia? The Camorra?"

His question was enough to make her insides twist. "Then we step aside and let the DIA do what they do."

As Colombo had mentioned, the antimafia investigation division had agents who had signed on for such dangerous work. Colombo had a daughter Ali's age, and Ali could see the gears churning in his head, concerned about the safety of his family.

"But if it was them," she said, "then we don't let their work go unnoticed."

Colombo stared at her, sucking a deep drag, letting the smoke trail out of his nostrils. She remembered watching him do that as a little girl, wondering if he did it consciously.

Colombo raised a hand and waved over Dante and Vinci.

The two men began walking over, and Ali took the opportunity to watch Daniele Dante. Back when Dante had been a plainclothes inspector like her father, he'd consistently outdressed those around him. When Ali had been in high school, she had complimented him on his fashion sense. That interest she had shown in his dress had somehow led to a level of trust and friendship between them. While her father and Colombo would be locked in a political argument or some other alcohol-fueled fiery conversation, Ali and Dante would have conversations of their own, often covering topics that would have been much too scandalous for her father's ears. She had always wondered if he was gay, more suspected it, but had never asked. Either way, it didn't matter, other than she had always felt comfortable around the man.

Now that Dante wore the marshal's uniform, with the gold-buttoned blue jacket, pants, and leather boots, he still moved with the same fluid grace of old, as if he were wearing one of his tailored Venetian suits.

"It's clear what we have to do," Colombo spoke to his two men. "I want the villa combed top to bottom again, this time with Vespucci and his team assuming we're looking at murder."

Dante nodded, looking Ali in the eye with a determined glare.

"I want to know what he was working on professionally," Colombo continued. "If it was mafia then we'll step aside. None of us will be involved in the case going forward. Understood?"

Ali nodded. Dante and Marco nodded.

Colombo pulled out his phone. "I'll need to speak to your superior down in Siena about you participating on this case."

"He'll be fine with it," she said.

"We'll let him be the judge of that."

"If he's not fine with it, then I'll quit. Then you can put me on the case without any trouble."

Colombo snorted. "A civilian on the case? That would be more trouble for me."

She opened her mouth to protest, but Colombo kept speaking, voice raised.

"I'll call him, and I'll smooth over everything. You're on the case, don't worry. Now give me his name and phone number."

She gave the contact information for the Siena police headquarters and Colombo entered it into his phone.

"Vinci," Colombo said, "you'll go to Rome with Ali, and to the offices of the Guardia di Finanza where Dino Falco worked. I'll make calls and make sure you'll have access to places and people for inquiry."

Marco nodded. His eyes darted to Ali and back, appearing to her like the idea shook him to his core. "Yes, sir."

"Is there a problem?" Colombo asked.

"No, sir. But you did want me to investigate our victim's next of kin."

"We'll put Tedesco on it. Not to worry."

"Yes, sir."

Marco Vinci still looked hesitant.

"I could go alone," Ali said. "He doesn't have to come. I have my own vehicle with me." She gestured to her Citroen.

"I'm in charge of this investigation and I say he does. If we are dealing with murder, then I want this man with you. This is your vehicle?"

"It is."

"Vinci will drive his car."

"Yes, sir," Vinci said.

She examined her car with a frown.

Colombo dropped his cigarette and stepped on it, apparently extinguishing the conversation with the gesture, because he walked away. "Keep me posted on everything."

She watched the smoke drifting up from the mangled paper and filter.

Marco remained with Dante, watching her. Dante stepped up and wrapped her in a hug.

She resisted at first, leaving her arms by her sides, then she wrapped them around the stiff cloth of his jacket, squeezing her old friend. The longer he held her the more her eyes welled up, until she found herself dripping tears onto his shoulders.

"Don't worry, Ali." Dante held her at arm's length, his gentle eyes staring hard into hers.

"Thank you," she said.

Marco was looking at the ground, shuffling his feet a few meters away.

Dante stepped aside. "I'll let you two plan your trip. I'll head inside. Please keep us posted, Ali. You have my number, don't you?"

She nodded, remembering the day Dante had given it to her before she'd driven down to Ancona, guilt suddenly gripping her for never using it.

"Then call me if you need anything." He turned on the heels of his boots and walked away, leaving her standing with Marco.

Marco peered at his cell phone, slipped it into his pocket, then forced a smile.

"So," she said.

"So."

"What time do we leave?"

They decided leaving the next morning was best.

"Okay. I'll see you then," he said, extending his arm like he was trying to keep the most distance between them as possible while still shaking her hand.

"See you then," she said, watching him walk away.

She went to her car, opened it, and sat down in the boiling hot air of the cab. Reaching for the gear shift, she winced in pain, raising her hand to look at her finger. There was a two-centimeter-long slice in the skin, still oozing blood. It wasn't dire by any means but would need a plastic bandage.

Putting the finger in her mouth again, she turned and looked at the Carabinieri building, catching sight of Marco disappearing into the front entrance. She saw a figure looking out a fourth-floor window. As she leaned toward her passenger window to get a better look at who it was, the figure turned and disappeared into the smoky glare that hid the interior of the building. After another few moments of staring at the spot, the figure failed to return.

She sat back, looking at herself in the rearview mirror. Was she seeing things? Not just the figure, who was probably a man looking out at the lake for a few moments in between meetings, but with everything. Was all this a farce? A lie constructed in her own mind, so she didn't have to face the truth that her father shot himself in the head?

Eleven years ago, her mother had driven to a mountainside parking lot for an unknown reason. And on that rainy night her vehicle had come out of gear and rolled over the edge of the slope, careening down until it started tumbling, thrashing down until it came to an abrupt halt on rocks a hundred meters below. Ali chose to hold the truth that her mother's death was an accident, because the other truth—the one that involved her father throwing her mother to the ground, and the dejected, defeated look in her mother's eye as she drove past Ali for the last time—was too hard to face. The truth that her mother had given up.

Was that what she was doing here with her father?

She focused her eyes again out the windshield. Pressing the clutch, she turned the key and shifted into gear.

"I need a cigarette."

10

Ali set her canvas duffle bag on the cobblestone sidewalk and looked up and down the street. Silvery puddles on the stone and asphalt reflected the pink sky above. The air was heavy, blotchy clouds hanging low, outlined with color from the rising sun.

Her cell phone lock screen read 5:57 am, a few minutes before Inspector Marco Vinci was supposed to pick her up outside the apartment building. She felt spry and fresh, having fallen asleep early and woken up an hour ago with a shower, and more importantly going with water last night instead of wine.

She was dreading the drive, which would take six and a half hours. If the map of Italy was shaped like a knee-high boot, Como was at the top and Rome was in the middle of the shin. About three-quarters of the way there they would be passing through the Tuscany region, and her hometown of Siena.

Maybe it was a better idea for them to drive down in separate cars as far as Siena, where she could drop her Citroen, and then ride the rest of the way into Rome in Marco's car.

That way she would have most of the time to herself.

And then what? She still needed to come back to Como and deal with her father's body. And if they really did figure out her father had been murdered? Colombo was overseeing this investigation, and he was here in Como.

The real issue was what six and a half hours in the car was going to be like. For the few minutes she'd known Inspector Marco Vinci she knew he was intelligent, compassionate to her situation, and definitely good-looking. She also knew it only took a second for all that to change. One grossly egotistical comment, one tone deaf remark and the whole trip would be torture.

You're driving down to Rome with this man, Ali. Just relax.

She eased the tension in her shoulders, looking up at the clouds skating past, listening to the city of Como awaken. The sound of bottles clashing loudly echoed through the streets as they were poured from a recycle container into the collection van. A few cars revved. Birds whistled in the trees above her.

At 6:05 am a black Audi S6 sedan came around the corner, swung a U-turn, and parked in front of her, the wheels crackling to a stop. The exterior of the vehicle shone like obsidian from the roof to the rubber tires. She couldn't see through the tinted windows, but she didn't have to wait long for the driver's side door to open.

Marco stood up into view. "Buongiorno."

"Buongiorno," she said.

He checked his watch. "I'm sorry I'm late."

He rounded the front of the vehicle and reached out for her bag.

"It's okay, I can get it."

"You can put it in the back seat." He opened the rear door for her and walked around to the other side of the car, slipping back behind the wheel.

He smelled like soap and a spritz of his now familiar

cologne. The car smelled like fancy new cars do.

She put the bag down in the back seat and got in front.

"Seatbelt on, please."

She put it on.

"Here we go." He let off the brake and accelerated hard down the road.

Marco drove aggressively, cutting in and out of traffic circles with smooth acceleration, braking for obstacles an instant before Ali would have, generally keeping his eyes glued to the road.

The radio was turned to a pop station, the music at a low, non-confrontational volume. All in all, he was doing well so far. But it had only been five minutes.

He smiled and looked at her. "In this country, you never know when somebody will show up."

She frowned. "Excuse me?"

He gestured to the clock, which now read 6:07 am.

"Oh, yeah. I was beginning to wonder."

"I personally don't like to leave people wondering, and I was glad you were waiting out front. Punctuality. It's a lost art in this country."

"I'm not sure it ever existed in this country."

He smiled, keeping his eyes on the road.

"You drive an Audi," she said, "You're into being on time. You must be part German?"

He laughed. "Italian through and through. In fact, my family is Roman, going back too many generations to count. At least, that's what my father tells us."

She nodded, looking out the window, trying to block out the things her father used to say. They were all bullshit anyway.

They passed through dense trees, alongside lush green terraced hills. Fog hung low to the ground, set aglow from the sun above, making her squint.

"How about you?" Marco asked.

"Where's my family from?"

His face dropped. "I'm sorry. Not a very good topic, is it."

"No. It's okay. My father was from Bergamo, my mother from Colorado."

"Colorado? Where is that?"

"The United States."

"Ah! Colorado! Cowboys and Rocky Mountains. That Colorado."

His enthusiasm made her smile.

"How in the world did your mother end up here?" he asked.

"She went to medical school in Massachusetts, came to Italy for a post-graduate program, where she worked with an NGO—a women's health clinic here in Como—and she met my father." Ali shrugged. "And she never went back to the states."

Marco smiled, still keeping his eyes on the road, still keeping the wheels between the lines, still wasting no time, still impressing her, if she was honest. Basso had once remarked she should have been a Formula One racer, but Marco Vinci genuinely had skills when it came to driving.

"And where is your mother now?"

"She's dead."

Marco looked at her, and the car swerved into the oncoming lane. "Shit." He corrected before she had to tell him. "I'm...so sorry, Ali. I did not know that."

"It's okay. She died in a car crash my last year of high school."

They rode in tense silence for a few minutes, Marco weaving the car down to the A9, where they slipped through the automatic toll lane and upped the speed, heading south toward Milan.

Six hours to go.

She had been casing the interior of the car, noting it was

just as clean inside as out, freshly vacuumed and smelling of Marco's scent, which was decidedly, thankfully, tasteful.

"You approve?" Marco asked, catching her in the act.

"It's a nice vehicle. You must be making the big bucks over there in the Carabinieri."

When he remained silent, she felt like she'd said something wrong. And she probably had, because making the big bucks at his rank and station couldn't have been possible, and they both knew it. Which meant the money was coming from somewhere else. Was he bothered with that fact?

A loud tone blared through the speakers, causing her to jump in her seat.

"Geez," he said, pulling his cell phone out of his pocket. "Sorry, it's a call."

The dashboard touchscreen read the name *Valentina*, a phone number listing next to it. A photograph of a smiling face, a stunningly beautiful woman with wavy brown hair cascading over her bare shoulders, also came onscreen.

Marco tapped his finger on the screen, then tapped his phone and put it to his ear.

"Where are you?" The woman's voice surrounded them, thanks to the Audi's many speakers.

Marco looked at the cell phone, tapping some more. The car swerved into the next lane, and this time Marco didn't notice as they came close to a car.

"Careful!" Ali called out, reaching for the wheel.

Marco dropped the phone and corrected back into his lane.

"What's going on?" Valentina's voice demanded.

"Nothing," he said. "What's happening?"

"Is that her?"

Ali turned to look out the passenger window, cocking an eyebrow.

"Yes, that was Inspector Ali Falco. You're on speaker phone right now."

"Ciao," Ali said.

"Oh, ciao. Have a good trip." The words were stripped of enthusiasm. "Call me when you stop for coffee or something."

The radio came back on.

Marco pocketed his phone, looking like he might jump out of the car at one hundred twenty kilometers per hour.

They were rounding the western outskirts of Milan, where the land along the Po River valley was board flat as far as the eye could see, which was to say was not very far, as torn blankets of fog still clung to the ground. The silence that had descended into the car was thicker than the outside mist. Five and a half hours.

They passed a sign reading *Autogrill—2 km*.

"Coffee?" he asked.

She smiled, nodding. "Now we're talking."

The mega-convenience store and restaurant known as Autogrill stood on stilts and spanned the traffic lanes that slid past below, serving both directions of traffic with pastries, coffee, food worthy of a Michelin star, and other delicacies and trinkets sourced from the local region.

Marco parked and they went inside through automatic doors, then up the stairs to the bar, which hovered above all lanes of the autostrada below.

"Espresso?" Marco asked. "You get the table, I'll get this round."

"Cappuccino, please."

She walked over and stood at a bar height table, waiting for Marco to navigate his way through the line and return with her drink.

The news on the nearby television was playing the day's biggest stories, and she was startled to see aerial footage of her childhood villa. Video showed a white van and two men wheeling a gurney out the front door of the villa, her father's corpse concealed within a body bag. Text streamed below: *Death on Lake Como. Former Carabinieri inspector commits suicide in his Lake Como villa over the weekend.*

More video, this time shaky, zoomed-in shots taken on the ground of polizia officers, a pair of plainclothes inspectors speaking to uniformed Carabinieri she recognized as Dante and Colombo.

"Here you go." Marco placed her cappuccino down.

"Thank you."

He glanced up at the television.

"It's plastered everywhere," she said.

He nodded, handing over a packet of sugar. "I know. I saw. Oh yeah, wait..." He walked away to the counter, picked up two plates topped with brioches and brought them over. "I got a chocolate and a plain."

"Plain please."

He put the plate in front of her and sat down, his eyes glancing at another television behind her. She saw the footage had switched to the case of the young woman pulled from the ground above Como.

She read the ticker. "You still haven't identified her?"

"We have. But we're not telling."

"Oh." She took a bite of the plain brioche and sipped her cappuccino, the two tastes melding together so perfectly that the troubles of the world, of her world, disappeared for a few moments.

White-clad forensic workers were shown taking pictures, picking through the soil, the ground around them stripped clean of the usual dense foliage that choked the forested mountainsides above Como. She knew from the articles that the cell phone company had been clearing the area for another cell tower.

"We have a positive ID through dental records, but she's not in any of the missing persons databases."

She frowned. "She was never reported missing? That's strange."

"Yeah." He lowered his cup from his mouth, eyeing the screen.

"What do you make of that?" she asked.

"My theory is those people who could have reported her missing didn't want to report her missing."

"Her family?" Ali asked.

Marco shrugged.

"Or she was checked out of the system," Ali said. "And nobody noticed she was gone. Or, rather, they thought she had just run away."

Marco nodded slowly. "Good point."

Now they were showing footage of Dante talking into a bushel of microphones. Behind the marshal stood Marco, standing at attention with arms clasped behind his back, flashes from cameras lighting his face.

The footage cut off and it went back to a newscaster in the studio.

"I have to make a phone call." Marco tipped his cup and wiped his mouth.

She nodded. *Valentina.*

"I'll see you out there." He left his cup and napkin and walked away, already skimming his cell phone screen.

She sucked down her drink and finished her brioche, taking her time. As she stood up, she checked her watch. Five hours to go.

11

Marco looked over again at the woman sleeping in the passenger seat of his car. Her dark hair was pulled into a loose ponytail behind her head, a few strands draping down and over her jaw, fluttering in the air coming out of his vents. Her eyelashes were very long, resting on the tops of her rose-tinted cheeks.

Keep your eyes on the road. And what are you doing? You're engaged to be married in a month.

Even so, he snuck another look. She had smooth tanned skin, a slight wrinkle in her forehead, as if she was having a bad dream. She probably was, with all she'd been through. To lose both parents, and both so horrifically.

It was a lapse of judgement not to look into her more thoroughly before the trip. He would have learned about her mother, and not put his foot in his mouth. There was just too much going on right now, with the wedding, and the case, and now this woman sitting in his passenger seat.

His eyes traveled down to the rest of her body, and its supple movement as the vehicle swayed. Her fingers were slender, hands loosely clasped together on her denim-covered legs.

No rings. She had that same scent as yesterday in the office, and now it filled the cab of the Audi, Valentina's scent not even detectable anymore.

He ripped his eyes off her, concentrating back on the road, shaking his head at the vile thoughts going through his brain.

You're engaged. To a beautiful woman.

An enraging, annoying, beautiful woman.

The road in front of him disappeared as he ruminated. Ever since he'd asked her to marry him, Valentina had turned into another human being, one he was having doubts about now. He'd been having the same thought for a few days—maybe they were just too different.

Valentina's parents were of and about money, and all the trappings it provided. They were well-respected, her mother in real estate development and her father in engineering. As far as Marco could tell, both of Valentina's parents had spent a lifetime of aggressively and successfully accumulating power, friendships in high places, and wealth.

Valentina had grown up in that environment, learning the ways of the elite, wearing the dresses, attending balls in villas along the shores of Lake Como. She had recently told him her father had set her up on a date with a politician's son, which had sparked a relationship that had lasted for three years.

Eventually, she'd left her boyfriend, or he'd left her, she didn't like to talk about it. But Marco did know, that after the relationship with the parliament member's son, Valentina had found Marco and pursued him with a fervor he'd never encountered in a woman before. He found it flattering, especially because she was so beautiful. She could have been a movie or television star if she wanted to. Her father had the connections with all the Mediaset and Rai production divisions, too.

Marco's own parents couldn't have been more different, both schoolteachers—schoolteachers who lived on modest wages, who lived in a small apartment in the outskirts of Rome, and not a palatial waterside villa.

Money had always been a topic of concern in the Vinci household, an idea that sparked debates and arguments between his mother and father, then Marco and his sister as they became old enough to shoulder some of the financial burden.

After his soccer injury, his parents had wanted him to go into banking, taking a job his father had lined up through a family friend in Lugano, a job that guaranteed money and prestige. But somehow the tearing of multiple ligaments in his knee that day had also allowed him to break away from his family's hypnotic obsession with money, or lack thereof, and pursue what he wanted to do—to be a cop. So he went into the military, attending the academy in Bologna, and now, here he was, doing what he wanted to do. And proving his father wrong.

His initial attraction to Valentina had been because she was a kindred spirit, also deviating from the obvious path her parents had set out in front of her, deciding she wasn't cut out for foreign relations and political science classes and all the inter-familial posturing. She was more interested in the simple passions she'd nurtured since she was a child: painting, drawing, and working with clay.

She had been a great artist and a passionate, loving human being.

But her love for art seemed to be dying a slow death, and with it her loving nature. And it had all started with Marco proposing to her last year.

Soon after their engagement, her daily painting sessions, or the time she'd spend every morning with her sketch pad, were suddenly no longer part of her routine. That's when the money had begun trickling into their lives, from her parents' bank accounts to theirs.

He had been angry when he'd learned about that first deposit into their account, the money growing from a four-figure, worrying, sum, to a five-figure astonishing number of Euro stretching their account by the seams. When he saw that money, he saw his father's approving nod in his imagination, and he felt like he was selling out. Like he was becoming the banker.

And Valentina? She had been happy, relieved, that she didn't have to worry about money ever again. Valentina had always been a strong woman, and he'd never gotten far by putting his foot down on issues, so he watched and waited, wondering if the money might have a positive effect on her art. Perhaps he'd been looking at it all wrong, and the source of money wasn't important. It was more important that they would be free to do what they loved in life.

But that's not what happened. Instead, she had taken a job at the Como Italian embassy office, working long hours with foreign men in expensive suits, their bank accounts making Marco and Val's artificially inflated bank accounts look like coin purses in comparison.

And then there was this car, which he loved, and which he would have bought in a heartbeat had it been with his own hard-earned cash.

His hands were sweating on the wheel.

He relaxed his jaw and rolled his neck, working out a kink in his shoulder.

He'd seen the calculations going on inside Ali Falco's brain as she asked about the car earlier. He realized now he'd never get over driving this lie. He would sell it when he got home.

His jaw tensed again.

And now this wedding. Damn this wedding. They may as well have been royalty with how much preparation and money was going into the ceremony.

He took a deep breath and looked out the window at Tuscany, the beautiful rolling green hills covered in wildflowers, stone agricultural buildings built by the common man hundreds of years ago perched on high outlooks or tucked among the tree-filled seams of the crinkled landscape.

Ali stirred, rescuing him from his thoughts.

He watched her wake up, stretching her arms overhead.

"Get some rest?" he asked.

"I think. Where are we?"

"We have about thirty minutes until we hit the outer edges of Rome."

"My God. How long have I been sleeping?"

"Two and a half hours."

She shook her head. "I'm sorry."

"For what?" He smiled.

"For not keeping you company on the drive."

"Don't worry about it. I had my thoughts."

Ali straightened, pulling down the sun visor and eyeing herself in the mirror. She had a mark on her face from where she'd been leaning up against the window. She rubbed it, trying to usher the blood back.

She felt mildly horrified that she'd been sitting there sleeping for all that time, probably drooling all over herself—she checked the door, she hadn't been, as far as she could tell.

"And how were your thoughts?" she asked, remembering what Marco had just said.

He shrugged, his face looking like he was back in them, and they weren't too pleasant.

She checked her watch. "Twelve-thirty. What time are we scheduled for meetings at the Guardia?"

"Thirty minutes."

She looked out at the thickening traffic, the buildings gathered in dense clumps and multiplying, the smog darkening the sky ahead. The tentacles of Rome had reached out to where they were.

"Do you think we'll make it?"

"I have confidence." He seemed to take that as a challenge, accelerating the car and passing a line of traffic in the left lane.

She felt refreshed after the rest, after such a strange last couple of days, with too much alcohol swimming in her system, too much stress, and too little sleep, but the uncertainty of what they were walking into was getting to her.

What would they find out? What had her father been doing? She remembered the final words she'd ever spoken to her father.

Either way. Accident or no accident, it's all your fault. I don't want to ever speak to you again. Stubbornly, Ali and her father had both honored her emotionally charged wishes for eleven years.

My God. Had they let that much time go by without either of them reaching out to one another? It was only a two-and-a-half-hour drive from Siena to Rome, where her father had relocated, and no time at all for a phone call or a text.

I'm sorry.

She shook her head, thinking of the text again, and the wound to his head, and the uneaten and half-prepared meal. What would they find down here? She had the feeling they were walking in the dark, straight towards a pack of waiting lions.

"You okay?"

She nodded. "Yeah."

"Can you pull up the directions on your phone?"

"Yes." She took out her phone, happy to be distracted by the here and now.

"I told you, I'm from here, you know," he said.

"So you said. And you need directions?" She smiled.

He smiled back. "It's a large city. There are numerous Guardia di Finanza buildings scattered across the seven-hills of Rome."

"I was only kidding."

They rode in comfortable silence for a beat.

"Where's Valentina from?"

"Bergamo."

She nodded, gazing out the window, kicking herself for asking the question.

"How about you?" he asked.

"How about me, what?"

"Do you have a boyfriend down in Siena?"

"No. Not at the moment." Or any moment within the last eleven years, she thought. Only the occasional alcohol-induced hookup.

More silence.

Ali reached over and twisted the radio knob, finding the song "Attenti al Lupo." She and her mother used to blast the song in the villa, singing at the top of their lungs, driving her father outside. "Do you mind?"

"I love this song." Marco reached over and turned it up.

She smiled, leaning back in her seat, the tension melting away, the sun streaming into the window feeling good on her skin, counteracting the cold air blasting out of the vents.

They spent the next twenty-five minutes finding their way to her father's branch of the Guardia di Finanza offices of Rome, Ali navigating on her phone, Marco following her directions, Ali trying to keep ahead two or three moves so they wouldn't get lost in the labyrinth of the ancient city streets, Marco following her orders with precise aggression.

Once they finally found the location, they began circling the area in search of a parking space.

Ali had known there were several branches of the Guardia di Finanza in Rome, having done an internet search the night before. Some of the buildings were ornately designed and decorated, lined with palm trees and gardens, terraced architecture covered in tasteful stone facades. Her father's building was not one of those places. The structure was drab, with salmon-stucco covering the exterior walls—eight stories of a box-shaped design containing a hundred windows, each dangling an air conditioning unit over pedestrians passing by on busy streets below.

"There!" Ali pointed at an open parking spot.

Marco slid into the opening front-end first, then straightened the vehicle out with a few moves and shut off the engine.

Ali got out and shut her door, stretching her legs and arms over her head.

The air was hot and humid, smog laden. Her skin itched. She straightened her shirt and pants, already feeling like she needed a shower after the long drive and now bathing in the Roman air.

They walked down the sidewalk along the building, taking in the space where her father had spent the last eleven years of his career.

The scents of concrete, asphalt, and exhaust perfumed the air, while the jangle of glassware from a nearby café punctuated the atmosphere. Cars sped past, the occasional honk of a horn echoing off the buildings.

They walked to the corner of the building and to a much busier street that ran along the front, joining throngs of pedestrians.

Marco led them up a long set of stairs to a pair of tall doors, waiting for her to enter first. She walked inside past him, and into an arctic pool of air that made her skin rise with goosebumps.

"My name is Inspector Ali Falco, Polizia di Stato." She laid her credentials on the reception counter.

"Marco Vinci," Marco said, putting his next to hers. "Carabinieri."

A stiff man dressed in an even stiffer uniform sat behind a glass partition. Bored looking to the point he appeared to be sleepwalking, he raked the creds back and checked them, typed on his keyboard, and slapped them back on the counter. He picked up a phone and ducked to the side, speaking softly into the phone.

He hung up, then pointed at the plastic chairs along the wall.

They sat.

"He seems nice," Marco said.

She crossed her legs and got comfortable, finding it difficult as her backside already hurt from so much sitting.

She eyed her watch, 12:58 pm. They had made the 1 o'clock appointment with two minutes to spare. Now they were at the mercy of someone else's idea of punctuality.

But the wait was only a few seconds. A door next to the reception window opened, and a man in a dark suit and tie stepped out. He looked to be her father's age, mid-sixties, with gray hair. His sense of style was off by a few decades, matching the era of his youth, especially his red glasses, though they framed kind, compassionate eyes.

"Ali?" he asked, hand outstretched.

"Yes." She stood and took his warm hand.

"You don't know me," he said. "But I knew your father very well. My name is Pietro. Pietro Garibaldi."

"Nice to meet you, Mr. Garibaldi."

"Please. Pietro."

"Ali," she said. "Uh, this is Inspector Vinci, with the Carabinieri."

Marco stood and shook his hand.

They stood motionless, Pietro still gently clasping her hand now with both of his, his eyes staring deeply into hers.

"You look so much like your mother. It's uncanny."

"You knew my mother?"

"Uh, no." He released her hand. "I'm afraid I didn't get that pleasure. But I've seen pictures." He motioned. "Come with me."

Pietro turned and led them down a long hallway with turquoise doors, many of them open, set among matching blue walls. The air was warmer here, taking on the scents of perfumes and colognes mixed with coffee. Florescent lighting buzzed overhead, as their shoes clicked on the shiny terrazzo floor.

As they passed one open office Ali could see a mound of paperwork on a desk and a sweaty man tapping on a computer.

Pietro stopped at an elevator bank and they got in. He pressed the fifteenth floor out of fifteen possible and they rode up in silence. The air inside the cramped space was hot and stuffy. Pietro's deodorant had worn off, or he'd forgotten to wear it today, or it was against his religion, and she was happy to be standing near Marco.

"This way," Pietro said as the doors opened.

They got out onto a brightly lit floor. Here the offices were enclosed in glass, revealing brightly lit interiors where uniformed men and one woman sat behind desks conspicuously devoid of paperwork, typing on computers.

Out the exterior windows Ali saw the Vittorio Emanuele II monument in the far distance, with its hulking white façade and massive columns stretching from the ground to the roof, topped with two massive winged bronze statues depicting goddesses, one on either side, majestic even in the smog-choked sky.

If her father worked in these offices, she admired his view.

They approached a corner room and Pietro stopped, gesturing for Ali and Marco to enter first.

There were three men seated around a shiny oval conference table, one wearing a green military uniform with gold buttons and general insignias on his shoulders, the other two muscular, hard-looking men wearing suits and ties. They stopped talking and turned toward them, though only the general walked around the table to greet Ali and Marco. The other two men stood by their seats, silent and expressionless. Their outfits said they were not military. Their builds and demeanor said they were dangerous.

"Hello, Signora Falco. My name is General Traviso."

She shook the general's hand. "Thank you for seeing us today." Ali nodded to the two men across the table, who nodded back in response, proving they were not robots.

"Please, have a seat." He gestured to the seats, then rounded the table and sat back on the other side.

Ali sat, her back sinking into puffed leather, noting that the general sat next, followed by everyone else. Marco sat next to her, Pietro next to him, the two other men back in their chairs across the desk.

The general looked about the same age as her father—early sixties. His eyes were forest green and unblinking, his nose distinctly Roman, his gray hair shaved tight, ears protruding and large.

"We've heard about your father, Signora Falco," he said. "I'm very sorry to hear about your loss."

"Thank you."

They sat in silence for a beat.

"I take it you've heard that he killed himself?" she asked.

The general blinked slowly, nodded.

"And that we have reason to believe his manner of death is suspicious."

"Yes."

Okay. So that was established.

The general looked down, and Ali saw the manila envelope in his large hands. He opened it with a precise movement, twisted it, then pushed it towards Ali.

She pulled the folder towards her and looked at the page. She read the sheet of paper, which she recognized as a government-issued annual pension statement. The name, Dino Falco, and date were circled with a red pen. No other papers were underneath it. "I'm confused. I don't understand."

General Traviso bobbed his eyebrows, keeping his eyes on the piece of paper. "Your father was on track to retire in September of this year. Less than three months from now."

"Okay. I was hoping you'd tell me what he was working on. Not when he was going to retire. I need to know who would want to make it look like he'd committed suicide."

The General nodded somberly. "I know what you're looking for. What I'm telling you is, we knew your father was going to retire for some time now. He put in for his date over a year ago."

The general stood, leaned forward, and tapped the piece of paper, his thick finger landing on a date from the previous April.

"I'm sorry," she said. "I still don't see your point."

"My point is we don't assign men who are months from retirement to high profile cases, especially ones that might get them killed, or put them in danger when they become civilians again."

She blinked.

The general's face hardened. "Do you know the last time an employee of the Guardia di Finanza in your father's division was assassinated by a criminal organization?"

"No."

"Thirty-two years ago," he said.

She shook her head, thinking that sounded wrong, but then remembered he had said *in your father's division.*

"What division was my father in?"

The General looked at Pietro.

"Cyber-crimes financial transactions division," Pietro said.

She looked at the two silent men next to General Traviso. "And who are these men if I may ask?"

"These two men work with the Direzione Investigativa Antimafia. I have spoken to Second Lieutenant Colombo about the suspicious nature of your father's death, and these men will answer any questions we may have. But we will not be using their names."

She nodded.

"Okay," she said, shaking her head, trying to get the conversation back on track. "But there is suspicion, real suspicion that my father didn't kill himself." She felt her face flush at the defiant tone in her voice, but there was no point in holding back. "What was he working on? I need to know. We need to know."

The General looked at Pietro again.

Pietro hesitated, taking a breath to speak, then let it out and shrugged.

Ali waited, but the man said nothing, just shook his head.

"Are you saying he wasn't working on anything?"

"We had a tax evasion case last year, about the time he put in for retirement," Pietro said.

"Okay, and what were the details of that case?"

"It was an Italian businessman from here in Rome." Pietro shook his head. "What can I say, the man was guilty, he knew it, everyone knew it. He's paying his debt, and had to serve six months in prison."

"Would he want my father dead?"

"He never knew your father existed, Ali. I was working on the case, too. We pushed the paper behind the scenes, did the calculations. That's what we do. We're admins behind the scenes. The lawyers were out there on the front lines, if you can even call that the front lines with this case. It was not a large amount of money. There was nothing outlandishly criminal about it. Just a troubled man who had made some bad decisions."

She stared at Pietro, then nodded. "And what else?"

Pietro shook his head. "We worked with these types of cases for the last ten years. It's how I met your father. He was very good with forensic accounting."

She sucked in a breath, remaining still in her chair. She had never known what job her father had taken with the Guardia, but she had always expected it to be more glamorous than paper pushing and forensic accounting. This was the man who was an inspector out on the streets of Como, telling her to be wary of any men who looked suspicious at school, around town, or near the villa, because they could have been out for revenge after getting released from a prison sentence her father had been responsible for.

"There was once a drug ring in Genova," Pietro said. "He helped tremendously with gathering the documents to prove the..." Pietro searched for his words, clearly patronizing her, "... the shipping bills of lading, the—"

"—He was behind the scenes," she said.

Pietro nodded. "Yes."

"I'm sorry, Ms. Falco," the general said. "Your father was a valuable asset to this organization. He was a good, likeable man. A good friend to Mr. Garibaldi here. But he was not in danger. Not here. Not with anything he was working on with the Guardia di Finanza. You can take my word. I have looked into this matter personally."

She nodded, feeling all the energy that had built in her body gone. She felt heavy.

Pietro cleared his throat. "I can take you down to my office, Ali, and we can discuss your father some more. I do have a lot to tell you about him."

She was staring at the wall behind the General. She blinked and nodded. "Yes. Thank you. Okay."

Marco stood. "Thank you for meeting with us, sir."

"You're welcome. Anything more I can do, please ask."

Ali stood, shook the general's hand, and followed Pietro out of the office.

Marco followed behind them to the elevator, where they rode down to the second floor.

Pietro led them down another cool blue hallway, with open doors revealing paper-covered desks.

He stopped at one of them and went inside. "This was your father's office."

She paused at the entrance, noting how tiny the space was compared to the room they had been in upstairs. There was a small window, the water-marked rectangle of glass showing a view of the building next door, an air conditioner unit covered in duct tape poking inside.

His desk was small, pushed up against the wall, because to put it sideways would have taken up too much space. There was a small bookshelf, with a picture propped on top: Ali, her mother, and her father, Ali no more than twelve years old, all of them laughing, gelato in their hands, the seaside of Liguria behind them.

She remembered that photo. It used to be in her mother and father's bedroom in the villa. She remembered that day. That happiness.

Her father was muscular in the picture, skin tanned.

Marco and Pietro remained silent, watching her.

She eyed the books, which seemed to be a collection of Italian accounting and tax law volumes. There was nothing on the walls, just the drab blue paint. Her eyes flicked to the desk, and a tiny clay bowl, an ashtray, painted pink and fired shiny in the kiln, a piece of pottery she'd made her father when she was seven years old...even though her father never smoked. It had been a family joke for their remaining years together.

A desktop monitor stood on the desk, the glass of the dated model display buffed to a fine sheen, reflecting Ali's image back to her. Her first impression of the office was it was sadly stark, devoid of life, but she remembered he'd always been like that. It had been her mother who adorned walls of the villa with pictures, and she had been the one to paint the walls with accent colors. Just like the clean, precise interior of his BMW, her father was right at home in this little nook of plainness. The thought comforted her.

The computer was left on, in sleep mode. She moved the computer mouse and the screen crackled to life.

"Oh," Pietro said, "he left his computer on."

"Does he usually turn it off?"

"Yes."

She looked at him. "Did he tell you why he was going to Como?"

"No. But he seemed upset. Like something had happened. I asked him if everything was okay. He told me, 'I'm not sure.'"

"He said that? He said, 'I'm not sure?'"

Pietro nodded. "He must have been in a hurry if he forgot to turn off his computer. He was very particular."

The icons glowed to life on the screen.

At first, she failed to recognize it, but then she saw the desktop image behind the icons, and time seemed to stop. The photograph was of a woman, taken with a zoom lens. The woman was Ali, and the photo was recent, judging by the length of her hair. She sat on a bench outside Siena, a wide smile on her face, a cigarette in hand, sitting next to Clarissa, who had her head back, laughing.

The tree above her in the photograph was in bloom with pink flowers, meaning it would have been taken in April or May. The shirt she was wearing told her for sure—it had been only a few months ago.

Had her father taken it? Had he hired someone to follow her and take the photo? He wouldn't exactly be rolling in money with this job. He had probably taken it himself.

"He visited you."

She looked at Pietro.

Pietro kept his eyes on the screen. "He would come back and show me the photographs. Like he was on some hunting expedition or something." A tear fell out of his eye, streaking down his cheek.

She turned back to the computer screen, now looking at it through the blur of building tears. She tilted her head back until the tears filtered back in. With a steeled resolve, she took the mouse and clicked on the email icon.

Marco and Pietro moved closer behind her. Both men kept silent.

"When did he leave?" she asked, waiting for the program to load.

"Let's see...it was Friday when I spoke to him last. We were going to go to lunch, like we always do, and he never came into my office like he usually does. So, I came in here to him, to see what was holding him up. He was sitting here. He had the newspaper spread out here on the desk, and he was staring at it.

"I snapped my fingers. Told him to wake up. It was time to go to lunch, and he just shook his head. He told me he had to leave to go to Como, and..." Pietro shrugged, "... he folded the paper, and got up to leave."

Pietro seemed energized by the attention Marco and Ali were giving him now. He continued to speak quickly.

"He said he was leaving. That was it. He wasn't talking about it anymore. I told him I'd cover for him, which really means nothing, I'm ready for retirement myself, that's why we're both down here in the pasture section. We don't do much these days. That's why they call this area the pasture. We've been put out to—"

"—*Corriere della Sera*?" Ali interrupted him.

Pietro blinked. "What other paper is there?"

"Do you know exactly what he was looking at? Which article?"

"He was looking at the front-page story. I remember, because I asked him about it. That girl that was pulled up from the ground up there in Como."

She looked at Marco.

Marco looked back at her, raising one eyebrow slightly.

The email application flickered on screen, fully loaded now. She bent over, putting a hand on the mouse and scrolling down, studying his emails. There were fifty, sixty, seventy or more unread new messages in the inbox.

She reached Friday of the prior week and slowed, paying close attention to each subject line. They were all marked as read, none of the subject lines jumping out as noteworthy, all the names and email addresses unrecognizable to her.

"Do any of these stand out to you?" Ali asked, reading each line.

Pietro bent over, squinting. He took control of the mouse, scrolling up and down, clicking on messages, reading the contents, closing them and going to the next.

She stood straight, watching patiently as he continued reading and clicking. After a few minutes he shook his head. "No. We get dozens of emails every day. It's a wonder the servers don't crash from needless communication overload. These are all from the usual suspects...litigation assistance...these here are from prosecution...nothing out of the ordinary. Every one of these are work-related. All boring subjects that have nothing to do with us."

Pietro took the mouse and scrolled. "But there's another inbox here." He clicked and studied the screen. After another search he shook his head again. "It's the same thing here."

"What about sent emails?" Marco asked, pointing to the screen.

He clicked on the tab and there were no sent emails to be seen.

"Is that normal?" Ali asked.

"As far as I know," Pietro said.

Ali sighed, standing straight, feeling her lower back muscles starting to tighten. "So, he was looking at the newspaper, reading about this dead girl in Como, and he said he had to go up there? Did he say why?"

"No. He didn't. And I asked him about it, like I said. I asked, 'Is everything okay?' And he said, 'I'm not sure.' I figured he had to check on that family villa of yours on the lake. I figured the article was reminding him of home. I would have pried more out of him if I could have. But, like I said, he was in a hurry."

"Did he make any phone calls?"

"None that I saw."

Ali rubbed her temple. "Is there anything else you can think of?"

Pietro shook his head with an apologetic expression. "I'm sorry. Nothing."

"It's okay." She smiled wanly.

"I'm very sorry about your father, Ali." His eyes welled with tears again as he squared off to her and put his hands on her shoulders. "He was such a good man. He loved you so much. You saw that photograph on his computer. He had hundreds of those."

She nodded, removing Pietro's hands. "Thank you. Thank you for your help."

12

"Ali, where's the fire?" Marco followed a few steps behind Ali as she moved quickly down the stairwell in front of him. With each flight, she opened more space between them. "Ali?"

She slammed her hip into an exterior side door, exiting the building out onto the sidewalk.

He caught the door before it closed and followed her into the blazing sun outside, watching as she walked briskly toward the side street where the car was parked.

He hung back, realizing she probably needed space. The stunned look on her face as she saw that computer desktop photo had been powerful stuff. The picture had clearly been taken without her knowledge.

Obviously, her father missed her and, though he was no psychologist, it seemed like she missed him. Whatever happened between them was unresolved and would stay that way now.

Marco looked down at the passing sections of sidewalk, thinking about his own father and how his death had left so much unresolved.

He rounded the corner and stopped, seeing she was waiting for him now. Her face was upset, but not sad. She was angry, her eyes narrowing into suspicious slits, glaring at him.

"What are you doing here?" She stepped up to him, poking a finger on his chest.

"I don't understand the question."

"Don't play stupid with me, Marco. Tell me why you're here? What did Colombo tell you to do when you were down here?"

"I'm supposed to help you look into what your father was up to before he came to Como, Ali. I thought that was clear."

She shook her head and turned around, walked away a couple of paces, and walked back, the suspicion still on her face as she looked at him again.

"Don't you think it's strange that he sees the article about the girl that's been dug up in Como, and he comes up to Como after that?"

"I did see that connection, yes," he said. "But I'm not sure why you're angry with me."

"I'm not angry with you."

"Okay."

She again paced away, then came back. "My father was an inspector in Como. In that same building you work in. Probably sat a few desks away from where you are now. You know that much, right?"

"Yes."

"Then you know he was good friends with Colombo and Dante. Pietro in there says my father was upset when he looked at the newspaper article, was so upset that he up and left for Como. Drove six and a half hours. Why? To kill himself?" She shook her head, walking away.

She turned around and came back.

"So, what do you think he was doing?" Marco asked,

genuinely curious now. "You think it was something to do with Elisabetta Sottocornola?"

"Who's that?"

Marco looked left and right, making sure they were alone. Foot traffic passed by unfazed by their presence. "We identified the body. That's her name."

"Okay." She looked away, then back at him, the heat in her expression renewed. "Colombo and Dante sat in that same squad room with my father. If he wanted to know about her, about that body, then he would have called them."

"Colombo and Dante," Marco said.

Again, she looked at him hard, trying to read something in his face.

He put up his hands. "I don't know anything more than you, Ali."

"Colombo and Dante never spoke to my father?"

"Not that I know of."

She shook her head.

"I'm telling you the truth. If your father spoke to Colombo and Dante about the case, then they didn't tell me anything. But they would have told me. They would have told you. Which means, they never spoke to your father."

After another few seconds of staring at him she nodded. "Let's go to the car."

Marco followed her, more confused than ever at her sudden shift. She wanted to leave now?

He clicked the key fob and opened the door, and she climbed into the passenger seat. A few moments later he sat behind the wheel, again finding her staring at him.

"Call Colombo."

"Okay." He fished his phone out of his pocket and made to open the door.

"On your car speakers. I want to talk to him with you."

Marco turned the car on and dialed the headquarters phone number, daring not call the second lieutenant's personal cell. A long tone rang in his speakers.

"Carabinieri," the female voice answered.

"Regina, this is Vinci. Can I speak to Colombo?"

"Colombo?"

It was highly unlikely that Marco would have asked for the second lieutenant on a direct line, and Regina's surprise was evident.

"I need to speak to him."

"He's in a meeting with the mayor."

"We need to speak to him," Ali said. "Now."

A pause. It felt like Marco's gut was being wrung by a pair of strong hands.

"And who is this?" Regina asked.

"This is Ali Falco. Inspector Dino Falco's daughter. We've learned some important information in my father's murder case, and we need to speak to Colombo now. Please let him know we're waiting on the line."

Ali sat back, flipping her hand. Marco held his breath.

"Please hold." The line clicked and there was a staticky silence.

Marco sat motionless, watching Ali as she stared with a hard jaw out the passenger window.

He leaned his head back, sucking in a slow breath.

The line clicked. Colombo's voice rumbled in the speakers. "Yes?"

"Sergio. This is Ali."

"Yes?"

"I have reason to believe my father left here, left Rome, because he was looking into the recovery of that woman's body up in Como. What was her name?"

She looked at Marco.

"Elisabetta Sottocornola."

"Elisabetta Sottocornola," Ali repeated. "Did you speak to my father when he came into town? Did he contact you?"

"No, he did not." There was no hesitation in the second lieutenant's voice.

Ali's mouth hung open. "And Dante? What about him?"

"No, Ali."

"Did you ask him? I want you to ask him."

"Yes, I did ask him. It's the first thing we asked each other when we found his body. We both wondered why he hadn't contacted us. We both wondered if we could have stopped him from killing himself if he had. I've asked Dante, Ali. We've spoken about it extensively."

Ali sat back and huffed a deep exhale. She closed her eyes and put her hand on her forehead. After a long silence she said, "He was upset and he came up to Como. He was upset about the woman's body."

The line crackled. "Okay."

"And I want to know what you know about it," she said. "I want to know everything my father knew about it. Why it would upset him. You must know. You were his best friend. You were his partner, for God's sake."

"Ali." Colombo's voice was sympathetic. "I do not know. I don't know what the connection would be there."

She lowered her hand, opening her eyes. Her gaze was devoid of life, staring out the window.

Marco watched as her eyes welled up.

She sniffed, then opened the door and got out, slamming it shut behind her.

Marco looked at Colombo's name still illuminated on his car's touch screen. "She left the car, sir."

"Where are you two?"

"We've just finished our meetings at the Guardia." Marco

told him about the meeting with the general and the DIA agents, and then the story of her father looking at the article in Friday's newspaper, and then leaving hastily.

"Is that so." Colombo sounded tired.

"Yes, sir. At least, that's what this man is saying. He was clear it was Friday's *Corriere della Sera*. We know that was when they printed that first big story."

"What else?"

"We checked his emails, there was nothing of value in there. At least at first glance. I think it's a good idea to get his full phone records."

"Mmm." Colombo said. "We're already working on it."

There was another, fainter, male voice behind Colombo's. Either the mayor's or Dante's, he presumed.

"What's next?" Colombo asked.

"I suspect we'll go to his apartment next."

"Keep me posted on what happens."

"How's our situation with the body?"

But the call had ended.

Marco sighed, noticing he'd missed two text messages from Valentina. He locked the phone, not bothering to read them, and put it in his pocket.

Ali sat on her heels, leaning against the wall of the building, closing her eyes, sucking in deep breaths of Roman air, trying to calm herself down.

Thoughts raced in her head, frustration churning them faster.

She tried to blank her mind like she'd learned in martial arts, but it seemed impossible.

She stared at the red backs of her eyelids, feeling the searing heat of the sun, ignoring the vision of her father's sunken face and the spatter on her childhood pictures.

I'm sorry.

The text message kept coming back to haunt her, clubbing her over the head.

The light dimmed and she sensed somebody nearby. She opened her eyes and saw Marco standing over her.

"Are you okay?" he asked.

I'm sorry.

He probably just killed himself. He was probably depressed about work, about that bland box he worked in with no view and no prospects of being useful to the brass upstairs, about the state of his relationship with his daughter. Maybe he was reminded of her mother's crash with that article and that had spurred him to drive to the villa. Maybe something on television had reminded him further and he'd shot the screen in frustration, or deep despair, then put the gun to his head.

"Ali?"

"What?"

"I said maybe your father's apartment will give us some clues."

She stared up at him, at the kindness in his eyes. He was genuinely telling her the truth, genuinely wanting to help ease her pain. She was certain about it. As for Colombo? Why would her father's old friend lie to her about her father contacting him or not?

She held up a hand and he took it, pulling her up.

For a moment they stood close, his warm hand still enveloping hers. And then he let go and stepped back.

"Well?" he asked.

She nodded. "Something isn't right. Right? I mean, still. I'm not just crazy."

Marco looked up at the building behind her, then back to

her. “I agree, one hundred percent, something is off. I’m just not sure what it is yet.”

“Thank you.”

He stared at her without expression, then turned away. “Let’s get going. Traffic will start getting bad soon.”

She walked behind him, gauging the line of cars travelling both directions. “How much worse can it get?”

Marco turned back to her, smiling ruefully. “Much, much worse.”

13

Her father's apartment building stood tall and narrow, adorned with stripes of multicolored tile. A small courtyard in front sat vacant, surrounded by a spiked iron fence and squat palm trees.

It had taken them twenty minutes to get to the building and five to find a parking spot, and now they stood outside the building on the sidewalk, looking up.

"Do you have a key?"

Ali shook her head. "I have the name of the building manager. He's expecting me."

She walked to the gate and pressed the electronic box. A list of names came up, and she navigated with the arrow buttons, passing her father's name to the name of the building manager she had spoken to on the phone the other day.

"Pronto?"

"Hello, this is Ali Falco."

"Ah, yes. Come in. I will meet you in the courtyard."

The gate buzzed and Marco pushed it open, motioning for her to go first.

The afternoon shade covered the cobblestone courtyard.

The palm fronds swayed in a gentle breeze, but the heat was still oppressive.

"Hello." A thin man trotted down the stairs into the courtyard. He was in his forties, wearing a t-shirt that had a sauce stain dribbled down the front. He wiped his hands on his jeans and held it out to Ali. "My name is Giuseppe, I am the building manager."

Ali shook his hand, vowing to wash it the second they got to the apartment as her skin stuck to the man's sweaty palm.

Marco nodded.

"I'm so sorry about your father."

"Did you know him?"

"Eh. A little bit." Giuseppe smiled sheepishly. At least he was honest.

"Can you please show us up?"

"Of course. Come." He turned and walked up the steps.

They went in through a set of doors into the main level, then to a small elevator.

"He was on one of the top floors. It's best we go up in the elevator."

They got in and let Giuseppe push the eighth floor. The elevator rattled, jolted, then continued smoothly.

"You live up in Como?" he asked.

"No, Siena."

"Ah! I have an aunt and uncle who live in Siena! Chiara and Pino Gandolino?"

Ali shook her head. "Sorry."

The manager pasted on a smile and pulled out his phone, mumbling to himself, poking and swiping the screen.

The doors opened on the eighth floor. The hallway was filled with the scent of cooking food. She had eaten only the half of the brioche this morning, and her mouth watered at the smell of sautéing onions and tomatoes.

They walked to the apartment door labeled 87 and stopped. Her heart fluttered with a nervousness that was becoming familiar. At least he had lived on one of the top floors and wasn't holed up in the basement.

Giuseppe cursed, trying a wrong key, then found the right one and twisted the lock. "Please." He pushed open the door and gestured for them to enter. "You can keep the key. I just ask you return it before you leave."

"If you could give us some time alone?" she heard Marco say as she walked down the entry hallway.

"*Si,* of course. Here is my card. If you need anything, please give me a call."

The door shut, echoing on the tile floor, off the plaster walls, plunging the entryway into darkness.

She walked out of the shadow and into a searingly bright living room. The main space was larger than her apartment's main room, which wasn't saying much, but it was bigger. There were four rectangular windows, uncovered and letting in the afternoon sunlight, heating the air to sweltering. She opened a window, letting in a breeze and the roar of the city.

Marco went to another window and pulled it up, and the effect was instant, letting in a welcome flow of air.

She looked out over the sea of buildings, relief washing through her at the view sprawled out in front of the windows.

"You can see the Coliseum from here," Marco said.

"You can?" She walked over to Marco at the other window, following his finger.

"There."

"Ahh...I can see it."

She leaned close, then realized she was pressing into him and backed away.

"It's nice," she said. "A hell of a lot better than his office."

A modest kitchen space jutted off the room, with a two-burner stove and a small refrigerator. Three chairs were tucked under a round table.

The walls were sparsely decorated, just a painting of a bouquet of flowers hanging above the table, a black and white framed photograph of downtown Como hanging between two of the windows. The living area featured a simple loveseat and a Barcalounger, with a small table between them, a coffee table, and a flat-screen television hanging on the wall. It wasn't exactly ready for Architectural Digest, but it was something. The space felt more alive than his office.

Marco edged down a hallway leading to a bathroom and another open door.

"Bedroom." He looked back at her, remaining where he was.

She stood still for the time being, searching the main room with what Basso would have called *an inspector's set of eyes*. There were a few envelopes on the table: a power bill, a water bill, internet, another water bill. Curious, she opened the statements and saw he was paying small fees for the Como villa power and water, too. It would have been easy, highly lucrative even, to sell the villa to the highest bidder, but he'd been hanging on.

Now, she assumed, these bills were hers. The villa was hers. What would she do with it?

She shook the thought away, deciding those difficult questions could come later. Marco watched her patiently.

She skimmed her eyes across the countertops of the kitchen, noting the neat arrangement of the knives, the covered toaster, the broom and dustpan hanging on the wall, the spotless tiled floor.

Marco was looking at his phone now, typing a message.

She walked down the hallway to the bathroom, flicked on the light and poked her head in, seeing a small shower and toilet, both neat and clean like the rest of the place. She ducked inside, shutting the door. "I'll be right out."

She flicked on the light and looked in the mirror.

The counter had all the toiletries one would expect a man to have, nothing more than the essentials. A big towel hung on a bar, a smaller one next to it. It smelled like her father's aftershave.

The scent pulled her into the past.

Staring into the mirror, she watched her mother stumble out of the door again. She saw her father crouched over her, throwing her bag.

Ali blinked and her own reflection materialized. Her eyes were red-rimmed, hair tendrils flying out of her ponytail like a tesla coil.

She sighed inwardly, recollected her hair, and put it up again.

Picking up the soap, she turned on the faucet to wash her hands, making good on her promise after the Giuseppe handshake.

She dried off and left the bathroom, finding Marco standing in the main room and not in the bedroom. He was letting her lead the way through the apartment, keeping behind her every move.

She nodded, suddenly feeling grateful for his presence.

Entering the bedroom, she found a modest space with a queen bed topped with two colored pillows, a matching duvet, and a painting of Venice on the wall featuring the same colors as the duvet. Impressive interior design compared to the family room. Probably all items found in the same section of IKEA.

There was a tapestry hanging on the wall above a small desk. Next to it, another window covered by opaque white drapes, bathing the room in soft light. She pulled them open to let in the full sun, then studied the wall hanging.

It was old, familiar-looking. She knew she had spent her childhood years looking at this tapestry but couldn't remember where. Somewhere in the villa, certainly.

She stared at it, mesmerized, realizing it depicted the hills surrounding Siena, not far from where her apartment was now. She recognized the snake-like double-row of cypress trees climbing along a driveway, a red-roofed stone villa topping the hill. The tapestry was probably the sub-conscious plant in her brain that had eventually drawn her to live in Tuscany.

"What is it?" Marco asked.

She shook her head. "Nothing."

Marco, however, seemed transfixed by the tapestry, too. "There's something behind there." He grabbed a corner and pulled it back.

Behind it hung a corkboard covered with pictures, a row of documents thumbtacked along one border, a photograph of...

She stepped back, a shock pulsing through her.

One of the photographs was a closeup of her mother's dead body lying on a gurney.

Marco dropped the tapestry back against the wall as if it were hot. "What is it? What?"

She took a deep breath, letting the shock dissipate. "Take it off the wall."

Marco reached up and unhooked the tapestry on either top corner and pulled it away from the wall, gently setting it aside.

Ali stepped closer, frowning at the spectacle beneath.

They stood in silence.

"Who is that?" Marco asked.

"My mother."

"*Madonna.*" Marco crossed himself.

It seemed to be a shrine to her, or rather, to her death. Another five photographs of her corpse were thumbtacked in line, each showing different angles of her battered body.

Ali stared with mute horror as she allowed her eyes to skim the photos. One picture showed the side of her mother's head, blood caked on the roots of her dark hair, a deep penetrating wound that pierced the skull, the wound circled with a black ink. The next two photographs showed closeups of her mother's bare legs, the skin scraped at the knees, the wounds again circled in black pen.

Two different photographs were tacked below this line, stills from black and white security cameras. In one, her mother stood talking with a young woman. Ali recognized the space as the reception area of the women's clinic where her mother worked. Her mother wore her doctor's smock with a stethoscope around her neck.

"These pictures are from my mother's clinic, where she worked."

Ali looked again at her mother lying on the gurney, her face wearing a peaceful expression, her lips perfectly unharmed and plump, seemingly still full of life. Unlike the misshapen, deflated, makeup covered version of her mother she'd seen at the funeral.

She reached up and put her hand on the documents affixed to the cork, flipping through the pages. The first packet of papers was a copy of the Carabinieri and Polizia reports of the scene of her mother's accident, the coroner's report second.

She read a few lines of the coroner's report, noting the name Dr. Sanfilippo, a name she didn't recognize from her visit the previous day. She stopped at the official cause of death, which read as accidental, followed by a list of her many, many injuries: fractured ribs, spinal cord injury, penetrating head injury, laryngeal fracture.

She moved to the next packet of papers, Polizia and Carabinieri incident reports, detailing the accident scene, the mangled state of her mother's car, the victim dead on arrival, dead when the rescuers finally cut her out of the wreckage with a hydraulic cutter, and so on.

Marco leaned close.

"What?" she asked.

He tapped his finger on one of the photographs—with her mother inside the clinic, walking with a young woman. "This is her."

"Who?"

"This is Elisabetta Sottocornola." He pulled the picture off the board and looked closer. "This is the jacket she was wearing. The pants. These are her shoes. This is the dead body we just pulled from the ground in Como."

Ali frowned, stepping closer still. "What the hell is going on here?"

14

Ali stood in the kitchen of her father's apartment while Marco paced back and forth, his body dipping in and out of the orange light slanting through the windows.

"*Si.*" Marco nodded again, phone still pressed against his ear. "Okay."

Ali sipped a glass of water, images from the bedroom discovery still swirling in her mind, implications forming, evaporating, then forming again. Her father had been suspicious of her mother's death. That's what the corkboard was telling them. He was suspicious of the injuries to her head and knees, so he'd circled them with black marker.

What did that mean?

She hadn't killed herself.

The thought was so profound, whispering quietly in her mind, daring not raise its voice.

Marco hung up and pocketed his phone. "They want us to take plenty of pictures of the board as it is now, and to bring it up with us when we return. We'll get a local Carabinieri unit to come seal off the place, just in case there are more clues in here we're not seeing."

She nodded.

The light coming in the windows behind Marco was a fiery orange as the sun set. The air was cooler, thicker with the scents of food as it flowed into the apartment.

"That's why he was in Como," she said. "That's why he was looking at the newspaper with such interest. Even though the newspaper didn't mention her name, he knew she was the same girl that was in those surveillance photographs with my mother."

Marco hesitated. "I think we've found some very interesting clues, Ali. What, exactly, do they mean? I think we have some work ahead of us on that."

She nodded again, resigned to that truth. But her mind got back on the hamster wheel, thinking again of the hole in her mother's skull, the black circle, the scrapes on her knees, the two black circles around them.

"And it's getting late," Marco said. "We've had a long day. I'm authorized to get us hotel rooms." He folded his arms. "How are you doing?"

She shook her head. "Fine. It's just a lot to think about."

"I think we should get something to eat. We haven't had anything since this morning. It will give both of our brains some energy."

She didn't kill herself.

"Ali?"

"Yes."

"I said I think we should go get some food. We'll come back later and pack everything up to take back tomorrow."

She nodded, suddenly feeling the cramping hunger for the first time in hours, although it had been there in the background all along.

"Come," he said, grabbing her gently by the arm and steering her to the door. "I know some good places to eat around here."

Ali followed Marco as he locked the apartment and left out into the evening air of Rome. The sky was an electric burner set on high when they reached the road below. Traffic buzzed more than ever. People choked the sidewalks, talking, laughing, hugging, kissing, arguing with explosive hand gestures.

Marco led them into the city on foot, weaving between stone buildings.

"I know a place near the Piazza Navona."

Ali took his word for it, trusting he knew where they were and where they were going, keeping close as they walked briskly under the fading sky.

After sitting in the car for so long, visiting her father's drab office, learning the depressing truth about his job, then discovering the pictures of her mother's dead body on display in her father's apartment, she was beginning to feel nearly dead herself. The walk felt good, pumping life back into her.

Marco set a brisk pace, leading them past fountains and statues, crossing streets choked with swift moving cars and scooters, passing open restaurants bursting at the seams with people, cutting through scents and sounds that multiplied Ali's hunger.

The enormous structure of the Pantheon came into view, rising immensely, injecting her with an ancient nostalgia.

They walked past the enormous circular building, along a narrow street lined with buildings, toward the hum of a crowd, as if they were walking through a tunnel into a stadium filled with people. And then the space opened up, revealing a sea of humanity.

"Piazza Navona," Marco said.

They walked into a long, rectangular space, lined with

buildings. Two fountains, with illuminated marble statues, rose up from the crowd.

Hundreds of people mingled: chatting, singing, loving, playing instruments, selling art, flashing cameras.

Ali knew the place, having been there as a child. She recognized the nearest fountain as the Fountain of Neptune. Water fell out of the marble sculptures, jetting from the mouths of cherubs into a glowing aquamarine pool. An obelisk reached for the sky at the center of the rectangular piazza, stabbing upwards from the next fountain.

"Pizza okay?"

Saliva flooded her mouth. "Please."

"Over here."

He led them down a side street off the piazza, to a restaurant with a patio terrace. Marco spoke to the host, who quickly grabbed two menus and led them to an outside table with views of the piazza.

They would pay a fortune for the table, she knew, but she was too tired, and too drawn in by the environment to protest.

The waiter came over and they ordered house red, sparkling water, and pizzas without looking at a menu, and then they stared out at the sea of humanity as it churned past and swirled into a vortex out in the piazza.

"I grew up pretty close to here," Marco said, pointing. "A kilometer or so in that direction."

"When did you move away?"

"When I went to the academy in Bologna. I got assigned up north after I graduated and haven't been back since."

The waiter returned, delivering the sparkling water and a carafe of red. He poured the wine for them, set one down in front of Ali, and left quietly.

She sucked down her glass before Marco had taken two sips, then poured herself another. Marco pretended not to notice, but she didn't care. She took another deep sip of her second glass, grateful for the feeling of relaxation that swept through her body.

"Piazza Navona. You said earlier you haven't been here in a while. Do you know it?"

"I just remember being here once with my mother and father. I must have been ten or twelve years old."

"It was built back in the first century A.D. The area of the piazza is a long, skinny oval, because it used to be an arena. Can you imagine the games they used to hold here? The screaming crowds. The violence." His eyes lit up.

"You like Rome," she said. "You miss it."

He blinked, sipping his wine. "I love it here. I hope to move back one day."

"Have you applied for a transfer?"

"Yes."

"But?"

"But nothing. It just takes time. It takes luck."

"And what about...Valentina? Does she like Rome?"

"She'll learn to like it if we get a transfer." His face darkened a little. He sipped his wine again as if to hide it, then pulled out his phone and glanced at the screen.

She left him to his thoughts and looked back out on the piazza, seeing the long, narrow space in a new light, imagining herself back two thousand years.

Marco pocketed his phone, his eyes returning to the here and now.

"What do you think?" she asked. "Would you have been the type of man to be out in that arena? Or a security guard, keeping the warriors safe from women flinging themselves at them?"

Marco laughed, and then his face turned serious. "I used to be one of those arena men."

"Oh, really? How so?"

"I used to play soccer."

"Ahh." She nodded, sipping her wine. "But?"

"I got hurt." He shrugged. "And now I'm a security guard for the arena."

She set her glass down. "I'm sorry."

"I'm not. Things worked out in the end."

"You still got the beautiful woman," she said.

He smiled, the mirth not quite reaching his eyes. Or maybe she was seeing things.

The waiter came by with two steaming plates of pizza, hers a margherita, his with salamino piccante.

Conversation halted while they ate, neither of them pausing once. When finished, Ali leaned back and set down her napkin, suddenly craving a cigarette as she tasted the smoke from passing pedestrians. Eyeing her nearly-finished second glass of wine, she decided to slow down, overcome by sudden fatigue.

"How are you feeling?" Marco's tone implied he meant in the deep, existential way.

"It's hard to explain."

"Try me."

"My father had pictures of my mother's dead body on his wall. Why?"

Marco said nothing.

"Because he was suspicious of those wounds on her head and knee?" Ali asked.

"It would seem so." Marco eyed the people next to them. They were lost in animated conversation. "And that was a picture of Elisabetta Sottocornola wearing the same clothing she had on when she was pulled from the ground last week."

"There was a timestamp on the bottom of that photograph that indicated it was taken the same night my mother died," Ali said. "Does that outfit in the picture mean this Elisabetta girl died on the same night my mother did? If so, that's extremely curious."

Marco's face went serious as he leaned toward her. "Please. I'd like to hear the story about your mother. I didn't want to pry before. I didn't want to be rude. Now, though, I need to know."

She nodded, sipping her wine, then allowed her mind to go back to that day.

"I was...coming home from school one afternoon. My boyfriend dropped me off before dinner. I was walking down the driveway when I heard some commotion. When I looked up, I saw my mother landing on the ground just outside the front door. Hard. Her bag flew from her hands, rolled away. I stopped in shock. Naturally I was concerned, and I called to her, but just as I said her name my father came out the door.

"The sight of him made me freeze. Because I'd never seen him like that. Never in my life. His face was so angry. He knelt and grunted in my mother's ear."

Ali picked up her wine, sipped it again.

"He was usually...always...a gentle and kind man. At first, I thought it was some kind of joke. That they were playing a trick on me or something. But then he picked up her bag and threw it, and I realized it was no joke.

"That's when he saw me. That's when they both saw me. I screamed at him, asked him what he was doing. He ..."

A tear slid down her cheek. She wiped it, closing her eyes. She had never told anybody about this until now.

"And then what?" Marco leaned forward, both elbows on the table.

"My father went inside, and my mother got in the car and drove away. When she went past me, she waved." The tears started flowing now. "I remember that wave. I'll always remember it. She was so sad. I thought she was...I thought she knew she was going to kill herself and that's why she was waving."

Ali put a hand over her mouth.

Marco reached out a hand. Ali wanted to reach out and grasp it, but she remained still in her chair.

"And then what?" Marco asked.

After another minute Ali composed herself. "And then I went inside to go talk to my father. I found him sitting on the couch, right where he was when...when he was found dead. He had a glass of wine in his hand, and he was staring at nothing. The television was off, the room was quiet, it was just him and his glass of wine.

"I asked him what happened. Why he did that. What did she do? I asked him. But he never answered. He just sat there, staring."

She picked up her glass and sipped again.

"And then what?" Marco asked.

She shrugged. "And then I called my boyfriend, had him come back and pick me up. I stayed out of the house that night. I planned on never coming back. I was so...so mad. I just couldn't believe what he had done. And then I was mad at my mother, for making him that mad, realizing she must have done something very bad to set him off like that. I just felt broken. It was like everything was broken."

Marco said nothing.

Ali stared into the past, the piazza and everything around her blurring into moving colors. "That night I got a late call from Colombo. He told me what had happened to my mother."

"She died that night," Marco said.

Ali nodded. "She was parked above Como, in a lot near the top of Monte di Lenno. Do you know it?"

Marco nodded.

"It was raining. Probably foggy. It was dark. Difficult to see the edge of the parking spaces, and she went over the edge. At least that's what Dante told me. That's what they were all saying, that it was an accident, that, somehow, she either forgot to put the car in park, or shifted back into gear, and she rolled down the mountain, down over the steep slope...and over the steep rocks...and landed a hundred meters below."

She picked up her wine, staring into the blood red liquid.

"They didn't have answers for...'what was she doing there or why?' They didn't have the knowledge I had—the memory of her fight with my father. They didn't see her face before she got into the car and drove away. The way she looked beaten. Defeated. Like she'd given up completely."

She closed her eyes, shaking her head.

"What is it, Ali?" Marco asked.

"The last time I spoke to my father was after her funeral. He tried to console me, telling me her death would have been instantaneous, without pain.

"And I told him the way she looked when she got in that car was proof it was with a lot of pain. I told him whatever she did, she didn't deserve to die because of it. And it was his fault, and that I never wanted to see him again. And that's the last time I saw him."

Marco said nothing.

"But I was wrong. I thought she had killed herself, but he didn't. Why didn't he tell me about all this? Why didn't he tell me he was investigating her death?"

She looked at Marco then out into the piazza, wiping the tears as fast as they came out.

She failed to staunch the outpouring. She felt completely exposed, telling this man she barely knew every dark secret of her past, letting her emotion flow out, ashamed at the public display.

"It's okay." Marco got up and sat next to her, putting his arm around her shoulder.

She felt dumb, but she also felt comforted, so she let it happen. He pulled her close and she allowed him to shield her from the world as she let the emotion drain out of her, letting eleven years of hatred, anger, hurt, sadness—all of it—release.

"I just don't understand why he didn't tell me."

"Is everything okay, Signor?" the waiter asked, appearing next to them.

Ali snapped out of it, pulling out of Marco's embrace.

He backed away, standing from the chair. "We'll take the check, please."

Marco sat at the other side of the table again. His face was red, his expression self-conscious.

The waiter came over quickly with the piece of paper, dropping two mints on the table.

She dug in her handbag for her credit card.

"It's on the Carabinieri," Marco said, waving her off. "Dante insisted."

She nodded, sitting back, grabbing a mint and putting it in her mouth. It was not a cigarette but would have to do for now.

They paid and left.

15

Ali and Marco walked through the throngs of people in Piazza Navona, threading their way toward the center, and the next glimmering fountain.

"Fontana dei Quattro Fiumi." Marco gestured to the ornate marble sculptures splashing water down into the shimmering topaz pool, an Egyptian obelisk jutting from the top into the darkened sky. "It was designed in the seventeenth century. It's supposed to represent the four great rivers of the world, and the influence of the Catholic church stretching to each one. Let's see...the Danube, Ganges, Nile, and the..." he frowned in thought.

"I think it's the Rio de la Plata, representing the Americas," she said.

Marco blushed. "Then you know all about the fountain."

"It's nice to hear it again." She smiled. "You really are passionate about the history."

"I don't know. My father was. He used to spout all these facts to us. I suppose I've turned into him, except I can't remember all the facts like he can."

She smiled, keeping her eyes ahead. "Tell me about your father."

"Well, he's...dead."

"I'm sorry."

"Thank you. He used to be a schoolteacher. My mother, too. She still teaches. Third graders."

Ali smiled. "That's great."

"My father used to be a professor. Not of history, ironically enough. But economics."

They walked in silence for a beat, exiting the piazza and heading down a side street, where the pedestrian traffic thinned out.

"What happened to him?"

"He was killed in a robbery. Murdered."

She looked at him, shock dropping her mouth open. "That's terrible."

Marco nodded. "It was in a bar. You know...a normal bar, not far from here, just like any other. He was standing there, having a glass of wine one afternoon, when a man came in and demanded the money from the barista. From what I hear, my father said nothing. Just stood there, minding his own business, not provoking the man in the slightest. The man apparently didn't like the way he looked, shot him in the chest as he was leaving."

"My God," she said, stunned into silence. "Did they...did they find the man?"

"No."

She shook her head and said nothing for a while. They crossed a street and continued walking in the same direction down a narrow alley lined with parked scooters.

"And that's why you went into the military to become a Carabinieri?" she asked.

He chuckled. "I would probably do more good becoming a

teacher. Maybe I could turn the bad guys around before they got into a life of crime. But this life is more exciting, don't you think?"

She said nothing, nodding.

"There is a hotel back by your father's place," Marco said. "After so much sitting in one day, I'm not sure why I'm so tired, but I'm exhausted."

She nodded, still thinking of a man standing with a glass of wine, a father, a teacher, getting shot in the chest for nothing.

"But, yes," Marco said. "I became a cop because of my father's death, if that's what you're asking."

She nodded.

"Why did you become a cop?" he asked.

"I..." she considered her answer. "I guess I always wanted to be like my father."

"How come you're in the Polizia and not the Carabinieri?" he asked.

"That's a good question," she said. "For the first eighteen years of my life I wanted to be like him, and then...everything happened, and then I didn't want to be like him."

"But you were still a cop," he said. "Inside."

"Yes. Exactly."

He nodded, like that explanation was perfectly sane.

"I've been thinking," he said. "I mean, I don't want to overstep my bounds."

He had her curiosity piqued. "What?"

"I think that your father had a good reason for not telling you about his suspicions surrounding your mother's death."

"How's that?"

"He had no proof, right?"

She looked at him.

Marco chose his words carefully. "What I'm saying is, what if he came to you with false hope? And then it turned out she really did...you know...that would surely drive you two even further apart."

She said nothing, considering the thoughts for the first time, putting herself completely inside her father's mind. They hadn't really studied the corkboard full of clues, but the gist of it was clear. Her father had suspicions about her mother's death. If he had proof her death was murder, they wouldn't have encountered the bulletin board, and she and her father would not have been estranged from one another for eleven years.

"I'm sorry," Marco said. "I shouldn't have said anything."

"No." She looked up at him. "Thanks. In fact, I think there's a good chance you're right."

They stared at one another for a beat, then continued walking.

"How do you like working for Dante?" she asked, changing the subject.

"He's a good man," he said. "Kind."

"Dante used to bring me gifts every time I saw him," she said, smiling at the memory. "When I was a child, all the way until I was a teenager, he always had something. He would put one hand behind his back and make me choose. And when I chose, I always chose right. No matter what. He always switched it behind his back to make me feel happy, playing it like I was some kind of psychic."

"He was close with your father?"

"My father and Colombo were close. Dante was ten years younger. They saw something in him, so my father and Colombo took him in, so the story goes."

"I think your father and Colombo were right."

She nodded.

"He gave me my chance a few years ago, hiring me on as inspector when I didn't have the experience of a normal recruit.

And now I'm the head inspector. It's been a good ride under him. I would do anything for that man, and for Colombo. Colombo is definitely...what's a nice way to put this."

"An asshole?"

He laughed. "I never said that. You did."

She smiled. "He's a good man, too."

Marco nodded, saying nothing.

"But he's difficult to work for?" she asked, prying.

"No. It's just that he keeps to himself more than Dante. He may be involved, but it's at a higher level, a level that we lower people don't see much of."

"Sounds like an asshole to me. I'll have to talk to him about that."

"Please do not say anything of the sort."

She laughed at the genuine concern creasing his face.

They walked. Marco may have been exhausted, but the tension release from Ali's earlier emotional breakdown had her feeling invigorated. Maybe some of it was being with this man. She dared not look over at him, fearing her eyes would give away her growing attraction to him.

Wake up! She pictured slapping herself across the face. *He's engaged.*

They continued without speaking, this time an edge of tension cutting into the silence.

She slowed. "Where are we going?"

"The car is this direction." He pointed ahead and to the left, at a building in front of them. "A few blocks that way. But the hotel is a few more blocks that way." He pointed in the almost opposite direction. "I figure we'll go check in first, then we can deal with the car."

The sky above them flickered and after a long pause a low boom shook the air.

"Looks like rain," she said, glancing up. Light reflected off low clouds above them. More lightning flickered, this time much brighter, illuminating the world around them like a camera flash.

Marco swiveled around, looking to her like he was lost.

"Everything okay?" she asked. "You do know where you're going, right?"

"Yes. I just realized we have a few more blocks than I thought. We came in from the other direction into the piazza, I thought a little walk would be good after the meal, but with the rain coming we should hurry." A bumping thunder rolled through the streets. "This way!"

The wind had freshened, carrying the scent of rain. They upped their pace from a brisk walk to a jog.

He led the way down another side alley, this one barely wide enough to let an Italian-sized car through.

A slice of dark sky was visible above between the buildings, swirling pregnant clouds sliding past. Another flash of lightning lit the alley, followed by a burst of closer thunder.

"I think we'll be getting wet," Ali said.

She looked over, slowing her jog to match his pace, noting he was favoring one leg.

"You're hurt."

"It's an old injury."

There was a crackle behind them, a crunch and twist of a tire on pebbles. A car had turned into the alley, headlights bathing the path ahead of them.

Luckily, they were nearly out of the small enclosure and onto a cross street. The vehicle behind them was almost scraping the building facades along either side of the narrow lane.

The air was electric, and Ali felt as if the hair on her body were lifting, which it probably was.

"This way." Marco hung a right turn onto a sidewalk along a two-way road.

A few cars drove past at Roman speed. The whoosh of their tires receded into the distance as another sound rose like a distant waterfall, growing in intensity, like a windstorm sliding down a forested mountain toward them.

A raindrop slapped Ali's scalp, heavy and cool, running down the side of her neck. Another, and then another splashed her, and then suddenly she was soaked, the sky opening up a deluge.

"Ah!" Marco looked at her, pulling his jacket up over his head to shield himself. He was smiling, and she laughed back at the absurdity of the situation.

Marco's eyes widened as he looked back over Ali's shoulder, startled by something behind her, his hand suddenly reaching out for her, clutching her shoulder.

She turned and saw a vehicle speeding towards them, half on the sidewalk, half off, windshield wipers swishing back and forth, headlights dark.

If she moved left, away from the road toward the building next to them, she would certainly be plowed down, so she jumped right, laying out over the hard asphalt of the street in a superwoman dive.

The vehicle slipped past, hitting her legs, twisting her body as she fell onto the road.

Pain exploded on her elbow and hip as she connected with the asphalt, but she barely registered any of it, instead thinking of the sickening thump she had just heard behind her.

16

Ali got to her feet quickly. The vehicle came to an abrupt stop a dozen paces away, brake lights flaring, lighting a bright red orb of driving rain.

Hurrying back to the sidewalk, she put a hand up as a visor against the water, searching the ground. A dark form lay in front of the vehicle's bumper. The headlights of the car were still off. What the hell were they doing off?

"Marco!"

Another car came out of the rain towards her, its headlights raking over them.

"Marco!"

The car on the sidewalk revved hard and the wheels churned, squealing on the wet pavement. It fishtailed then bounced as it returned to the road and accelerated away. Only then did the headlights flip on as it swerved around a parked car and around a tight corner at breakneck speed.

She turned and watched the other vehicle pass without slowing, harmlessly, and oblivious to what had happened.

"Marco!"

She walked toward the unmoving lump on the sidewalk,

and as she got closer, she saw it was a garbage can, demolished, the debris inside strewn everywhere and soaked by the rain. She released her breath, relief washing through her.

"Ali!" Marco's voice came out of the rain. "Here!"

She searched the darkness, and the next flash of lightning revealed a dark patch up against the side of the building.

Marco sat with his back against the wall, holding his leg.

"Are you okay?" She hurried over, kneeling next to him.

"I'm fine! Are you?"

"I'm okay!"

"You went the other way," Marco said. "I couldn't grab you. You dove the other way. I thought you were hit!"

"I thought you were hit!"

She looked down the road, seeing no vehicles, only the cone of light from a streetlamp a block away looking like a spewing faucet.

"Here." She held out a hand and he took it.

She pulled him up, Marco grimacing with bared teeth as he stood.

"Are you hurt?"

"The old injury I was talking about. My knee. I tweaked it when I jumped."

"He had no lights on," she said. "He was coming right for us."

Marco said nothing, shielding his face, looking down the road. The rain started driving harder.

"Let's go!"

They jogged another two blocks, and despite the limp, Marco moved quickly as he led them through the maze of streets.

With each alley they entered, Ali took in the scene with a vigilant eye, ready for more quick action. Her mind kept going over the way the car had turned on its headlights after it had almost rammed them. There was no way anybody could have been driving around in that rain without lights like that. It must have been deliberate.

A couple minutes later they reached a narrow building sandwiched between two larger ones, the hotel finally emerging as a safe haven, lit by a green and blue neon sign that read *Pagina*.

Marco opened the door and Ali followed him inside. They stood on a wicker mat, splashing each other as they patted off the rain from their heads and shoulders, sniffling, both breathing heavily.

It was almost silent compared to outside, only the faint sound of a radio playing Vivaldi spilling from a back room.

A clerk appeared behind the counter, eyeing them with a welcoming smile tinged with horror. "Buona sera! Wow, you were out there in this? Come in!"

"I'll check us in." Marco stepped to the counter, his shoes squeaking on the marble floor.

"Are you looking for a room?" the clerk asked.

"Si, signore."

Ali remained by the window looking out, seeing no sign of the vehicle, only rain and empty streets.

"...I was confused, you have no luggage," the clerk was saying.

"We left it in the car for now."

"Ah, well, you're in luck. I have one more room. King-sized bed."

Ali turned, seeing Marco had turned to look at her, too.

"Only one?" he asked. "Are you sure?"

"Yes. Is that a problem?"

"We were hoping to have separate rooms."

The clerk nodded, eyeing them. "I understand. Not together.

Okay, let me check my computer." He put a finger on the side of his head. "Yes. I'm sure. Only one room."

Marco nodded. "I see. Okay. Um...can you tell me where is the nearest hotel?"

"It's three blocks down. I tell you what, I will call him for you. Save you a walk in the rain. He's my friend, I can ask if he has any rooms. One can stay here, one can stay there. Although his rooms are all shitholes." He laughed and dialed the phone, his mirth disappearing.

Marco stood patiently as the clerk yelled into the phone.

"Si? What?...none at all? Va be...si. Bene." The clerk hung up. "He doesn't have any rooms. It's a busy night tonight, you know. You're here on the week of the Roman Cultural Celebration, you know that, right? You can try elsewhere, but I think you should go north at least a dozen blocks, or out of the center of the city at least. You are going to have bad luck anywhere. You are lucky even getting a room here. I had a cancellation earlier."

"Do you have rollaway cots?" Ali asked.

"Of course."

She looked to Marco, then outside. It was still raining.

Marco nodded, slapping down his credit card, still looking none too sure about the prospect of spending the night in the same room with her. Probably wondering what sweet Valentina would say. Ali, however, couldn't have cared less. She needed a warm shower as soon as possible.

The room was on the third floor, spacious and warm, with a king-sized bed in the center of the space. The floors were black and white checkered tile, the walls bright yellow, with a painting of a naked woman lying seductively on her stomach hanging on the wall above the headboard.

"I will get your cot and bring it up in a flash," the clerk said.

They watched him go.

"I'm beginning to wonder if there was anybody on the other end of that phone call he made," Marco said, focused on the painting.

Ali ducked inside the bathroom. There was a corner shower, large by Italian hotel standards. Two towels hung next to it, and next to them two fluffy robes.

"We need our bags." She held out her hand. "Give me your car keys."

"I'll go get them."

"Your leg hurts. I'll go."

"You have no idea where we are, or where it is."

"I have a cell phone, and a map app." She pulled out her phone, relieved it flickered to life with the tap of her finger and wasn't dead by drowning. Although they were in the center of one of the biggest cities in the world, her cell service was abysmal, and the app didn't load.

The hotel owner came into the room pushing a folded cot on wheels. "Here you are. There are pillows and sheets inside the wardrobe there."

Marco handed him a soaking ten Euro note and the clerk turned to leave.

"Do you have internet?"

"Of course, the password is on that sheet of paper on the nightstand. Is that all?"

"Thank you," she said.

The owner eyed them both, a smirk tugging at the corner of his mouth, then turned and left.

"You stay and set up the cot," Marco said. "And then get yourself a hot shower. I'll be back in five minutes."

He tried to push past her, but she stepped in front of him.

They stood nose to nose, so near she could smell the after-dinner mint coming off his breath.

"You're hurt."

"I'm fine." He stared at her, unblinking, something behind his eyes looking like it was yearning to come out, like he might lean forward and kiss her. He held his phone out in front of her face. "That way I can make a phone call in the car, too. I haven't spoken to Valentina since this morning. She'll be worried."

He walked around her, brushing her shoulder.

"Be careful out there."

"I will."

"I'm serious. I don't like what that car did. That was crazy."

"You think he was deliberately trying to kill us?"

"You don't? Why would a car do that? Its lights were off, it almost ran us over on the sidewalk."

"If he wanted to kill us, he failed miserably. A couple of gunshots would have done a better job."

She shook her head. "Who knows, maybe that's exactly what the driver was going to do when he came to stop. Another car was coming. Maybe that's what drove him away, or he would have gotten out and started shooting."

"Why?"

"Because we're getting close to something? I don't know."

He said nothing for a beat, then, "I'll be careful. I have my Beretta."

She flipped a hand, realizing there was no winning. "Fine." She stripped off her jacket and threw it over the desk chair, then pulled off her shoes, then her socks. She unbuttoned her pants and paused at unzipping the zipper. Marco stared at her.

"You leaving or what?"

He blinked, turned, limped out, and shut the door behind him with a soft click.

She sat on the edge of the bed, rolling her neck, seeing

herself in the wall mirror opposite the bed. She looked like a wet cat, mangled hair sticking to her scalp, strands lashing to her forehead. Her face looked cold and dead, skin pale, smeared liner painting dark circles around her eyes.

She went into the bathroom and turned on the shower, finished stripping the cold clothing off her body, and climbed inside—the warm water cascading down her body, thawing her flesh, soothing the ache in her bones.

17

Ali snapped out of a dreamless sleep and sat up. The silken sheets slipped off her shoulder. A breeze fluttered the drapes, painting shifting patterns of sunlight on the opposite wall. A car honk echoed outside, coupled with the sounds of passing traffic. The rain had drained out of the sky sometime overnight, revealing pieces of blue outside.

She sat cross-legged, surveying the room. The cot had been pushed up against the opposite wall, the sheets ruffled and pulled aside.

Marco was gone and the sound of running water came from behind the closed bathroom door.

After Ali's shower last night, she had found her bag sitting on the bed, and Marco's on the floor next to the still-folded cot. Marco had come in to drop off their luggage, but was nowhere to be found. After putting on her pajamas she made up the cot, then debated which bed to take as her own.

Now she felt a sliver of guilt for taking the big bed, but him pulling rank had pissed her off, so she'd slipped between the sheets, falling asleep much faster than she'd anticipated, half wondering if Marco would end up sleeping in the car anyway.

She hadn't even heard him enter.

The water stopped running, and the bathroom door clicked. Marco walked out with just a towel around his waist. He saw her and froze.

"Okay," she said, averting her eyes.

"Shit, sorry. I...forgot to bring my underwear into the bathroom. I mean, I brought the rest of my clothes, just not my...I'll just get my bag...sorry..." He walked in front of the bed to the window, picked up his bag, and walked back to the bathroom.

She snuck a glance, eyes tracing his muscular body, noticing he was hobbling just as much as the night before. There was a black bruise on his knee, with an angry red scrape that oozed blood.

"My god, your leg."

"Oh, yeah." He went into the bathroom and shut the door.

She got up and changed quickly, then went to the window and opened the drapes. Outside a scooter sped past, cutting through a large puddle left over from the rain. Scattered cotton ball clouds hung motionless in a powder-blue sky.

Her phone told her it was 7:25 am. Her elbow was stiff from where she'd landed on the pavement last night.

The memory of almost getting run over and killed came back to her, igniting anger within.

She thought again about the car. Strangely, she had remembered more details as her mind calmed last night, as she lay in bed waiting for sleep. It had been an Audi, she realized, with tinted windows. It had an Italian license plate. She could have sworn the province code had the Rome stamp, and she had seen an HE, or an HF, and then 87...and following that a stream of numbers she couldn't recall.

With the windows so dark, she hadn't gotten a look at the driver.

Marco emerged from the bathroom again, this time in pants, a shirt, and holding a pair of socks.

"Did you dress that wound?" she asked.

"I washed it."

"And then just put your pants on?"

He shrugged in response.

"You should put a bandage on it."

"I don't have a bandage."

"I do."

"Okay." He stepped away, sitting on the edge of the bed. He straightened his knee, wincing. "And I don't know what to think of that damned car last night."

She told him about the license plate numbers she remembered as she dug in her bag for a bandage, a tube of antiseptic gel, and handed it over.

"It might be enough. We'll check the database." He stood up and walked into the bathroom, leaving the door open. "All the more reason to get back up to Como. They want us up there with that corkboard ASAP."

The thought of sitting in the car for another six and a half hours revolted her. "I need a coffee."

"You and me both. First things first though, we need to stop by your father's apartment again this morning."

"Why is that?" she asked.

"I spoke to Dante last night. He wants us to do a final walk-through to make sure we didn't miss anything. The locals are going to seal it up today."

She checked her watch. "Then let's go."

. . .

Fifteen minutes later they were walking the streets of Rome with overnight bags slung over their shoulders. Ali welcomed the exercise as they swerved around puddles.

Marco's limp was still pronounced and painful looking, but subsided as they progressed, his pace speeding up after a couple blocks.

They ducked into a bar and picked up espressos and brioches, eating them standing up among dozens of patrons on their way to work or beginning a morning of sight-seeing, then continued to her father's apartment building.

She still had her father's set of keys, using one of them to get into the electric gate in front of the courtyard.

They took the elevator for Marco's sake, otherwise Ali would have liked to use the stairs, pushing her legs harder before the drive.

They reached the eighth floor, went to her father's apartment, and twisted open the lock.

The lights were off, and with the outside light hitting the exterior of the building at an opposite angle, the apartment was dark.

She flipped on the light switch, seeing a large cardboard box on the floor inside the main room.

She walked into the living room, frowning at the conspicuous box. A couple of framed pictures were stacked inside. She looked around, noticing empty spots on the wall where the pictures had hung.

"It's my father's things." She reached in, pushing aside the rolled-up rug depicting the Tuscan landscape scene that had hung over the corkboard, a hinged box lying underneath it, a pair of belts, some leather shoes, two felt hats. Beneath all of it, a stack of clothing, folded neatly.

Marco stood with his hands on his hips, looking down. "What the hell?"

There was a rattling of the front door, and it squeaked open. Marco put a hand on his gun and edged around the corner to look down the hallway at whoever had entered.

"Buongiorno," a voice called.

"Buongiorno." Marco took his hand off his gun, his posture relaxing.

The building manager came to the end of the hall. "You're back."

"What is this?" Ali asked.

The manager pulled his mouth down, shrugging. "Those are your father's things."

"They're all packed."

"Yes." The man's face blushed. "I have a prospective tenant that is interested in the apartment. I was...hoping to clean up and..." he shrugged again, putting his hands together. "There's another box in the bedroom with his clothing. The apartment was rented furnished. So, the furniture stays."

"Later this morning, Carabinieri inspectors will be here to seal off this property until we deem it fit for release." Marco squared off with him.

"How long is that going to take?"

"I said, as long as we deem fit. Now if you don't mind, please leave us."

The manager's nostrils flared, looking clearly displeased. "Yes. Of course."

The manager turned and left, shutting the door behind him.

"Can you believe the nerve?" Marco asked.

Marco's pocket started chiming. He stepped away, looking at his phone, immediately bringing it to his ear. "Vinci...yes..."

Ali left him to his phone call and walked into the bedroom, seeing it was just as it had been the day before, minus the rug and a single painting removed from the wall. Another cardboard box sat on the floor, filled with stacked clothing.

Marco walked in, pocketing his phone.

"Who was that?" she asked.

Marco hesitated. "Dante."

"What's wrong?"

Marco opened his mouth. Closed it. Then he pointed at the box. "We can bring this stuff back with us."

"Are you sure?"

Marco nodded, picking up the box and walking out of the room.

She followed him into the living room, where he set the box down next to the other one. His face seemed troubled.

"What's wrong?"

Marco looked at her.

"What?"

"There's been a...development in the case."

"My father's case?"

"Elisabetta's," Marco said. "And your father's."

"Okay."

"When we found Elisabetta Sottocornola's body up on the mountain, we also found a watch near her body."

She frowned. "I hadn't heard about that."

"We never told the media about it. You know how it is, we didn't want to give all the clues to the public, in case somebody came forward. The watch was badly damaged by the elements, covered in rust and dirt. The forensic team has run tests on it, checking for any organic material that may have survived. Cleaning it up."

"And what did they find?" She narrowed her eyes.

Marco's mouth hung open, no sound coming out.

"What?" She was about to jump out of her skin. "What did the watch tell you?"

"There was an inscription on the bottom. One that read... just a second." He pulled out his phone, swiping, then reading off the screen. "To Dino Falco. You are the love of my life."

He turned the phone, showing a closeup picture of the back of a silver watch lying on a white table.

She blinked, looking at the picture. The inscription read exactly as he'd said, staring her in the face.

"It was your father's watch, Ali."

She walked to the window, seeing none of the city outside. Instead, she saw her father's watch, the twenty-year-old memory emerging from the depths of her mind.

"What the hell am I supposed to think of this?" she asked. "Why would she have my father's watch with her?"

Marco shrugged. "Colombo wants us to come back up as soon as possible. He says there's more."

"More? What more?"

"I don't know."

She glared at him. "Do they think he had something to do with Elisabetta's death? Is that what they're saying?"

"I don't know," he repeated.

She shook her head, turning her back on him.

"I can take you to the train station. I know the Freccia Rossa leaves at just after ten for its morning run. You'll get there quicker and easier on a high-speed train than driving back up with me. Dante would pick you up from the train station up in Milan. Or you can ride up with me if you would rather do that. It's up to you."

"I'll go with you."

18

Her father smiles, placing the metal band around her wrist, clicking the clasp shut. "It fits you perfectly."

She raises her arm, and the heavy watch slides up to her elbow, the heavy metal raking across her skin.

"What time is it?" he asks.

She twists the face to see. "Umm...I don't know."

Her father laughs, gently pulling the watch back to her wrist. She has to flex her muscles to keep it balanced between her hand and forearm.

"It's half-past seven. Almost your bedtime."

She frowns. She was having so much fun and he always ruins it with talk of bedtime or school.

"But that doesn't mean we have to go to bed yet," he says, ruffling her hair. His eyes go wide. "It's been one minute. Now what time is it?"

"Um...seven thirty and one?"

He laughs heartily, and she laughs too, clapping her hands, and with her enthusiasm the watch falls off her arm and lands on the ground with a sharp crack.

. . .

Ali snorted awake, feeling the vehicle come to rest.

Marco turned off the engine and looked at her. "We're back."

She straightened in her seat and saw they were in the Como Carabinieri headquarters parking lot. The sky was dark outside, the windows streaking with water, the patter of rain drops hitting the metal roof.

"What time is it?"

"It's two-thirty."

She was so groggy. She'd spent the first two hours of the drive staring out the window at the countryside in silence, the last four in a dead sleep.

"Ready?"

She nodded.

They got out, grabbing their bags from the back, the corkboard from her father's apartment, and an umbrella Marco had stashed in the trunk.

Once inside they went up the elevator, getting out into cool, humid air smelling of coffee.

In the squad room, they passed rows of desks, slowing at a desk with a nameplate perched on the desktop reading *M. Vinci.*

"You can drop your bag here," Marco said.

"Vinci! You asshole!" A man in uniform approached. "They cut Lapida. He was already cut when you made that bet. You cheat!"

"It's not a good time, Salvaggio."

The man straightened at Marco's glare, noticing the corkboard in his hand, then looked at Ali with an apologetic smile. "Oh. I'm sorry. I..." The man nodded and walked away.

"Sorry about that," Marco said, leading her down the hallway beyond his desk, carrying the corkboard. They walked to Colombo's office and knocked.

"Come!"

Marco twisted the knob, revealing Colombo, Dante, and Dr. Vespucci sitting within. They stood as Ali and Marco entered.

"Ali," Colombo said. "You two made it okay. Please. Take a seat. You remember Dr. Vespucci?"

Ali watched Marco prop the corkboard at the front of the room next to Colombo's desk as she sat. Vespucci shuffled away to stand near Marco along the back wall.

Dante sat next to her, Colombo across from her. The leather of her chair was warmed and flat from Vespucci's backside.

A plastic evidence bag sat conspicuously on the desk in front of Colombo, inside of it a watch—presumably the watch in question. Her father's watch.

She reached out and picked up the bag, dangling it in front of her, turning it, putting her fingers on it through the plastic. She stared at the silver metal, which looked as clean as if it had been purchased yesterday from a vendor.

Through the bag she could read the inscription on the back.

To Dino.

You are the love of my life.

Ali didn't know the story behind the words etched into the metal, but it seemed to be a confession of her mother's love for him. The only memory she had of the watch was being four or five years old and dropping it, cracking the crystal face.

Hadn't she? She looked at the face of the watch, seeing it was perfectly intact. Either she was making up the memory of her dropping it in her own mind, or her father had fixed the watch face.

Other than that, she had no recollection of him wearing the clunky piece of jewelry. She could recall his wedding ring easily enough, with its bands of different metals woven together, but not the watch. He'd never been a watch kind of guy, as far as she knew.

"It's a watch your father got from your mother," Colombo said.

She twirled the bag, looking at the black face and silver numbers. It was made by IWC. Expensive. Not as expensive as watches could get, but decently pricey. Probably going in the thousands, even back when it was purchased, decades ago.

She set it back on the desk, the metal knocking on the wood.

She folded her arms and sat back. "And?"

"And it was found near Elisabetta Sottocornola's body," Colombo said. "Buried next to her."

"So?"

Dr. Vespucci walked to the corkboard and pulled off the closeup photograph of her mother's injured skull, with the circle of black ink around the wound. "Last night, after we heard about these pictures you found in your father's apartment, I pulled the autopsy report for your mother."

Vespucci put a manila folder on Colombo's desk and opened it up. He picked a glossy photograph off the top, closed the folder, and set it on top next to her father's photograph.

"We found the wound on your mother's head was identical to that of Elisabetta Sottocornola's. You can see here...the pattern of indent in their skulls are of the same shape, applied with similar force. The rounding of the object here on the back, the squared off, deeper indentation into the bone at the other end."

Ali leaned forward, following Vespucci's index finger, seeing immediately that it was true.

Vespucci left the photos atop the manila folder and stepped back. Colombo put the photos back in the folder and handed the file back to Vespucci. For a moment they sat in silence, listening to the rain hit the window.

"Ali." Dante's voice next to her was low, soft. "Inspector

Vinci told me you learned that he was reading the newspaper article, and then he left Rome in a hurry."

"Yes." Ali looked at him. "So?" she asked again.

Dante stood and walked behind her, taking the floor next to Colombo, gesturing for Vespucci to move aside. "Did your father push your mother down that night they had the argument? Did you see him push her? Or did she fall on her own?"

"She fell hard. I could have been seeing things, but I think he pushed her. Why?"

"Did you ever ask him about what their fight was about?"

"Yes."

"And what did he say?"

"Nothing of substance."

"What did he say, Ali?"

"He told me he made a mistake. He said their trust had been broken, and that he'd been wrong. He wouldn't give me the details."

Accident or no accident, it's all your fault. I don't want to ever speak to you again. Ali remembered delivering the words with an acid tone.

"After all these years," Dante said, "he never spoke to you about it again?"

"We haven't spoken since...not since after the funeral."

Dante nodded. "Because you were understandably upset with him. More than upset. You suspected, as we all did, Ali, that her death was not a mere accident. We had six seconds of crash data on your mother's car. She didn't have a seatbelt on, the steering wheel had not been manually turned, the brakes had not been applied. Her automatic transmission had been shifted into drive, the brakes let off, and she coasted over the edge."

Ali said nothing.

"The next day your father confessed to us they had been in a big fight," Dante continued. "The biggest. And he was very upset. Despondent. He didn't speak to us about it, didn't come into work for weeks after that. It looked like it could have been a deliberate death to everyone. Like suicide."

She sat motionless, feeling like she was being poked by the words. For twelve years she hadn't heard any of this spoken outside her own head.

"Of course, there was no way to prove it. We chose to call it an accident, for the sake of everyone involved."

Ali remained silent.

Dante gestured to Vespucci. "Tell her."

Vespucci cleared his throat. "We've figured out that Elisabetta Sottocornola was pregnant at the time of her death. I found remains of an early-stage fetus."

Ali narrowed her eyes. "Okay."

"Your mother's medical clinic worked with women," Dante said. "With the underserved female population the system had passed over, such as illegal immigrants, and women who didn't have documentation for other reasons. The poor, living on the street. Women like Elisabetta Sottocornola. Look at this photo."

Dante pointed at the corkboard. "Elisabetta came to your mother. Look at the time stamp. That's the night of your mother's death. That's the outfit we found on Elisabetta when we pulled her from the ground."

"I noticed," Ali said.

"The same night of your mother and father's fight. What time was that fight between your mother and father, Ali?" Dante asked.

"After school. I don't know, six-thirty, seven at the latest."

"So, a few hours after school."

"Yes."

Dante pointed at the picture again. "The time stamp says 8:11 pm. This is after the fight. Your mother must have left the house and gone to the clinic to see Elisabetta. What did you do after that fight, Ali? Did you stay with your father at the villa?"

She shook her head. "I left. I called my boyfriend, and he came and picked me up."

"And then what?"

"And then you called me later that night, telling me about her death."

Dante folded his arms. "You don't know what your father was doing after you left." It wasn't a question.

"I know what you're thinking," Ali said. "You're thinking my father was involved in all of this. In Elisabetta's death, and... with the matching wounds on their heads...my mother's death." She shook her head. "And I don't believe it."

Again, silence, only the soft tap of rain on the windows. Colombo stared through the desk in front of him, saying nothing, despair coloring his expression.

"Nobody knows where your father was that night, Ali," Dante said.

"So?"

Dante folded his arms, looking down at his shoes, but not before his eyes moved to the watch on the desk.

Ali cleared her throat. "Let me get it straight what we're saying here. What you're trying to allude to. Are you suggesting my father got Elisabetta Sottocornola pregnant? And my mother found out about it because she was Elisabetta's doctor? And...maybe the cause of this fight that night that I witnessed, was my mother confronting my father about it? That my mother was Elisabetta's doctor, and found out the father of her child was my father?"

Ali scoffed. "But he was the one who was upset. Why would he be upset if he was cheating on my mother with a street urchin and my mother found out? If that were the case, my mother should have been the one that ran him out of the house, not the other way around." Ali chuckled. "She would have beaten him over the head with her shoe. He would have been the one getting in the car and leaving, not her."

She looked at Dante. "But he was the one angry. Very angry. It was like she had done something. Not the other way around."

"And you don't know what that is," Dante said.

"No. I don't."

She looked at Vespucci. "Do you have a weapon that made those indentations on their skulls?"

Vespucci shook his head. "This is all very new. Just hours old information."

She stared into nothing. "Somebody hit her. My mother. And then put her in the car. Is that what you're saying?"

"It would have to be that way," Dante said. "They originally thought the wound on her head had something to do with the crash, but now matched with Elisabetta's, it's certainly the case they were both hit over the head."

"And you think my father did it. That he hit both of them over the head and pushed my mother over the edge of that parking lot in her car...and then killed Elisabetta and buried her, drove her to the other side of the lake, and buried her near Brunate. Where he dropped his watch in the process."

Dante looked at her apologetically. "It could look that way, Ali. You see it."

"I don't remember him wearing this watch ever. I mean, I do. But I dropped it when I was a little girl. I cracked the face of it. There was a big slice through the center of the face. And he never wore it after that...at least, I don't remember."

They looked at her, saying nothing.

She tried to picture her father doing all those things, the psychotic episode he would have had to have been going through to carry it out. This was a man who threw fish back after catching them because he didn't want to clean them with a knife. And he was smashing two women over the head? One, being the love of his life. The other, a streetwalker he was seeing on the side. Pushing one over a cliff, and burying the other in the ground?

"You know how infatuated my father was with my mother." She looked at Colombo. "It seems so unlikely he would have a mistress on the side. This is crazy. There must be another explanation." She looked at Vespucci. "Can you do a paternity test on the fetus to find out if it was my father who got her pregnant or not?"

Vespucci shook his head. "The fetus was very early stage and the DNA has been too badly damaged."

"What about my mother's clinic? Are there files still available? We could see what my mother wrote about the case."

"Your mother's clinic no longer exists," Colombo said. "After her death it was converted into a physical rehabilitation center, then later subsumed by the hospital next door. I've asked. They have no records of anything."

She looked at the corkboard, with the reports and pictures. "Look at that," she said. "My father was investigating my mother's death, was he not?"

The room remained silent.

"I asked a question. Does it not look, clearly, like my father was looking into the suspiciousness of my mother's death?" She stood up, went to the board, and picked off the other picture of her mother with the black circles. "This one of her legs. He was interested in the scrapes on her knees. Why? And the hole in her head?"

Vespucci shrugged. "Your mother's car was badly damaged, all of the glass broken out of their frames. Your mother had no seatbelt on. Dr. Sanfilippo did mention the wounds. He suspected the hole and scrapes could have been injuries from the ground. As the car rolled, your mother could have collided with rocks and dirt through the broken windows." He put up his hands. "That's what he wrote. He did not have all the information we did of course."

"I don't think my father did it." She looked around the room. "We're missing something. In Como. Not down in Rome. It's up here. That's why my father came up here. And I tell you what, I think somebody doesn't want us looking into it."

"What do you mean?" Dante asked.

Colombo narrowed his eyes.

"Somebody almost ran us over in Rome. They tried to hit us with their car. The night after we went and saw my father's office." She turned to Marco.

Marco straightened. "She's right, somebody almost hit us. I'm not prepared to say it was premeditated."

"And the watch?" Dante's voice was low with sympathy again. "We have him at the site of Elisabetta's burial."

"We have his *watch* at the site of Elisabetta's burial," she said. "Not him."

Dante put his hands behind his back, dropping his head solemnly. "And then there's the text message."

"Which we've already talked about," she said. "Somebody could have sent me that message."

Dante sucked in a slow breath, gesturing to Vespucci and Marco. "Can you please give the second lieutenant, myself, and Ali a few moments, please?"

The two men shuffled into the hallway. The door clicked shut, leaving Ali sitting across from Colombo, Dante standing by the window. Ali sat still, defiance lifting her chin.

"What?" Ali asked.

"Like we said, Ali," Dante said, "your father never told us about any of this." He gestured to the corkboard. "I agree, yes, at first glance, it looks like he was investigating your mother's death. And, please, don't get me wrong. That is the first idea we are inclined to entertain. But..."

"But what?"

"But what if this is something else? Marco told us you found this hidden behind a tapestry hanging on the wall. Why would he hide this?"

She chuckled without mirth. "I don't know, maybe in case he had company and they saw he had pictures of his dead wife hanging on the wall?"

Dante nodded. "Maybe. Yes."

She looked at him, then at Colombo. "But what? You think it's some sort of sick shrine to my mother's and Elisabetta's death?"

"Or your father making sure it could never be tied back to him?" Dante asked. "Maybe he was covering all his bases? I don't know. And what if he knew he lost his watch that night? What if he suspected he dropped it during the struggle, but what he was reading in the newspaper was that evidence never showed up at the crash site. We didn't tell the press about the watch. It wasn't in the article. Maybe he came up here...maybe he was so upset...because he knew the watch would damn him. He wanted to see if we had it."

Colombo kept his eyes on his desk, letting the marshal speak.

Dante continued. "He reads about it in the paper, and he knows the watch will implicate him if we find it. He comes up, maybe with the intention of meeting with one of us, snooping in on the investigation, to see if the nightmare is true."

Ali closed her eyes, listening, the words now feeling like they were clubbing her over the head.

"And maybe he was watching the news that night?" Dante continued. "Maybe he looked at the screen and saw the news speaking of the 'other evidence' we had found and weren't sharing with the public. We didn't tell the media about the watch, but we did tell them we had other evidence we weren't sharing just yet. Maybe he saw that and he got angry, and shot the television. And then..."

Dante trailed off. He turned and gazed out the window. Water swept down the glass in sheets now, bending the green light of the forest outside.

After a few moments he turned to Ali. "That's an inspector talking to an inspector. Those are all my thoughts. And now I'll never forgive myself for sharing them." A tear slid out of his eye, streaking down his cheek.

"What kind of investigation did you do after my mother's death? Did you interview any locals?"

"Nobody saw anything," Dante said. "It was raining hard that night. There weren't many people out."

"Did you interview my father? Did you suspect him at the time?"

"We didn't interview him," Colombo said. "Not officially. We had no reason to suspect he was involved in any way."

"He told us he had been in an argument with her," Dante said. "He was destroyed. We left him to his grieving."

"And now things are different," Ali said.

The two men lowered their eyes.

She stood and turned to the door. "I'm going to go."

19

Ali sat on the balcony of Chiara's apartment, sipping a heavy glass of wine, staring at the lake through the buildings.

The rain had subsided, leaving the city wet. A long thin cloud hung low over the lake. The sun had dropped below the mountains to the west, cooling the evening air as the light dimmed.

Her phone vibrated, buzzing the table next to her. Basso. She let it go to voicemail. She had spoken little to Marco as he'd driven her back to the apartment, hadn't returned the wine shop attendant's smile as she bought the two bottles of red, hadn't acknowledged the man in the courtyard who had tried chatting her up. She wasn't in the mood to start talking now.

Earlier she had sat on the couch inside and turned on the television to fill the silence, to supply her with external thoughts, but the noises and images coming from the electronic box only aggravated her. She eventually shut off the TV and went outside.

The darkening city below vibrated with life. The Wednesday evening rush hour was winding down, people were taking to the street to grab an after-work drink, citizens of all ages walking, chatting, laughing. Living.

She felt dead. Maybe that wasn't it. But she did feel alone. Growing up an only child, then losing her mother, she'd gotten used to the feeling over the years, but now her loneliness had reached a new depth.

So why was she ignoring Basso? She picked up the phone and tapped his number.

"Hello?"

"Hey," she said.

Basso cleared his throat. "I was leaving you a voicemail. I just wanted to check in on you. I spoke to Ferrari a little while ago. He spoke to the second lieutenant up there in Como and got all the details of what's been going on, and he filled me in on the gist of it."

Ali said nothing.

"Are you there?"

"Yes."

"Okay. I just...I just wanted to call and let you know I'm here for you if you want to talk."

"Thank you, Roberto." And she was thankful to hear his voice. "I'm doing okay. Not great, obviously. But okay."

"Okay."

They sat in silence for a beat, until Basso said, "Listen. I also called because I wanted to let you in on the developments that have been going on down here."

"Developments?"

"Yes. About the foot chase through the city, and the cell phone videos."

She closed her eyes, shaking her head. "What about it?"

"Fabiano's father, the piece of shit. I fought for you, Ali. I did. You know I did. I told Ferrari everything that happened, that the guy deserved it. Hell, even Carrera, that Carabinieri sergeant who was leading that troop is not throwing you to the wolves. His version of the story is that the perp was taunting you. But the footage from the cell phone doesn't tell enough of the story. The local media is sensationalizing it as heavy-handed policing, and Fabiano's father is fanning the flames."

Ali stared out at the cloud rolling over the lake. She fished out a cigarette from her pack and lit it.

"Ali, are you there?"

She exhaled. "What are you saying, Roberto?"

"I'm saying Fabiano's father was pushing for your removal. But Ferrari pushed back. Your job is safe."

"But?"

"But you're not making inspector. Not this time around. Ferrari already told me Fabiano's in. You're out. I just wanted to tell you."

"Okay, thank you, Roberto."

"You're welcome."

They sat in silence for a beat, static crackling in her ear as she smoked her cigarette.

"It sucks," Basso said. "I'm not going to enjoy working with that squeaky little bastard."

She smiled wanly. "It's okay."

"It's not okay. It's bullshit, Ali."

She said nothing.

"What are you going to do about your father? I heard there is new evidence. I'm so sorry I had to tell you this news about Fabiano when you're already dealing with such bad news up there."

Her phone vibrated in her hand, and she saw on the screen that Ferrari was calling her on the other line. She sent the call to voicemail and put it back to her ear.

"Are you there?" Basso asked.

"Yes. Listen, I have to go."

"Call me if you need anything, Ali. Anything at all."

"I will. Thank you, Roberto." She hung up.

She sat still for a few minutes, taking in the information.

Ferrari texted her: *Please give me a call when you get a chance. We have to talk.*

Not anytime soon, she thought, putting her phone on the table next to her.

She snuffed out her cigarette in the ashtray, stood up, and leaned on the balcony, looking over. Five floors below a young couple strolled hand in hand, and she wondered what Marco was doing right now. He was probably choosing tablecloths for his wedding reception. Probably making love to his beautiful fiancée.

She thought of his bared torso as he had come out of the bathroom.

Shaking away the thoughts, she walked inside and saw two pieces of mail had been shoved under the front door.

One was an envelope addressed to Chiara, the other a postcard advertisement for a travel agency, with a picture of a tropical beach, the bold message reading, *"What if?"*

She picked them up and put them on the kitchen table, then stared at the photograph, picturing herself standing in the sand, the sun tanning her skin, the warm sea water lapping at her feet. What if she went on a vacation? Got away from everything?

Then what? As if she'd be escaping anything. It wasn't going to be that easy.

She thought about living like this, day after day, thinking of the horrible tragedy her family had become, and the anxiety started up again, accelerating her breathing. She felt just like she had in the weeks following her mother's death.

She eyed the ad again. *What if?*

What if her father hadn't done it? What if her father hadn't killed her mother? What if her instincts were spot on, that her father was looking into the murder of her mother? And Marco was right, that her father hadn't told her about his suspicions about her death because he didn't want to give her false hope?

She thought back on how things had gone down after her mother's death.

"You're still angry with me, Ali."

"No shit."

"Because of what you saw when you came home from school."

"Yeah, something like that. What could she have done that made you so angry, Daddy? Did she cheat on you? Is that it? That's the only thing I can imagine. What did she do?"

Her father shakes his head. "I'm sorry, Ali. I thought our trust was broken, but I was wrong."

"So you did think she was cheating on you?"

Her father closes his eyes. Tears stream down his cheeks.

She is enraged at the non-explanation. "It doesn't matter. What matters is you handled it wrong. You pushed her down. You broke the trust." She stabs her finger toward her father. "She trusted you to never lay a hand on her, and you pushed her down. You humiliated her in front of me. And she gave up because of it. You killed her."

"I don't think she killed herself, Ali." Her father shakes his head again, this time with conviction. "No way."

But there is doubt in his eyes. She can see it. "Either way. Accident or no accident, it's all your fault. I don't want to ever speak to you again. I'm leaving tomorrow."

Ali blinked back to the moment. Sweat trickled down the side of her face. She wiped it away, seeing the piece of mail again.

That doubt in his eyes...had that been him holding back a disturbing truth where he'd clubbed her mother over the head and pushed her down a mountain? A truth where he'd then murdered a young woman and buried her in the ground?

No. It couldn't have been. It had been doubt about her mother's death. He was holding back his suspicions she'd been murdered. Ali had not exactly given him the space to talk in that moment, or for eleven years after for that matter.

She went to the sink and poured out her wine, no longer willing to muddle her mind. Not until this was figured out.

What if?

She began pacing the apartment, thinking back on that night, but this time from her father's point of view. After the fight, her father had gone and sat down on the couch. Ali had left him there at the villa, walking back up to the gate to meet Matteo, who was coming to pick her up.

That left a perfect gap for him to leave and do the disturbing deeds she was trying to exonerate him from. She shook her head, going back to the question.

What if?

But if he hadn't killed her, then he either stayed home, which gave him no alibi, or he went somewhere else. There really was no way to know.

But then a thought came to her, and she stopped pacing. Maybe she didn't know where he'd gone after he got drunk, but where had he gotten drunk in the first place? Probably the same place he always went to have a drink after work.

She put on her shoes, tying the laces tight, readying herself for a long walk along the lake.

20

Como sat on the southern tip of the lake. Ali made her way north through town toward the shore, following the cool breezes skating off the Alps and over the water, cooling her body as she stepped quickly with purpose and destination in mind.

She weaved through the streets, past shops and crowded bars filled mostly with men, past pizzerias and restaurants with their mouthwatering scents. At the water's edge, she turned west onto the Passeggiata Lino Gelpi, the walking path that rounded the southern tip of the lake and veered north into the distance, hugging the lapping shores.

She was invigorated, her legs moving, her blood circulating, her mind clearing from the depressed fog it had been in all day. Was the pub still there? She put that thought out of her mind, enjoying her surroundings.

The dark blue sky was cooling to black overhead. She passed fragrant flower beds, lovers sitting on benches, elderly men chatting. The floatplanes were all tied up, the airport docks darkened on the other side of the lake. A couple of boats were still out, stitching wakes on the still water, their wakes lapping against the elevated walkway.

She continued past the Como Stadium, brightly lit but silent—it must have been a soccer practice and not a game—and she thought of how she used to walk here with Matteo, although at a much slower pace, arm in arm with her high school love.

A few minutes later, making her way up shore, the Villa Olmo came into view, enormous and regal, its ornate rooftop sculptures lit brightly, surrounded by palatial grounds fit for the aristocracy who used the property for hundreds of years until the city of Como took it over in 1927.

The gate was closed, a sign indicating the gardens were closed after dark, which meant this was the end of the line for the Passeggiata Lino Gelpi. It didn't matter to her, though. This was her destination, or rather, the road that came in here from her left, perpendicular to the water's edge.

Holding her breath, she turned and looked up the road, and with a wash of relief she saw the brightly lit streetlamp illuminating the sign clear as day.

Riccardo's Pub.

It was still there. That was half of the job done. Now she needed to find somebody in there who knew her father.

She walked up the road and found the pub entrance was propped open, letting out laughter, music, and the aroma of food.

She walked in past the two men, pausing to take in the scene.

Her father had taken her here on a few occasions, and it was just as she remembered. A rectangular bar divided the room into two spaces. Stools lined the counter, about half of them occupied by men of varying ages. They all looked up at the wall-mounted televisions, eyes glued to the football match between

Barcelona and Inter Milan. Tables ran along the windows, one taken by a family with two young kids.

"You want to eat?" A young, heavyset man behind the bar nodded to her as he poured a pint of beer into a mug from a tap.

She nodded.

"Welcome. You can sit here at the bar or take a table. Your pick."

"Thank you."

She considered her options, then sat at the bar and ordered a bottle of sparkling water and a menu.

"Ready to order?" The bartender sat the glass in front of her.

"Bolognese, please."

"Good choice."

She sipped her water. Her legs were heavy from the walk, the pressure of the seat on her backside feeling like a firm massage.

She observed the pub's other two employees, one an attractive woman about her age, dark hair pulled back, chatting with the men like they were all annoying uncles. There was a very young teenager no more than thirteen years old, wiping tables and shuttling dirty dishes to the back. The bartender was no older than Ali.

None of these employees would have been old enough to work here eleven years ago, so she examined the clientele.

One man she recognized across the bar, though she wasn't sure where from. She pegged him in his early to mid-sixties. He wore a white shirt and a blazer, a pair of gold-rimmed glasses, and an expensive watch sparkled on his wrist.

The man looked at her, his eyes flickering with recognition as well. He raised his glass, nodding, his face blank.

She nodded, keeping eye contact with him. He was the right age.

He gave her what looked like a sympathetic nod and shifted his interest back to the game. How did she know him?

The bartender came over and topped off her sparkling water. “Food should be here soon.”

“Thank you. Excuse me, but you didn’t work here eleven years ago, did you?”

The bartender laughed, whipping out a towel and wiping the counter in front of her. “Look that old, do I?”

“No. Actually, you don’t.”

“Why do you ask?”

“My father used to come here. I was hoping to talk to somebody who might have known him. Eleven years ago, to be exact.”

The bartender pointed at the man on the other side of the bar, the same man she thought she recognized, who was now looking at her again.

The man looked at the bartender, and the finger jutting in his direction. “What?”

The bartender turned back to Ali, ignoring him. “That’s my grandfather. He opened this place thirty years ago. Now he’s the mayor, but he doesn’t do squat for work, really. And at night he sits there drinking Prosecco, watching football, while his kids and grandkids do all the work.”

“Oh,” she said, recognizing him now as the man who had been in Colombo’s office when she had barged in on the meeting the other morning.

The bartender’s grandfather, the mayor, shook his head and looked back up at the game. He screamed at the nearby television as a slow-motion replay showed a player landing hard on the turf.

“If your father was a regular here, he would know him.”

The bartender held out a hand. “I’m Giulio.”

“Ali.”

"Ale?" he asked, saying the short name for Alessandra.

"No. Ali."

"That's an interesting name."

"It's short for Alison. My mother was American."

"And your father Italian through and through if he came into this place, I take it?"

She smiled. "Exactly."

"What was your father's name? Nonno!"

The mayor turned to them, ignoring the action on the screen. He leaned forward to hear better.

"Dino," she said. "Dino Falco."

"Nonno! You know Dino Falco?"

The mayor looked at Ali, his face turning kind. He nodded. "I knew your father, Signora Falco."

"Can we talk?"

"Please. I would be honored."

She got up and walked around the bar.

The old man had turned on his stool, watching her approach.

"I'm Ali."

"Riccardo." The mayor stood up, smiling gently.

They shook hands. His was a rough, loose leather glove, warm in hers. "I was very sorry to hear about your father."

"Thank you." She took the seat next to him. The mayor sat after she got comfortable, looking up at the television with a grumble. Inter was losing one-nil, and the clientele was getting angrier by the second.

Giulio wiped the counter space in front of her, and she set down her water glass. "Thank you."

Riccardo glimpsed at the screen once more, but the old man was clearly preoccupied with the new woman sitting next to him now.

"You've heard the new theories, I take it?" she asked.

Riccardo eyed her, his expression curious. "New theories?"

"The watch?"

"I have heard about the watch. But they hadn't cleaned it yet."

"Never mind." She sipped her water. "I would like to ask you about my father."

"Of course. What would you like to know?"

"You say you knew him?"

"He came in here just about every day after work for more than twenty years, until...until he moved down to Rome. I knew him very well."

Giulio came back with a steaming plate of pasta Bolognese and set it down in front of her. The red sauce, enriched with ground meat and vegetables, sent fragrant steam to her face.

"That's what your father used to order." Riccardo smiled.

She looked at the plate.

"I remember you," he said.

"Yeah, I kind of made a scene the other day. I apologize for that."

"I mean, you used to come in with him when you were little." Riccardo laughed. "He used to tell me 'Don't tell her mother.'"

Ali smiled, still remembering the place, but not the man sitting next to her.

"Did you know my mother?"

"I think I met her once, maybe twice. But with how much your father used to talk about her, I feel I knew her well." He smiled, looking back up at the television, shaking his head. "He used to talk about her a lot. I never understood how a man could love a woman so much. As for me? My wife could move to Africa and, eh, I would be fine."

"Nonno!" Giulio chastised as he poured a drink nearby.

Riccardo ignored his grandson. Instead he looked down at the untouched plate of pasta in front of Ali.

"Eat. I made it myself."

"You made it?" Giulio shook his head.

"It's my recipe."

"It's Nonna's recipe."

"Make yourself useful." He held out his glass. "I'll take another Prosecco."

Ali smiled and forked the pasta into her mouth. The flavor was amazing, the pasta consistency perfect. The taste brought back a memory of her sitting with her mother and father in a restaurant in Montalcino, looking out on the sunset, the shadows between the rolling hills growing longer while they ate. Smiling. Laughing.

"You like it?"

She nodded. "It's excellent. Thank you."

She ate in silence out of respect for the man next to her, and because she had been hungrier than she could remember in a long time. When she was done, she wiped her mouth on her napkin and set the fork down.

"Grappa?" Giulio asked, offering the grape liqueur often sipped after meals as he pulled away the plate.

"No. Thank you."

She watched Inter Milan continue to struggle on screen, listening to the men of the bar grow increasingly irritated, increasingly drunk around her.

"You know about my mother, right?" she asked. "I mean, what happened to her?"

Riccardo kept his eyes on the television. "Yes. That was a tragedy, that night. Your father was here when he got the news. It was very disturbing." He looked at her. "I'm sorry. I'm sure you know well how disturbing it was, my child."

"When he got the news?" Her body pulsed with excitement. "He was here when he got the news of what?"

"Of your mother's accident."

She stared at him. "When exactly was he here that night?"

"Well, I remember he was here twice that night. After work, and then he came back later."

She could barely contain her breathing. "I'd like to know the exact times. You said he came in after work. When was that?"

"It was early. I remember he was waiting for me to open, sitting out there in his car. And when he came in, he was very upset. He had many more than his usual two or three drinks."

"But then he went home," she said.

"That's right. He left for dinner. We tried to stop him from driving, but he wouldn't listen. He..." Riccardo made a fleeting gesture with his hand, then sipped his Prosecco.

"And it was what time he went home for dinner?"

He shrugged. "Around six or seven."

"And you say he came back. What time was that?"

"Oh, I don't know. An hour later? Maybe two?"

"So eight or nine," she said.

Riccardo nodded. "Yes. You look troubled."

She shook her head, turning back forward in her chair, electrified by the revelation. She had uncovered the alibi. He was innocent.

She quickly turned to the mayor, making him jump in his seat. "You're sure?"

"Yes. Positive. Why, child? What is going on?"

She shook her head. "Sorry. I'm just...what else? What else can you tell me about that night?"

"Uh, well, like I told you, he was upset."

"And he stayed here? He never left, other than that hour or two?"

"Yes."

"How long did he stay? I mean the second time."

"Until he got the call, my child."

"The call about my mother's death."

"Yes. A colleague from the Carabinieri called him on his cell phone."

"When was that?"

"Eleven. A little after."

"How do you remember so clearly?"

"I drove him where he needed to go. It's not a night I'll forget."

"You drove him to the scene of my mother's accident?"

"Yes."

"And he was here the whole night before that."

Riccardo frowned. "Yes, I told you."

"And then what happened? I mean, when you got there, to the scene where my mother was killed?"

Riccardo shrugged. "I left him there, and I drove back. They all knew him. I was forgotten, as it should be. I got back in my car and left, assured by one of his friends that he was taken care of."

Ali put both her hands on the bar.

"What is it, child?"

"Are you willing to tell the Carabinieri about what you just told me?"

Riccardo raised his eyebrows. "Why do you need me to tell—"

"Just, are you willing to tell the police what you just told me?"

"I'll tell the queen of England. I don't care."

She nodded. "Thank you."

"You're welcome. Although I'm not sure what for." Riccardo picked up his glass and took a drink.

She watched as the man set the Prosecco down and look up

at the football game.

"Could I have the check now, please?" she ased the bartender.

"You are not paying for that," Riccardo said. "It is on me."

"Thank you."

She took a final sip of sparkling water and stood. She began to walk away but stopped and came back. "Do you know why my father was upset that night?"

He looked at her. "You don't know why?"

"No."

"I'm not sure it's my place to tell you."

"Either you tell me, or I'll never know otherwise."

"Some things are better left unknown."

"Not this." She waited.

"He said your mother was having an affair."

She nodded, the news not surprising her. What else could have put him into that rage? What else could have had him drinking so heavily? She just wished she had heard it from her father.

"With somebody he was very close to at work," Riccardo said. "He kept saying he was betrayed. You know how it is when people get really drunk, they start repeating themselves. And he was saying that a lot that night. I'm sorry to be the one to tell you this." He looked back up at the game.

"Did he say who?"

Riccardo shook his head. "Just that he was betrayed."

She sat thinking of one man, the only man it could have possibly been. "I appreciate you telling me."

Riccardo nodded, keeping his eyes on the game. Inter scored and the bar erupted in cheer, but the mayor sat, motionless.

When the noise finally died down, she patted him on the hand. "Thank you for the talk. And I'll be getting in touch with you again, like I said. It's very important they know what you told me."

"Why? What is going on, Ali?"

She shook her head. "I wish I knew."

She walked away, out the front entrance, turning down the sidewalk toward the lake.

The air was dead still and warm. A flash lit the sky, along with everything around her, turning night into day for an instant. A few seconds later a thunder rolled somewhere behind the mountains.

Shit. After living nineteen years of her life up here she should have learned to always carry an umbrella.

She walked to the end of the street and onto the Passeggiata Lino Gelpi. The water was still and black, pinpricks of light from the other side stretched into bright spears. She pulled out her cell phone and unlocked it, considering who to call with the bombshell of information she'd just learned.

Colombo had never been a number she stored in her phone, nor Dante's. That left Marco, whose number she had added before the Rome trip. He was a soccer player in a former life, or so he'd said. He would probably be watching the game. She thought of the beautiful Valentina, and what she would think of Ali's call.

A car door shut somewhere behind her, and she absently looked back, then back at her phone to scroll through her contacts.

She would call Marco. If Valentina had a problem with it, well, then that was Marco's problem, not hers.

She turned back around again, realizing nothing had happened after the car door had shut. There were no headlights flipped on, no brake lights flashing. And there was nobody in sight.

Her eyes landed on a dark blue Audi parked under a streetlamp halfway up the block. The license plate drew her gaze. It had the ROMA stamp, and when she recognized the number sequence, starting with HF, followed by a stream of numbers that began with 87, her heart jumped into her throat.

Then there was another flash, quick this time, and she saw a figure standing next to the parked vehicle, hidden in the shadows of the foliage next to the sidewalk.

The night went dark again. She hadn't been looking directly at the spot, but she swore she saw a man—very large, very muscular—and he had been looking directly at her.

21

She stood rooted, body tingling, phone clutched in hand, not daring to take her eyes off the spot.

There was another flash, and this time it wasn't lightning, but a fist-sized flare within the shadow. She held her breath, watching as a man lit a cigarette, illuminating a hairy face with a scar slashing a bare streak through the beard. His eyes were locked on her, never looking at the flame licking the still air in front of him.

The lighter went dark, leaving a glowing cherry that lowered to his side.

Her heart pounded in her ears. The way he'd been staring at her, she had no doubt she was being hunted right now.

Her eyes skipped back up the road, toward Riccardo's Pub. No patrons smoking cigarettes outside, no cars passing on the busier road beyond it.

She snuck a glance down the length of the walking path. The brick walkway extended to the south, sweeping a long, lonely arc around the lake, threading in and out of black shadows devoid of movement. She was alone with this man.

Maybe she was being paranoid. She considered walking up

the street, giving the man a wide birth, but the way he lurked in the shadows said he was there for her. And then there was that license plate.

More of her father's words came to her. *Ali. Listen to your instincts. I have put bad men in jail. Men who might want to hurt me, or those I love. If you see a man, or men looking at you strange, you run. Do you hear me? You run.*

This was real, and she needed to start moving fast. But she also needed to call for help.

She began walking down the walkway, raising her phone at the same time. She woke the screen with a press of the side button, tapped the contacts button, and scrolled her recent calls for Marco's number, aware every millisecond counted.

A noise ripped her eyes to the spot where the man stood, then she twirled when she heard another noise right next to her. Suddenly the sound was all around her, the night hissing with the sound of rain hitting the ground, the lake, and trees of the Villa Olmo behind her. The cold drops hit her, sending shivers up her spine.

The man moved toward her, coming out into the light, walking fast, flicking his cigarette into the street. He wore a tight-fitting black shirt and black pants, muscles rippling beneath the athletic fabric. He was menacing-looking on all accounts, his head shaved, wet from the rain and reflecting the light of the streetlamp, his eyes slanted pools of shadow aimed in her direction.

Her gun! The revelation came with immediate disappointment as she remembered her Beretta was back in Chiara's apartment.

Something metallic glinted in the man's hand, a silver blade. The sight was like a taser to her spine.

She ran.

She ran as fast as she could down the pathway, raising the phone and pressing the call button.

The sky opened up, hitting her with a wind-blown sheet of rain across her back as she pressed the phone to her ear. Her legs pushed as hard as she'd ever exerted them. Her free arm pumped back and forth to give her more forward momentum. She could barely hear the ringing through the tiny speaker pressed to her ear, and the act of holding it to her face was slowing her, so she pressed the speaker button and began pumping both arms.

With dread, she looked over her shoulder.

He was there. The man was no more than a few meters away, moving like a seasoned athlete, his muscular legs propelling him toward her with stunning speed.

"Pronto?"

Marco's answer to her call was smothered by the rain, the heartbeat pounding in her ears, and an involuntary squeal of panic that escaped her throat.

The man moved so fast.

He reached out with a large hand, the other hand by his side fisting a backwards-turned blade.

"Help!" she screamed.

The man grabbed her shirt, his hand clamping hard on her shoulder.

She gave up on running, instead coming to a dead stop and ducking sideways.

The man collided hard with her hip, rolling past her in a heap of twisting, muscle-bound limbs. Her arm straightened and her sleeve was ripped clean off with a sharp tearing sound.

She didn't see the man land, because she turned and ran in the opposite direction, but not before hearing him grunt as he landed hard on the pavement, limbs slapping and scraping, audible through the driving rain.

Now she was running back toward the Villa Olmo, and the road to Riccardo's Pub. Hope drove her forward, pushing her legs as fast as they could go. Her lungs burned. Her throat burned.

"Ali!" A voice came out of the phone still clutched in her hand.

"I'm being attacked! I'm at the Villa Olmo!" She didn't bother putting the phone to her ear, she just raised it to her face and shouted. "At the edge of the lake!"

Footsteps splatted behind her, the sound materializing out of the roar of rain. She turned and saw him coming, legs thrusting, thick muscles hardening as his feet hit the ground. My God, he was an Olympic-level sprinter.

The same move wouldn't work again. She needed a weapon, damn it. She looked on the ground.

Her vision bounced, her lungs cycled, a howl escaping her throat with each exhale.

There was nothing. No metal bars. No discarded knives or guns to help her now. Only the smooth pavement bricks of the Passeggiata Lino Gelpi. Despair overtook her, then grim determination. She would have to draw on her Krav Maga training, using her hands, knees, elbows, fingernails, teeth, whatever it took to kill this man.

His hand slapped onto her back. "Gotcha!"

This time she turned sideways without slowing, jumping off the path towards the lake. Instead of landing in the frigid waters of Lake Como, however, she landed on sand.

Her feet gave way underneath her and she fell, twisting, her side and back slamming against rocks as she rolled.

She sat up, trying to get to her feet, watching the man jump down after her through the shimmering curtain of rain.

To her right she saw the glowing screen of her phone, lying amid the rocks and sand, too far to reach. The rain hitting the water was so loud behind her, she couldn't hear if Marco was talking or not.

"I'm at the Villa Olmo!" she yelled again.

The man darted toward the phone, swept his leg back, and kicked it.

Tiny needles poked her all over her face, in her open eyes, as a blast of sand and rock hit her. Ducking to the side, she brought her hands up and clenched her eyes shut, feeling tiny granules scraping across her corneas. The last thing she had seen was her phone sailing over her shoulder into the lake behind her.

Then strong hands grabbed her, twisting her, disorienting her, like she was sitting in a car during a collision. And then she was on her back, and the man's weight sagged hard onto her, his breath suddenly close to her ear.

"Perfect. Let's take a little roll on the beach." His breath was fast, hot on her face, smelling of rancid meat. "Nobody's out. Let's take advantage of it, shall we? Let me take care of you before I take care of you."

His hand grasped her breast through her shirt and squeezed. He pushed down on her chest, squeezing the breath out of her. Her ribs felt like they were cracking.

"So nice," he said, kissing her face with an open mouth. "You taste so good. This is going to be the best job I have ever had."

She squirmed with all her might, kicking her legs up underneath him, trying to make a dent in the concrete statue sitting atop her torso. Her arms were pinned beneath his knees.

His mouth still sucking on her face, the beard scratching her, his teeth scraping her skin, she screamed. Or tried to. All that came out was a pathetic sounding whimper. There wasn't enough air in her lungs.

Blinking, the rain washed into her eyes, but the sand that was still under her eyelids scraped mercilessly.

His mouth separated from her face with a sucking noise. He sat up, straddling her, and then grasped her other breast, both now in his oversized hands. As he shifted his weight, she managed to free her arms upward, extending them over her head.

She tried to wrench his hands free, but it was no use.

If he has both hands on me, where's the knife? The thought made her open her eyes despite the pain. Her vision was too blurry to see anything. She reached up, clawing toward his face, but he leaned back and moved just out of her reach.

She tried digging her fingers into his lower neck, but it was like trying to poke rock. His arms were thick lumber and just as unbudging, his chest two massive river boulders. Her eyes were focusing now, and she saw each of his muscular, deeply tanned arms bore a tattoo depicting an Egyptian eye.

He laughed quietly, barely straining himself as she thrashed under him, punching him with pathetic blows that took all her might.

Desperately, she changed tack, and although it went against every instinct in the moment, she relaxed, stopping the struggle, laying her arms again above her head, as if offering herself to him. Blinking again, she could see the metallic glint was in his mouth now. He'd put the knife in his mouth to free his hands.

His grip on her breasts eased up slightly, and he began massaging her chest instead of whatever hate-filled thing he was doing before.

She relaxed more, her chest heaving up and down as she caught her breath. She let out another whimper, one that could have been interpreted as pleasure, if the man's brain were just that small and misaligned with reality.

Slowly, she turned her palms to the ground and felt around, slowly as to not draw his attention away from her chest, for two rocks that would fit in her hands. With cold, numb fingers she felt the ground, pain flaring in her wrists as she turned them awkwardly to clutch two rounded stones.

He was getting aroused now, his breathing turning to rhythmic grunts. He leaned down toward her again, the blade between his teeth moving closer to her face. Taking advantage of his relaxed arms and closer proximity of his head, she brought both the rocks up at the same time.

He was faster.

He pushed down, slamming her back hard against the ground before she could sit up anymore. The effect created a whip in her arms, and she slammed him hard on the head with both rocks. Two hollow thuds emerged from the sound of rain, coupled with a grunt of pain.

"*Cazzo!*" He let go of her, clutching his head.

Ignoring the stabbing pain of the sand, she kept her eyes open and focused on the hilt of the knife. Reaching out with a lightning movement, she grabbed the handle and pulled the blade free from his teeth, then pushed it up into his thick, muscle-bound neck.

The steel must have been surgically sharp because the blade slid quicky and smoothly into his flesh.

He spasmed, his body jerking, and then his arms slammed down hard, swatting her arms away to one side. Both her arms wrenched so hard, her lower body still stuck to the ground beneath the man's weight, she felt her spine might twist apart. Somehow, she kept hold of the knife, and through the tears and rain she saw the blade rip free of the man's neck at an angle.

Hot blood sprayed onto her. Falling backwards, clutching his neck —he fell sideways, splashing onto his knees at the water's edge.

She got up, ignoring all the pain, and moved away as fast as she could.

Back up on the walkway, she turned and looked. He was on all fours still, and through the rain she thought she saw a steady stream of dark liquid falling from his neck. He clutched his neck with a hand, and when lightning flashed she saw blood streaking over the Egyptian eye tattoo.

She panted, teeth bared, entire body flexed and ready. Where was the knife? She wanted to go back and find it, to pick it up and lunge onto his back, blade first, severing his spine in five places, killing him, ending the life of this disturbed beast.

But the man was now moving with horrifying, panic-driven speed, making guttural noises that stayed in his chest, slapping water against his neck. He turned towards her, fear and rage rippling in his eyes. He looked caught between coming after her and tending to himself.

The wound had to be mortal, she probably cut his carotid artery, but she couldn't be sure from this distance, looking through the ever-increasing wall of rain that fell from the sky.

She just needed to get the hell out of there. So she did.

22

Ali woke to the sound of voices echoing in a great hall.

She lay on her back, staring up at a fluorescent light, its casing filled with dead bugs.

"She's still sleeping," a voice said.

She sat up, pulling off a paper-thin wool blanket, the truth of the situation coming back to her. She was not in a great hall, but rather on a cot in a tiny room in the Como Carabinieri building, having slept after a long, drawn-out night.

Sitting sideways on the small bed, she winced at a sharp, pulling pain in her side.

Lifting her shirt, she checked the cut slashed across her abdomen that had been stitched up by the emergency room doctor last night. She peeled off the tape and gauze, checking the wound underneath, and saw the five neat stitches that had sewn her shut were still holding strong, though they were leaking a bit of blood and she would have to change the bandage.

Things could have been worse. Much worse. The cut was superficial, not deep. Last night she hadn't even noticed it until Marco had said something. She must have been slashed when she'd stabbed her assailant's throat and the man had reacted by slamming down onto her arms. The blade must have nicked her.

Things could have been better, though. She had been showered by the man's blood last night, and there was no doubt some of it had mingled with her own. She could only hope the rain washed any disease off her faster than it could take hold inside her own body.

She shook her head at the thought, only to be frozen by the memory of the man straddling her, his large, impossibly strong hands groping her chest. The angry scar on his hairy face. The certainty she was going to be slashed to pieces, defiled on the shores of the lake, left in a dead heap of body parts for people to find the next morning.

No. She would have been found more quickly than that. Marco had gotten there fast, but it wouldn't have been quick enough if she hadn't gotten lucky with the rocks. She'd made it. She'd survived.

She stood quickly, moving, keeping her mind in the now.

How long had she been out?

She wore a gray t-shirt with Carabinieri written on the front, the same slightly damp sports bra from the previous day, and a pair of large sweatpants she'd gotten from Marco.

She stretched open the neck of the shirt and looked down to assess the damage on her chest, finding discolorations roughly the size of a psychotic killer's fingers that were tender to the touch on and around her breasts.

A set of keys lay on the counter, and she recognized the keychain as the one to Chiara's apartment. Her phone was in the lake, she reminded herself. She would have to remedy that.

"We found nothing. No blood. No sign at all that anything happened."

The words drew her down the hall to the entrance to the

squad room. She stood in the doorway and saw Marco speaking to another plainclothes inspector dressed in a suit. They had their backs turned, silhouettes against the bright sun coming in through the windows.

"I'm telling you, it's like nothing happened," the man said to Marco. "It's all been washed by the rain."

"There's the cut on her. The bruises," Marco said. "Are you saying she's lying?"

"No. I'm just saying there's nothing there."

"Bring a K9 unit out there."

They both stood up, both turning around and straightening at the sight of her.

"Ali," Marco said.

She nodded.

The man with Marco looked down, sheepishly. "I'll keep you posted." He walked away, leaving her with Marco.

"What time is it?" she asked.

"Nine," Marco said. "How are you feeling?"

"I'm okay."

"Are you sure? How about your cut?"

"I'm fine."

He stared at her for a beat. "Can I get you a coffee?"

"Please."

"Sit down if you want." Marco gestured to his desk, then went to the coffee station to prepare an espresso.

She sat, taking his chair, keeping her upper body board-straight to minimize movement of her bandage.

Dazedly, she watched the squad room operate for a while, noting how much busier things seemed up here compared to Siena. Phones rang. People walked past, delivering memos and reports to and from desks. People laughed. People frowned, lost in their own problems.

Marco returned with two espressos, delivering one with a packet of cane sugar and a plastic stirrer.

"Thank you." She poured in the sugar, deciding today wasn't a day to deny herself small pleasures, and sipped the coffee.

"I'm supposed to tell Dante and Colombo when you wake up. They want to talk."

She looked down the hallway toward the two closed doors.

"But we can sit here for a few moments and enjoy our coffee," he said, smiling.

Memories came back from after the attack. She had run back to Riccardo's Bar to make the call to the police, and then to the Carabinieri, unable to call Marco since her phone had been kicked into the lake. Two uniformed Carabinieri got to her first, but Marco had not been far behind, along with another three Carabinieri units and two Polizia vehicles.

Marco had been so kind, so protective. He had been the one to notice she was hurt, had taken her to the hospital, had heard every word of her story: concern, anger, and compassion morphing his face as he listened.

And then he had brought her here, giving her warm, dry clothing and the bed to rest on.

She looked him over. His bloodshot eyes had rings beneath them. He wore a pressed suit and tie, but all night he'd been running around with her wearing his pajama pants and a sweatshirt, soaking himself in the rain as he ran down to the lake shore to find her assailant. Of course, he hadn't found the man because the man had somehow disappeared.

"Thanks," she said.

Marco tilted back his espresso cup. "For what?"

"For everything last night."

"I just wish we caught the bastard."

"I heard what that other man said. That there was nothing he could find on the lake shore."

"Tedesco?" Marco shrugged. "The rain seems to have erased everything as far as blood evidence. There was no knife. The important thing is you're okay."

They sat in silence for another couple minutes. She sipped her espresso, taking fractions of an ounce in her mouth at a time, savoring the morning ritual she would never take for granted again. When she was done, she set down the cup. "I'm ready if you are."

Using the armrests, she pushed herself up, her legs feeling extremely sore. She hadn't run much last night, but she couldn't remember running that hard, ever.

Shaking the memory of the man gaining on her like a predatory animal, she walked with Marco down the hallway, stopping to knock on Colombo's door. He twisted the knob and walked in first, Ali next.

"Ali!" Colombo stood quickly from his desk. Dante was sitting across from him, also rising from his chair.

Dante hurried toward her. "My God, are you okay?"

"I'm fine. I'm fine." She put up her hands, waving them back.

"You need a coffee," Colombo said. "Marco, get—"

"He already got me a coffee. Please. Relax."

They backed off, eyeing her like she was a house of cards in a windstorm.

"Please." Colombo gestured to one of the seats on the other side of his desk.

She sat, doing the same stiff upper-body routine.

"Does it hurt?" Dante asked.

"It's just tight," she said.

Dante sat down next to her. His eyes were also tired, searching her like a concerned father.

Colombo looked pale. "We'll find the bastard that did this," he said.

"You haven't found him yet?" she asked.

They shook their heads.

"I'm pretty sure I cut his carotid when I stabbed his neck. He would have needed medical attention fast."

Colombo sat back, sighing. "You may have been close, but there's no way he drove out of there with a severed carotid."

"Or if you did cut it, he probably had somebody else in the car with him," Dante said. "Somebody who stayed back, saw what happened, and helped him get into the vehicle after you left. Or..." he said, spreading his hands, "you didn't hurt him bad enough to stop him from driving away."

"But you're okay," Colombo said, sternly. "That's what matters."

She nodded.

For a moment nobody moved, then Dante reached over and slid a hand into his leather briefcase and pulled out a photograph. "Was this him?"

Dante put the picture in front of her. It was a color mugshot, face slashed with a fresh, angry red wound that was barely scabbed over, pulling his face into a grotesque half smirk that failed to reach his dead, black eyes. She instantly recognized him as her attacker.

"That's him. How did you...?"

Dante pulled the photograph back. "Your description of his appearance, specifically the tattoos, was enough to find him. The license plate you gave sealed it for us. His name is Pino Greco. He has a very long rap sheet, mostly down south. He's a suspected assassin with the De Sanctis clan."

She frowned. "Camorra?"

Dante nodded.

"It was the same man who tried to run us over in Rome," she said.

"Marco told us that much," Dante said.

"Why is a Camorran assassin trying to kill me?"

Colombo sighed with a quiver in his breath. "This is highly alarming."

"It is," Dante said. He looked at Ali. "And we have a lot of people looking into it."

"We're checking on all medical clinics in a hundred-kilometer radius," Marco said. "His car was already gone when I got there. Whether he drove himself or not, there's no way he could get very far with such a wound."

"Maybe somebody with medical training drove him," she said.

She hadn't even thought of looking into the vehicle to see if anyone else was with the man. Terror had seen to that.

"We'll find him, Ali."

She turned and met Dante's determined glare. She nodded. "And what about Rome? We were led to believe my father was into, literally, nothing down there. But the Camorra seems to think otherwise.

"Perhaps it's time to pry harder into his affairs in the Guardia di Finanza," Colombo said.

"And the mayor," she said. "Riccardo Saleza. The owner of Riccardo's Pub. You heard what he said about my father the night of my mother's death?"

Dante and Colombo nodded. "We heard what you told Marco."

"There's no way my father killed anybody that night. He was drinking in that bar the whole time."

"The mayor is coming in this morning to speak to us," Dante said. "He will fill out an official report."

"Good." She nodded, elated. "So, there you have it. My father's not the killer."

Dante and Colombo remained silent.

"What? You don't believe it?"

"We believe it, Ali," Dante said. "We just have more questions than answers now. That's all. If your father didn't do it, then why was his watch found at the scene of the crime?"

She nodded, locking her eyes on Colombo. The man was staring at his desk. "I don't know," she said. "Somebody would have had to been close to him to get that watch. They would have had to be in our villa, or...friends with him."

Colombo's gaze snapped to hers.

She remembered what Riccardo had told her about her father's state of mind that night. *He said your mother was having an affair...with somebody he was very close to at work...He kept saying he was betrayed.*

"He was very upset that night," she said, holding Colombo's gaze.

She had done a lot of thinking last night, sitting in that emergency room, driving around with Marco, remembering those words Riccardo had told her. The conviction that whoever had been cheating with her mother must have been involved in all of this grew within her. And the more she stared at Colombo, the more she put the pieces of the puzzle together, the more she saw her father only being that upset, that disturbed, if it was his best friend who'd betrayed him.

Colombo's eyes narrowed, as if he were reading her thoughts.

She stared back, defiantly. "He was upset. And he was drinking. Riccardo said after a few drinks he was very vocal about it."

"Maybe Riccardo doesn't know what he's talking about." Colombo's voice was low, his face expressionless.

They stared intently at one another now.

"What's going on?" Dante asked, looking between them. "What's happening right now?"

Colombo held her gaze for a moment longer, then blinked, straightening in his chair. "I need to speak to Ali alone." He stood, buttoning his jacket. "Come, Ali. We'll get a coffee."

"I told you, I already had one."

"Then we'll go get you another one." He flicked a look back at Marco. "You join the search for our knife-wielding assassin. Dante, I'll be back. Call me when the mayor arrives."

Dante stood, and all three men walked to the door, leaving Ali sitting alone in her chair.

"Are you coming?"

She looked over and saw Colombo waiting alone.

Again, they stared at one another.

Colombo swung the door shut behind him, his mouth upturned in a grotesque-looking sneer. "What is it, Ali? You think I had something to do with this?"

She swallowed, her eyes dropping to the gun on his belt. Quickly she stood up and faced him, her fists clenching at her sides.

Colombo shook his head, dropping his eyes. "You are wrong Ali. Now let's go get a coffee so I can explain why."

23

Ali and Colombo walked out of the parking lot and headed down the sidewalk, thick foliage brushing up against them on one side, traffic streaming past on the other.

Ali remained a dozen steps behind him, staring at his back, curiosity pulling her forward as if she were hooked on a string. Colombo slowed pace for a moment, looking at her over his shoulder, then continued onward. The old man was moving fast, swaying back and forth, looking like he was pushing his body's limits.

They reached the bar and Colombo passed it, ducking around the corner of the building. She followed, finding him in the middle of the sidewalk.

He faced her with wide, hard, eyes. His face was flushed, his forehead sweating.

"What's going on?" she asked.

"Why was your father upset that night?" Colombo asked. "That's what you'd like to know?"

"Yes."

"And you think your mother was cheating on your father with me?"

"I never said that. How did you know that?"

"But that's what you think, right?" Colombo asked.

"He was drinking that day because he was upset," she said. "He was upset because somebody at work was...with my mother. He said it was somebody close. That he was betrayed."

"I did not, ever, sleep with your mother!" Spittle flew from his lips as he spoke. His whole face shook as he stomped his foot down. "We were not having an affair! Nothing of the sort! Never!" His face was bright red, his words choking off in his throat. She stood stunned at his fervor.

He looked side to side behind him, hands reaching out, as if looking for a place to sit before he collapsed. Ali reached forward, clutched one of his arms, and led him to a step near the doorway to the building next to them.

Colombo sat, wheezing, digging in his pocket, eventually pulling out a handkerchief and blotting the sweat running off his forehead.

"Okay," she said. "Okay."

He leaned his head back, sucking in breaths, looking at her from the corners of his eyes as she sat down next to him.

"Are you okay? Are you having chest pains?"

He waved her off.

A pair of men walked up. "Everything okay?"

She looked again at Colombo, still wondering the same thing.

Colombo waved them away with utter annoyance.

"*Grazie,*" she said, gesturing them onward.

They sat in the morning sun, the light breeze lapping against them. Ali's body tensed, ready for action as she listened to Colombo's strained breathing.

But eventually he calmed, and with a controlled voice he said, “Your father was very upset because he thought I was having an affair with your mother. There’s a big difference between that and me *actually* having an affair with your mother.”

“Okay. So, why did he think that?”

He shook his head. “When your mother died, a few days after, your father confronted me about it. I was taken aback completely. I loved your mother and father. I always have. And I would never do that to him. He was my best friend. I would have given my life for your father. I almost did in fact. He was my brother, from the day I met him in the academy in Bologna. We were inseparable. And I loved your mother in turn. I would never hurt either of them.”

He turned his head toward her. “I have a wife and children. I love them very much, too. Ali. I’m telling you right now, just as I told your father. I was not having an affair with your mother.”

She nodded, sure the man was telling the truth.

He chuckled, leaning on the door behind him. “Madonna. Look at me. You think a beauty like your mother would have anything to do with this man?”

“But why did he think that? What was my father so upset about?”

A tear fell down Colombo’s cheeks. He began sobbing like a little boy, his breaths choked off with his stuttered words. “Your father’s birthday was later that month. I was helping your mother prepare his surprise party. Your mother and I had been meeting in private, a couple times after work, another time at lunch. He caught me on the phone with her once, and I played it off terribly. I think he must have seen us out...he must have gotten ideas.”

“That’s why they were arguing?”

Colombo’s face went slack. “I’m sorry.”

"Over a stupid surprise party?"

Colombo said nothing, just stared back at her.

"So, he confronted her about spending time with you...and that's what started the fight?"

Colombo remained silent.

"Why didn't she just tell him the truth?"

"That's why your father was so upset with himself afterwards, Ali. He told me later, before he went down to Rome, that she had tried to tell him, but he was too enraged to listen. He had pushed her down, and that had shut her down. She had just gone silent, and she left. And your father had done it all in front of you."

Ali thought of her mother leaving that night, remembering the dead look in her eyes as she climbed into the vehicle.

"My father never told me about that."

"He was too ashamed, Ali."

She stood up and walked to the edge of the sidewalk, looking out on the steep mountains lining the lake.

Either way. Accident or no accident, it's all your fault. I don't want to ever speak to you again. It was a wonder her words hadn't killed her father right there on the spot that day.

The reason he had been upset was the missing piece that enraged her for all these years. The secret she knew her father was keeping that he wouldn't tell her. It was the wedge between them that couldn't be removed.

She put herself in her father's shoes with this new information. He would have been filled with shame for his actions that night.

"Stupid, stubborn son of a bitch," she said. "He could have just told me. I would have been angry, but I would have at least understood."

She tilted her head to the sky.

"But, no," she said, turning. "This stupid fight between my

mother and father was not the cause of her death. You sneaking behind his back with my mother to plan the party was not the cause. My father flying off the handle didn't cause all this pain. It was the person who hit my mother over the head with a blunt object before pushing her car over the edge of the mountain. It's the same person who hit Elisabetta over the head and buried her."

She turned to face Colombo, still seated on the step.

"Did you do those things?" she asked, point blank.

His face soured. "Of course not, Ali. My God, no."

She stared at him. As his expression relaxed, she could see he was still hiding something.

"What are you thinking about? Right now. You're hiding something from me."

He blinked, shaking his head. "I..."

"You what?" She sat down next to him. "You what?"

"And the watch?" he asked. He looked away from her, his voice turning into a whisper. "The watch needs to be explained."

"You still think he did it? After all this, you still think he did it?"

"No, I just..." he trailed off.

"There's an explanation waiting." She stood back up, pacing on the sidewalk. "I don't know, maybe my mother had it for some reason, and maybe Elisabetta stole it from her. Didn't you guys say she lived on the streets? I mean, that's why she was at my mother's clinic, right? Because she didn't have support. She couldn't afford help from anybody else."

Colombo nodded, but his look was still distant.

She sat down next to him again, feeling her stitches pull. "Somebody else is responsible for all of this. Otherwise, they wouldn't have tried to kill me last night. They wouldn't have killed my father and tried to make it look like suicide. They're still alive, while my mother and father are not.

"It has to do with Elisabetta Sottocornola's body being exhumed. The timing lines up. Elisabetta was pulled from the ground, and my father came up here. He was intrigued by the appearance of Elisabetta's body, because he had been looking into her eleven years ago."

"Yes." Colombo said.

"So why didn't he call you?"

Colombo shook his head. "We have not spoken either, Ali. Not since he accused me of being involved with your mother. He apologized to me, then went down south to Rome. I had reached out to him a couple times and got no response."

"I want access to everything you have on my mother. All the original reports, the original coroner's report. I want access to everything you have on Elisabetta Sottocornola. I want in on it all."

He nodded, reaching in his pocket, producing his phone. "I'll make the call now." He leaned forward to get up, grunting.

Ali hooked his arm and helped him stand.

"Thank you."

Ali watched as he made a call. He spoke briefly into the phone and hung up. "Okay, Vinci will be your official liaison. As long as you are with him, you have full access to everything we have, past and present."

She took a deep breath. "Thank you. I want to start with looking at the original coroner's report for my mother."

"That would be on file at the coroner's office. Call Vinci. If you need me to talk to him, tell him to call my cell."

"Thank you." She gestured to the coffee shop windows. "Did you want to go inside?"

Colombo eyed the building. "I could always use another espresso."

She turned to lead the way back to the front of the building.

"And Ali?"

She paused and turned around. "Yes?"

"I heard about what the man did to you last night. Until we find him, I want you to be very careful."

She nodded, her eyes matching his sincerity. "I will."

24

The afternoon heat rose off the sidewalk in waves. With no trees on the street, the exterior of the coroner's office bore the full brunt of the afternoon sun. Sweat slid down Ali's side underneath her blouse and suit jacket.

That morning Marco had given her a ride back to Chiara's apartment so she could have a much-needed shower, a change of clothing, a proper meal, and a rest. She also stopped at a nearby grocery store, which sold electronics, and purchased a burner phone. She pulled it out of her pocket now and checked the screen, the cheap plastic device revealing it was 3:36 pm and Marco was six minutes late.

On cue Marco drove past slowly, waving, looking for a parking spot, another vehicle following closely—Dante's BMW sedan. Both vehicles rolled past, then disappeared around the corner and into the side parking lot.

When they parked and walked around the corner Dante seemed perfectly comfortable in his uniform buttoned around him despite the heat, walking with the supreme confidence one would expect of the marshal. Marco walked a few steps behind, holding a manila folder and his phone, distracted by the screen.

"Sorry we're late," Dante said. "It was my fault. I wanted to offer my help and told Marco to wait for me, but then I got stuck on a call."

"That's okay," she said. "It's only been a couple minutes."

More than a couple minutes, but the apology counted for something.

"Shall we? It's hot out here." Dante walked up the stairs to the entrance of the building.

Marco motioned for Ali to go next, then waved the manila folder to her. "The copies of your father's files you wanted."

"Thank you," she said. "It will be good to reference those with the originals here. So, any sign of the assailant?" she asked, walking up the steps.

"Nothing yet," Marco said.

Dante stopped at the tall metal door. "We'll get him."

"And did you speak to the mayor?"

"Yes."

"And?"

"And his testimony puts your father at the bar most of the night."

"There's no way he could have killed my mother, or Elisabetta Sottocornola."

Dante nodded. "It appears that way."

She didn't like the way he said the word *appears*, as if there could be another explanation, but said nothing as Dante pulled open the door, deciding this wasn't the place or time.

Ali entered first. Nothing had changed inside since a few days ago. The reception area was still just as stagnant and hot as outside, the scent of body odor from the tired-looking man sitting behind the desk still permeating every molecule of air.

Dante wrinkled his nose and walked to the clipboard on the counter. Scribbling his name he said, "We're here to see Vespucci."

The man behind the desk worked fast, making a call, mumbling into the receiver, and pressing a button, all within a few seconds.

They went to the elevator and rode down to the basement. The elevator opened and they got out. The air in the hallway was still every bit as cold as she remembered, but the embalming fluid stench didn't bother her so much this time knowing she wouldn't be seeing her father's corpse. At least, not in person.

They walked into Vespucci's office. The coroner was seated at his desk looking at his computer.

"Ah!" He stood. "Marshal. Welcome. Please, have a seat."

They sat, and Marco set the manila folder on the desk in front of them and opened it, fanning out collated and stapled copies of her father's files from the corkboard.

Ali carefully slid the coroner's report from the stack of papers. She opened the cover sheet, revealing the photograph of her mother's corpse lying face up, grateful the color had been leeched from the photograph in the copying process.

The other men watched her in silence.

She flipped the page to the next photograph, which was a close-up of her mother's skull, and the hole, and the black circle that had been drawn around the wound.

"Can I see this original photo from the original autopsy report?"

Vespucci sparked into motion, pulling a file from the edge of his desk. Like a casino dealer he splayed out a series of photos and sheets of paper.

He pulled the photo in question and set it down next to the copy.

Ali looked at the original, numbing her mind, not allowing the vivid color of her mother's hair and skin to break her.

"Dr. Sanfilippo made a special note of this wound."

Vespucci scanned the report. "He could not explain what caused it." Vespucci flipped a page. "But he doesn't seem overly concerned about it, other than it likely contributed, or was the cause of your mother's death."

"That's concerning enough, isn't it?" Dante asked.

"Well, yes. But what I mean is, he does not speculate it was caused by a weapon. He speaks about how it could have been caused by rock. But, then again, he goes on to say he found no stone or mineral fragments in the skin."

"Which is probably why my father circled the wound," she said. "It's suspicious."

"And your father was right to be suspicious, as we know now." Vespucci put another photograph next to her mother's scalp closeup. "Here we have Elisabetta Sottocornola's scalp. This picture was taken a few days ago."

Elisabetta's scalp was dark, dirty, looking like it had come from an Egyptian tomb, only a wisp of hair on leathery patches of skin. A dark hole in the bone yawned open in the center of the picture, looking nearly the same shape as the wound in her mother's skull.

"Elisabetta's wound is even deeper," Vespucci said. "It doesn't look exactly the same at first glance, but here...you can see the line here, the indentation, and then the puncture of the skull at the end." He put one finger on Ali's mother's photograph, another on Elisabetta's.

"Tell her about the weapon," Dante said.

Vespucci stood, plucked a long, black, metal tire iron from the shelf behind him, and placed it on the desk with a soft clank. The tool's paint was glossy and still had a price tag stuck to it.

"I bought this at the hardware store yesterday," Vespucci said. "It's not exact, but almost, so close a match I'm willing to bet it was a tire iron that made the marks on your mother's and

Elisabetta's heads. It's long, and then it bends at an angle. Here's what would have made the indention. And this lug at the end would have made the holes in their skulls."

Vespucci glanced at Dante, then cleared his throat. "It would have been used with a lot of force. And ..." He sat back, leaving his sentence hanging.

"And what?" she asked.

"And there are other marks on Elisabetta's head. Similar marks." Vespucci eyed Ali. "She appears to have been hit multiple times."

"And my mother?"

Vespucci nodded, pulling out another piece of paper. "There were numerous hematomas found on your mother's head. They were assumed to be caused by the violence of the crash. But now we suspect otherwise."

Dante's voice was low. "I think she would have been unconscious after just one of the blows."

There was no way the man could have known that, but she was thankful for the gesture.

She rolled her neck, feeling a knot forming. "I want to talk about my father now."

"What would you like to know?"

"You did a gunshot residue test on his right hand, correct?"

"Yes."

Marco and Dante both moved in their chairs at the same time, as both of their phones chimed.

She watched the two men eye their cells.

"What is it?" she asked.

Marco put his phone to his ear. "Si?...si." He listened, closing his eyes, something akin to revulsion creasing his brow. "Send the address to me."

He hung up, slowly putting the phone back in his pocket. "I think we need to come back to this meeting a little later."

“Why?” Ali asked.

“They found the clinic your assailant went to last night.”

“And?”

“And it’s not good. They found the doctor who worked on him. Dead.”

25

An unassuming storefront property in a strip mall like many others dotting the outskirts of Como, the *Clinica San Pancrazio* was a small medical clinic off the tangential highway between Como and the A5.

Ali had ridden with Marco in his Alfa Romeo cruiser, following Dante. As they approached the mayhem, she counted two Polizia cruisers, three Carabinieri Alpha Romeos, an ambulance, and a nondescript white van she assumed was forensics.

The traffic sliding by was sluggish, the drivers and passengers all gawking at the promise of something terrible and unknown that must have happened inside.

Ali followed Dante and Marco into the parking lot, through the herd of flashing vehicles, and underneath a fluttering line of crime scene tape. A soldier in Carabinieri uniform stepped forward and spoke with Dante, marking on his clipboard, nodding, stepping back out of the way.

Ali followed Dante and Marco around the barrier and inside, where a trio of forensic workers stepped gingerly, snapping photographs. Following the aim of the lenses, she saw the blood coating the floor.

Inside the clinic there was a clean desk sitting on black and white tile acting as a reception area.

A few paces beyond, at the cusp of an entryway to a back room, there was a pool of blood, and within the crimson lake, a man dressed in a white doctor's smock lay on his side, arms splayed out.

One of the crime scene workers came up and nodded. "Sir. This way. There's more in the back."

More of what? Ali wondered. Certainly, there could not be more blood. It was all here.

The man pointed behind them, to another door that led off the reception room. It proved to lead to a bathroom with two entrances, one to the reception area, one to the back room. Both doors inside the restroom were open, serving as a hallway for crime scene workers to get to the rear of the clinic, rather than navigating over the body.

They stepped through a starkly clean bathroom, and into a back room, which looked to serve as the one patient room in the clinic. Here the air was hotter, circulating less, the smell of fresh death hanging in the air.

And there was more blood. A gurney sat in the middle of the room, a spotlight above it shining down on sheets soiled with dark-maroon stains.

"Our doctor's name was Gianfranco Camposto," the crime scene investigator said.

Another inspector, the one who had told Ali to keep behind the tape, walked up next to her.

"A cleaning crew came in just over an hour ago and found the victim," the inspector said.

"And how are we sure it was him, our man, who did this?" Dante asked.

"There are some photographs the doctor took on the data pad, sir." The forensic worker pulled off a glove, dug into the white uniform, and produced his personal phone. "I took pictures of the pictures, so we wouldn't have to handle the tablet anymore."

"Let me see them," Dante said.

The man swiped, tapped, and presented the phone.

Ali leaned to see. The first photo was a closeup of an unconscious-looking man, eyes closed, naked from the waist up, religious tattoos of crosses and Madonna and Jesus printed dark on his heavily muscled torso. His arms had two Egyptian eye tattoos, one on either forearm. It was their man with his bearded face and angry scar cutting diagonally through it, just in case they needed triple proof.

The forensic worker swiped, showing more photographs of photographs found on the data pad. These pictures were closer inspections of the wound Ali had inflicted with the man's own knife. There were x-rays, an extreme closeup inside the wound made by a special imaging scope.

"I think it was bad," the forensic analyst said, "but obviously not bad enough to kill him. No severing of the carotid, which is the only reason he was alive. He looks unconscious in these photos, but obviously he woke up at some point. He took one of the scalpels off that cart there and slit our victim's throat. We've been told the doors were locked when the cleaning crew came, so he must have stolen the doctor's keys and locked up after himself."

"We found the assailant's vehicle outside," the inspector next to Ali said. "It's parked along the side of the building."

"Show us," Dante said.

The worker led them past the gurney, keeping a wide berth, and into a short back hallway leading to another open door leading outside.

They streamed out into a side alley, where the dark-blue Audi sat parked up alongside the opposite curb.

Here a tall, fabric-lined, chain link fence separated them from the traffic streaming by.

The vehicle doors were open, revealing the black leather interior. Another white-clad forensic worker snapped photographs, backing out of the way as Dante approached.

Marco and Ali followed, and Ali leaned to get a look inside. Red on black didn't show up well at first glance, but the more she studied it she saw the smears of blood on the steering wheel.

"He drove," Marco said. "He was alone."

"He must have stolen the doctor's car after he left here," the other inspector said.

"And we're looking for that vehicle now," Dante said. It wasn't a question.

"Yes, sir," the inspector said. "A brand-new Alfa Romeo Giulia. Black. We've put out a BOLO."

"Anything of interest found inside?" Marco asked. "Phone? Electronics?"

"No sir."

"Keep us posted." Dante turned and walked along the side of the building back to the swarm of emergency vehicles parked in front.

Ali tilted her head back, grateful to let the warm, humid air smelling of exhaust and distant food scrub the death out of her nose.

"So now what?" Marco asked.

They stopped in a three-person huddle at the edge of the lot. The shadows were growing longer, the sun white-washing Dante's face.

Ali couldn't help but stifle a yawn. Her body felt like it weighed a thousand pounds, held up only with extreme effort. The cut on her abdomen hurt and felt like it was sweating profusely. She looked down, startled to see blood seeping through her shirt.

"You have to get that taken care of," Marco said.

"I will."

"You will," Dante said. "And you'll get some rest. You look like you were attacked last night, only rested for a few hours on a god-awful cot in a back room at Carabinieri headquarters, and have been running around all day since, probably without adequate food or liquids."

She gave a wan smile. "Sounds about right."

He nodded at Marco. "You take her home, and don't take your eyes off her tonight."

"Yes, sir."

"My car's at the coroner's office," Ali said.

"And it will stay there," Dante said. "At least for tonight, until you're looking better to drive. Get some rest."

She snuck a sideways glance at Marco. He looked less than enthused with his assignment.

"I don't need to be babysat," she said.

Dante frowned. "You don't need to be babysat. But you need somebody to watch over you while you get some much-needed rest. Do we need to go back in there for a reminder why that is?"

She shook her head. The vision of the doctor lying face down, eyes open, arms sprawled in a pool of his own blood, would remind her for some time.

26

Ali walked out into the apartment building hallway.

"Wait."

Marco put a hand on her shoulder, stopping her. Quickly, he stepped in front of her, gun at the ready with a two-hand grip. He swiveled side to side, creeping his way down the hall, checking around a blind corner, then came back.

She watched, vaguely aware that the elevator door closed into her, hitting her shoulder.

Marco came back and pushed the doors open, grabbing her by the arm and helping her out.

"Are you okay?" he asked.

"Yeah."

"You don't look like it." Holstering his Beretta, he took the box of pizza and plastic bag from her and led her down the hall.

They had spoken little since leaving the brutal scene at the doctor's clinic, stopping twice on the way to her apartment, once for pizza, the second time for first-aid supplies from the pharmacy.

The silence was fine with Ali. She didn't feel like talking. Her energy was sapped, and she seemed to be running only on subconscious commands.

Her brain was preoccupied with thoughts of her mother, and the dead man lying in his own blood. Her mother had worked in the same type of place, albeit bigger with a total of five doctors in house instead of just one, but she had been the type of person who would have left home to go tend a patient in the middle of the night. She wondered if that's what had happened to the murdered doctor. Had he been married? Did he have a family? Had he left them to do a good deed, getting repaid with a slashed throat?

She thought of her attacker's face over her, his hands grinding into her chest, and another shiver washed over her body.

Although her teeth chattered, she felt hot, sweat beading out of every pore on her body.

"Which apartment?" Marco asked. "You said fifteen. There is no fifteen on this floor."

She blinked, shaking her head. "Look at the key."

"It says sixteen."

"It is sixteen."

He went to the door marked with a 16 and looked at her. "You're pale as a ghost."

"I'm okay. I'm just hungry."

"Step aside." Marco motioned for her to lean against the wall, and she realized he was taking precaution that somebody could have been inside the apartment.

Oh yeah, good point, she thought, her face hanging slack as she watched him move.

She wanted to crawl into her bed and close her eyes. What was he doing here? She felt so sluggish. Her cut stung, feeling wet with the sweat.

Marco dropped the plastic bag and pizza box on the hallway

floor, pulled his Beretta again, and inserted the key. With fluid movement he twisted the lock, then the knob, pushed open the door, and stepped inside with gun raised.

She peeked around the corner, watching Marco move quickly out of sight, come back, and go out onto the balcony.

"Clear." He holstered the gun and drew the curtains closed for every window.

She picked up the pizza box, feeling dizzy as she stood upright, and stepped inside. Setting the pizza box on the kitchen table, she almost knocked over the bottle of wine and the half-drunk glass she'd left standing next to it.

Marco grabbed the bag from the hallway, shut the door, and locked it.

He said something, steering her toward the bed.

She let him lead her, frowning, staring at him, wondering if this was some sort of sexual advance.

"You need to lie down. You're going to pass out."

"I just need to sit." She flipped away his hand, then walked over and sat heavily on the couch.

Marco watched Ali sit on the couch. She leaned back with the force of a very drunk person who had mis-timed their movements. Her eyes were glassy, and her skin was whiter than the marble floor.

He dug out the ibuprofen he'd purchased at the pharmacy, poured out two from the bottle, and gave them to her with a glass of water. "Take this." He watched her swallow, then asked,

"Are you really hungry?" he asked. "Or are you just saying that?"

"I ..." She shook her head. "I was just saying that."

"Come." He put out his hand. "You have to lay down."

She reacted slowly, eventually scooting forward and standing.

Her shirt had a much larger blood stain now, and she winced, clutching her wound with her free hand.

"Try not to touch it." He led her to the bed, then opened the sheets for her.

She slipped off her shoes, then lay down. "It's so dirty in here," she said. "I'm sorry."

He put the sheets over her as she murmured, "It's filthy." She shivered, her teeth clicking in her mouth.

"It's okay. It's not dirty." He meant it. She had a couple of dishes sitting in the sink, and the bottle of wine sitting on the table, but other than that the place was cozy and neat, smelling like flowers and whatever fragrance she spritzed herself with. She was delirious.

He plucked a throw off the couch and draped it over her.

Staring at him, she squirmed under the sheets. A few seconds later she pulled something out from under the covers and threw it on the ground.

He looked down at her pants lying at his feet.

"Aren't you going to kiss me?" she asked.

"O-kay. Uh...just go to sleep." He continued straightening the sheets, avoiding her glazed look.

"I have to clean your cut." He walked to the kitchen table, picked up the plastic bag of supplies and brought it back to the bed. "But you're freezing. I'll probably..."

When he returned, her eyes were closed, her breathing deep, mouth parted slightly. He reached down and swept the hair off her forehead, feeling her burning hot skin.

He stared at her for a beat. "I'll probably wait until you're awake to clean your cut, even though you need it. Because that would be creepy for me to clean it right now, especially since you took your pants off. Right?"

He looked around. Nobody was there to answer.

She whimpered slightly, smacking her lips, eyes still closed.

"I'm going to wait." He sighed, walking back to the kitchen, setting the bag back on the table. He got her a glass of water, brought it to the nightstand, and set it down.

But why was she so feverish? He needed to clean the wound. To just let it sit there and fester while she slept in a pool of her own sweat would have been negligent. Right?

The apartment answered him with a shrug.

"Screw it," he said. He gathered a bowl of warm water from the kitchen and a clean washcloth from the bathroom closet, then came back to the side of the bed.

"I'm going to clean your wound now."

She whimpered slightly, turning her head to display her long, slender neck.

For a few more moments he stood, staring at her slow, rhythmic breathing, and then he reached down and pulled up the covers at the side, carefully folding them, exposing her arm, with a slender hand, noticing for the first time her nails were unpainted and kept short. Chewed, undoubtedly.

He pushed aside the blanket and sheet, exposing her leg and torso, her leg a smooth lane of bare skin that led up from the dark depths of the bed by her feet, ending at the strip of white silk of her underwear. Quickly he covered her leg with the sheet, keeping only the portion of the blouse splotched by blood exposed. The wound was on her right side, nearest him, which was a good thing.

He cleared his throat, reaching forward. "I'm going to pull up your shirt now."

She smacked her lips.

He lifted her shirt, slowly.

Her arm shifted, but remained by her side.

Come on, she needs the wound cleaned. Look at her, damn it. That's the problem!

Ignoring the argument going on in his head, he lifted the shirt to expose the wound. It was caked in blood, some of it seeping from a shoddy stitch at one end. Either the doctor hadn't been experienced or she'd been moving around too much all day. Probably a combination of both.

He removed the bandage very slowly, to minimize the pain of the tape pulling on her skin. That took what seemed like an hour. Then he dipped the washcloth in the warm water and got to work dabbing away the blood.

"Nnnnnnn," she frowned, her eyes still closed, and tried to roll sideways away from him.

"It's okay," he said. "It's okay." He reached up to pet her forehead, pausing before touching her skin. "Just relax," he said instead. "Just relax."

She rolled over onto her side, exposing the full backside of her silken underwear, which he quickly covered up. "Damn it," he said under his breath.

Without further deliberation he moved in again, pulling the blouse up, kneeling over her and making quick work of wiping away the blood. He added a dollop of antiseptic gel and applied another bandage. He climbed off the bed, covering her with the sheet and blanket.

In the kitchen, he poured himself some water and drank it down greedily, taking a second and third glass of the cool liquid, then opened the pizza box, unveiling the pizza inside.

Sitting at the table, he stared at the wine, ignoring its call. He could have used a glass, or three, but he needed to stay vigilant for this woman.

He blew through one slice in less than a minute, then stood, pacing as he ate a second. The walls were sparsely decorated, with just two framed photographs of landscapes: Tuscany in summer, with its rolling hills covered in grass, and Ligure, with its jagged shoreline surrounded by the shimmering Mediterranean. Both places Marco loved, places he had longed to live in at one time or another.

He grabbed a third slice, sucking down another sip of water, and went out onto the balcony.

He had to admit he loved the city, with everything it had to offer. But he had to get the hell out of here. Especially now.

There was a noise at the front door, shocking him to attention. He slipped back inside, setting the piece of pizza down and pulling his gun. Keeping his eyes on the crack of light seeping under the bottom of the door he waited for more movement, more sound. A couple of envelopes had been shoved under the door. That must have been the noise he had heard.

A moment later he heard faint footsteps leading down the hallway, and then a woman and a man speaking jovially.

"Ah, Signora Giovanni, you are taking Pippo for a walk?" the voice said, loud enough for Marco to understand clearly.

A dog growled.

The woman said something unintelligible, a door closed, and the conversation seemed to be over. He heard the faint clicking of dog claws as they tapped past, the elevator sliding open, and then the hallway went silent.

He holstered the gun, picked up the envelopes, saw they were junk mail for a woman named Chiara Bartolomeo, and set them on the counter.

It was then he noticed the cardboard box sitting against the wall, the one filled with all of Ali's father's personal belongings, scraped up by that scumbag landlord down in Rome. The guy had no shame, swooping in so quickly to turn over the property to the next renter. Marco had barely stopped himself from wringing the guy's neck.

He walked to the living room area of the studio apartment,

peeking around the corner to see how Ali was doing. She was still turned to her side, the profile of her face dark against the white pillow, one hand tucked under her chin. Her hair was splayed out on the pillow. With a sigh he went back outside to the balcony.

A pack of cigarettes sat on the small table outside. He'd never started up the habit.

Staring out at the city, he got the feeling somebody was staring back at him. He scanned every darkened nook and cranny in view, waiting for movement, a sign of a maniac staring back, but saw nothing.

He resisted turning around and going back into the apartment, walking back over to that bed, and staring down at that beautiful face again.

Guilt twisted in his stomach as thoughts of Valentina came rushing in again. She had been so angry this morning, so devastated at his proposal to postpone the wedding. He wondered where she was. He pulled out his phone and saw she still hadn't called or texted.

Who was he kidding? She would never call again. Not after the things he had said. Not after the admission he didn't love her anymore.

He slipped back inside, ate another piece of the pizza, leaving half for Ali when she woke up.

She made a noise, another whimper, like she was having a bad dream, or she had awoken and was confused.

When he turned the corner, he saw her lying on her other side now, and this time her whole face was covered by her hair.

He walked over and stopped, listening to the rhythm of her breathing. She was still in a deep sleep.

He reached down and brushed aside her hair, exposing her face, those long eyelashes resting on her cheeks, the full lips moving gently, as if she were speaking to somebody, as if she were whispering secrets to him. He pictured lying next to her, his head resting on the next pillow, receiving those whispers.

He backed away, shaking his head, making his way back into the kitchen.

Madonna. He needed a glass of wine.

27

Ali takes the ball and throws it, watching it bounce off the rock wall of the villa. The uneven surface of the stone sends the rubber ball shooting left and down, skipping hard off the grass and past her, tumbling down the slope of the lawn, over the erosion line, onto the sand, and into the shallow water of the lake.

"Six to four!" Cristina's yell is fueled by triumphant joy.

Ali wades into the icy water, plucking the ball out of the small waves, and runs back up to the lawn.

"Your turn." She hands the ball to her friend.

Cristina has been getting so lucky, with her bounces always coming straight back. Surely Ali's luck will change, and she'll win this latest competition between her and her friend, especially since Ali is the better athlete.

She watches Cristina throw the ball, and immediately knows she will score a point on this one.

"Ha!" she says, watching the ball fling sideways out of Cristina's hand, her friend's clumsiness finally showing itself. The angle is too much, the bounce will be sent into the trees!

But then Ali's face drops as she watches the ball's trajectory. It's heading straight for the window on the second floor, and as if in slow motion, she watches the ball punch a hole into the multi-colored glass, disappearing inside.

In horror, they both put their hands over their mouths, and they watch a jagged shard of the stained-glass window fall, smash into pieces, tinkle down the rock façade, and land on the grass.

For what seems like minutes, hours, they watch the window continue to disassemble, falling similarly over the edge, sometimes inward into the villa, crashes echoing out.

"What is happening!" Her father's voice booms from inside.

Cristina turns to Ali, her face blanched, her eyes already tearing. "I'm sorry, I'm sorry, I'm sorry!"

The front door squeals, and her father storms outside, stepping off the porch onto the grass.

"Damn it!" He reaches down and grabs his foot, kicks at something as he walks full speed toward them. "What happened?"

Cristina shrinks back, taking up position behind Ali. Cristina's own father is very mean, she assumes Ali's father is the same, and he looks like it the way he storms towards them, eyes looking incredulously up at the window and back at them.

"Ali? Speak!"

"I...we were throwing the ball and I threw it through the window!"

Her father arrives, studying her face, and Cristina's behind her. He looks up at the wall, and the black cavity that used to be a stained-glass window. A final shard breaks free and tumbles to the ground.

Her father keeps his back turned to them, studying the house, and again they wait for what seems like minutes.

"Well, that's not good," he says, turning to them. "You didn't mean to do it, did you?"

Ali shakes her head.

Her father nods. "Okay, you two. Come in and get your ball. We have some serious cleaning up to do."

. . .

Ali jerked awake. The sheets beneath her were soaking wet, wrapped around her limbs like vines keeping her lashed down.

She flung aside the bedding and sat up, getting her bearings. She recognized the small night light plugged into the wall, her nightstand next to her, the glass atop it. It was all hers. She was home.

She grabbed the glass of water off the windowsill and downed it, noticing the shape of the vessel in her hand was foreign. Since when did she have water glasses like these?

She didn't. She wasn't home. She was in Como. In Chiara's apartment.

Reaching over, she flicked on the light and got up, storming into the kitchen, her throat parched and demanding more liquid. After her third glass she looked down, seeing a large red spot on her shirt.

And the memories, the reality of the situation, came back to her. She twisted quickly, seeing Marco lying on the couch, his eyes open and staring at her.

"What the hell?" The glass clattered into the sink as she dropped it and pulled her shirt down to cover her exposed underwear.

Marco turned his head, putting a hand up to block his sight. "Sorry."

"Damn it," she said, marching back to the bed.

She opened her luggage, pulled out a tee-shirt and sweatpants and went into the bathroom, slamming the door behind her.

When she took off her shirt, she was alarmed to see a blood splotch the size of a pasta bowl had soaked through the fabric.

So much blood. She had seen so much blood over the last few days: the blood on the wall next to her father, the blood on her mother in the coroner's photographs, the blood pouring from her attacker's neck, the blood pooled under the murdered doctor. When was it going to stop?

She splashed water on her face and stared at herself in the mirror, deciding she looked decent. The whites of her eyes were clear, her skin full of color. Strength had returned to her limbs.

She remembered the first aid supplies they'd stopped to purchase last night. They were nowhere to be found in the bathroom. Then she realized the bandage over her cut was perfectly clean, slightly damp from sweat, but devoid of blood.

Slipping on her clothes, she padded outside, stopping at the sight of Marco sitting at the kitchen table.

Eyes tired, hair disheveled, he was stifling a yawn when she arrived. "I'm sorry. I should have said something. I thought you knew I was here."

"And I wanted to flash you my ass for a few minutes?"

His face went red, hands resting on the table as he looked down.

"You cleaned my cut?"

"Yes," he said, looking at her. "I was concerned. There was a lot of blood. You were delirious with fever. I wasn't going to let you lay there without cleaning it and giving you a fresh bandage."

"And you decided to take off my pants in the process?"

"You took off your own pants."

She blinked, horrified. "Oh."

"You were underneath the covers when you took them off. I didn't see anything. And I didn't look, I mean, I didn't see anything when I lifted the covers to put on the bandage."

"Well, that's good."

"Yeah." He flicked a hand, stood up, and walked back to the couch.

She tried to think back. She remembered coming in, sitting

on the couch, feeling heavy, getting up, but couldn't remember the act of going to sleep, of lying in the bed and falling asleep.

Marco laid down on the couch and faced away from her. He had no blanket. His shoes were on the floor near the front door. She walked to the bed and pulled off the throw that had been flung aside, brought it to Marco and draped it over his legs.

"Anyway," she said. "Thank you for cleaning my wound."

"You're welcome."

She walked back into the kitchen. The oven clock read 12:13 am. She felt completely rested. And ravenously hungry.

Marco had corked the bottle of red, placing it on the counter. The wine glass was scrubbed clean, along with two bowls and three plates she'd left in the sink, now neatly propped on the drying rack.

"There's some pizza in the refrigerator," he said, his voice still muffled by the back of the couch.

She opened the refrigerator and pulled out the pizza box. Without bothering to heat it, she grabbed a piece and ate.

She uncorked the wine, poured a glass, grabbed the box of pizza, and sat at the table.

The drapes were all drawn, and the effect was claustrophobic. But she remembered the way Marco had cleared the hallway and the apartment when they had arrived. There was still that mad knife-wielding man out there.

Her eyes landed on the box from her father's apartment. She had brought it up from her vehicle earlier and had been meaning to go through it but hadn't had the time or energy. Now that she had plenty of both, she picked up the box and put it on the table.

"Careful."

She looked over, finding Marco had turned around and was watching her.

Ignoring him, she opened the box.

The framed photographs that had been hanging on her father's walls were stacked neatly along one side.

The first picture was of her and her parents standing in sand next to the water's edge in Liguria, waves breaking behind them, all three of them squinting as the summer sun beat down, Ali was tanned, a skinny twelve-year-old in a bright yellow swimsuit, her mother young, vibrant, stunning in her bikini, her father as thin as he ever was, his skin also tanned dark, wearing a proud smile.

She pulled out the next photograph. The faded color photo showed her father standing next to Colombo, arms wrapping around each other's shoulders, easy smiles on their faces as they stood on her father's old Riva boat.

There was a photo of her mother in a winter coat, standing on a mountain in the Dolomites, skis buckled to her feet. One picture showed Ali, no more than eight years old, wearing a backpack. She kept digging, feeling the sadness deepen inside of her. Then she found a ball tucked into the corner of the box.

She stared at it, then picked it up, turning the heavy rubber in her hands.

Remembering the dream, she felt her father's presence there with her. Tears welled in her eyes, and soon she couldn't lean over without dripping them into the box. A warm hand landed on her shoulder, squeezing gently.

She stepped back, closing her eyes. She turned to walk away but collided with Marco. At first, she stutter-stepped to the side, but his arms wrapped around her, rooting her in place. They stood motionless like that, Marco's arms around her, hers hanging by her sides, and just when Marco released her, seemingly self-conscious about the embrace, she reached up and wrapped her arms around his torso.

The ball dropped to the ground, rolling away.

Marco returned the embrace again and they stood in each

other's arms, Ali's ear pressing to his chest, hearing his heart race. She squeezed, gentle but firm, and Marco did the same, responding to her instantly.

Her heart hammered, too, and she felt her breathing quicken.

And then he unwrapped his arms and stepped back, averting his eyes as he went to the kitchen sink and poured himself a glass of water.

She stood, wiping her face with her forearm, then split in the opposite direction, walking to get a tissue from the bathroom.

When she returned, she found Marco lying on the couch again, staring at the ceiling.

What had just happened? Was that an act of compassion for her loss, or something else? Something more?

Shaking off the strange, exhilarating encounter as best she could, she walked back to the cardboard box. She knew more pain sat inside the cardboard enclosure, but she didn't care. She had to face it.

She pulled out the next picture, this one showing Ali's mother in her white coat, a stethoscope draped over her neck. Her smile was so beautiful, so radiant that the picture seemed to give off heat.

A small box inside caught her eye. It was small, the kind one would store jewelry inside of, perhaps some of her mother's jewelry, or her father's rings, or...

The logo inlaid on the top of it made her breath catch.

IWC Schaffhausen.

She put the photo aside, reached in, and picked up the case.

. . .

Marco lay on the couch, staring at the ceiling, feeling an ever-increasing tightness in his chest. He was a complete idiot. What was he doing?

You're an asshole!

Valentina's words from this morning's fight slashed across him, like she was right here screaming in his face again.

Look at me, though, almost taking advantage of a woman in such a vulnerable state, and not even twenty-four hours after breaking it off with a woman I've been with for seven years, ending a six-month engagement, vaporizing the months of wedding plans and the money that had already been paid.

Maybe he was an asshole.

He had to pull himself together and act like a respectable man in this situation, not...not whatever he was doing.

He looked over to Ali as she sifted through the box on the kitchen table. Her hair cascaded over her face, keeping her beauty in broken shadow.

Did he just break up his relationship for this woman he'd barely spent more than two days with? Is that what he'd done? Ended something real for a crush? If that was the case, then he'd made a mistake. He didn't even know this woman. She didn't even know him.

But no. It hadn't been Ali. She had been the catalyst for him making the final cut. He broke it off because Valentina was trying to make him somebody he was not. For God's sake, after telling Valentina about his role in the new Elisabetta Sottocornola case she had spoken about him getting into politics. Politics? Why? Because he looked good on the TV screen near the podium, she had said. Which would have been okay in itself, but she'd gone as far as to set up a meeting between him and a former parliament member friend of her father's to discuss specific steps to make it a reality. And there was the way she spoke of trying for kids within two years, three in total by the end of the decade. The way she had been planning his life after the wedding with such detail, with no regard to what he wanted, had disturbed him deeply.

Valentina had turned into somebody else. Or he'd just been blind until now. Either way, he wanted no more of it.

He realized Ali was staring at him, her face contorting, looking at an open box in her hand.

"What?"

She shook her head, looking at the object in her hand.

Marco walked over to see that inside the box, tucked into a black felt interior, a platinum watch gleamed, identical to the one they had found in the ground next to Elisabetta Sottocornola's body.

He frowned. "My God. It's the exact same."

But the match wasn't exact—this one had a huge crack in the crystal face, distorting the image of the hour and minute hands beneath.

Ali ran a finger over the crack. "I remember doing this. I dropped the watch. I did this. I thought it was just a dream or something. But I remember." She pulled the watch from the felt restraint and turned it over, moving underneath the overhead kitchen light.

Marco stayed close, watching the light lance off the inscription beneath:

To Stefano.

You are the love of my life.

He frowned deeper, trying to comprehend what he was looking at. The inscription they had found on the watch near Elisabetta Sottocornola's body had read:

• • •

To Dino.

You are the love of my life.

"I ... I don't get it." Ali turned over the watch again.

"That makes two of us."

Marco saw there was a folded piece of paper in the box, tucked out of sight against the edge. He took the box and with his fingernails he pried the paper loose. He gave the paper to Ali, taking the watch from her in exchange.

She unfolded the thick cardstock. "It's from Colombo."

Marco saw slanted black ink he instantly recognized as the second lieutenant's scrutable handwriting.

"My Dearest Friend Dino. Your gift was too much, but I humbly accept it with great honor. I know you would have done the same for me if the situation were reversed. You know I've always loved this watch. But now you constantly asking me what time it is has become unacceptably annoying. Happy Birthday my friend. Sincerely, Stefano."

She lowered the note, looking at the watch again. "So...this is my father's watch? Colombo gave the same watch to my father for his birthday?"

Marco pointed at the letter. "'I know you would have done the same for me if the situation were reversed?' What does that mean?"

She thought back. "Colombo told me earlier today that...he would have given his life for my father. And that he almost did." She shook her head. "I didn't know what that meant at the time, and I never did get to ask him about it. We were too busy talking about other things."

She stared at the note again. "So...my father got a watch

from my mother. And he gave it to Colombo after Colombo saved his life, leaving my father without a watch."

"And so Colombo gave him the same watch as a gift, identical in every way except for the cheeky inscription on the back," Marco finished her thought. "It would have upset your mother, though, right? She had bought the watch for your father, had it inscribed to him, professing her love for him, and he gave it away?"

"No. It wouldn't have upset her." She smiled, shaking her head. "In fact, if she knew how much Colombo liked the watch, she would have insisted on it. The awkwardness of the inscription would have made her laugh." She turned over the watch, pointing at the writing on the bottom.

"So...it was Colombo's watch found next to Elisabetta," he said. "Not your father's."

Ali's smile vanished, her eyes darkening. "He's been lying right to our faces. I can't believe it."

Marco pulled his phone from his pocket, seeing it was now twelve-thirty a.m. It didn't matter. The man had been betrayed, too. They all had. He would want to know right now.

"I'll call Dante."

28

"Yes sir, we're sure. Ali says she remembers dropping the watch and cracking the face. This is the watch Dino Falco has always had. Not the one we found in the ground."

Ali watched Marco pace her apartment, phone pressed to his ear. She could hear the tinny scratch of Dante's voice coming out of the ear speaker.

"Doesn't he remember any of this?"

Marco lowered the phone slightly. "What?"

"Put me on speaker."

Marco tapped the button and thrust the phone toward her.

"Daniele?"

Dante's voice filled the apartment. "Ali. I'm here."

"Do you know about Colombo saving my father's life?"

"I...don't know all the details. But I know Colombo was shot by someone. He took the bullet, and somehow the bullet was meant for your father. Colombo pushed him just as he was going to be shot and took the bullet in his hip. I was a rookie in the department at the time, but it was a big deal. Colombo got a medal for his bravery. It's one of the reasons he moved through the ranks so quickly."

"How is that possible that I never heard about that?" she asked, pacing the room. She remembered being very young when she dropped the watch, four or five years old. Her father apparently kept a lot of life details to himself, especially monumental ones like these. Then again, his silence fit a pattern—Colombo had been hurt on his behalf. Of course he would have kept the story quiet.

"If it's any consolation," Dante said, "I never heard much about it either, and I was in the department with them. They kept it close, whatever the details were."

She paced to the window and back, hefting the box in her hand. "But what about this watch? You never saw Colombo wearing this watch after that incident?"

A long pause. "Colombo has always been a watch connoisseur. He has at least ten watches in his collection. And we're talking about what, twenty, twenty-five years ago when he would have been wearing it? I'm sorry. I don't remember specifically. Again, I was a rookie back then. Your father and Colombo were ten years on the force already when I joined. I wasn't exactly rubbing elbows with them until later in my career."

Dante breathed into the microphone as if he was walking, the speaker rustling. "Anyway. I want to see this watch. And..." He stopped speaking, or his voice cut out.

Marco looked at his phone. "Are you there, sir?"

"Yes. I am here. I was just...I am thinking, give me a second, please." Dante said nothing, and they waited.

Ali felt like she was hopped up on five espressos, her body thrumming with anticipation. "We need to speak to Colombo," she said.

Still, Dante didn't speak.

"Sir?"

"I'm just looking through some photographs," Dante said.

Ali frowned, looking at Marco. "Of what?"

"Oh God. Okay, listen. I need to meet with you two as soon as possible. Meet me at your villa."

"The villa?" Ali asked. "Why?"

"If I'm right, there is something there I need to show you. It could explain a lot. If I'm not mistaken, it could explain everything."

"Okay," she said.

"Bring the watch and the note. And for God's sake, bring your gun this time, Ali."

The call clicked off. Marco pocketed his phone, eyeing her. "Are you up for leaving?"

"And figuring out what happened to my father? To my mother?" She went to her nightstand and retrieved her Berretta from the drawer. She checked the gun, tucking it into her holster, and put the holster on her belt. "Let's go."

29

"Is that him?" Ali leaned toward the windshield, squinting. A vehicle was parked along the wall in front of the villa, lights off.

As if on cue, a web of lightning crackled above, and everything—the lake to their right, the iron spike-tipped wall, the villa, the overgrown trees, and Dante's BMW sedan—was illuminated as if it were one in the afternoon, and not one in the morning.

"It's him," Marco said. His Audi coasted forward, headlights blazing against Dante's parked vehicle.

Dante's brake lights blossomed as they approached.

She rolled down the passenger side window as they slowed next to him. Dante sat, a cigarette wedged between his fingers, smoke wafting into the still air, his face pale in the dashboard lights.

"I'll follow you in," he said, waving them forward.

"Pull up there." She pointed. "I'll get out and push open the gate. The code doesn't work."

Her feet swished through damp grass, mud soft underneath

from the previous night's downpour. She grasped the cool iron gate and slid it along the rails, wide enough for the cars to slip through.

As she walked back to Marco's car, she felt a huge drop of rain slap her head. Another drop smacked against the top of Marco's Audi, and then a dozen of them at once. She ducked into the vehicle and shut the door. Within seconds the torrent began.

Marco muttered a curse, muffled by the sound of the drops drumming the roof of the car, as he flicked on his windshield wipers and pulled through the gate. Ali thumbed the house keys in her pants pocket as they crawled down the road. The outside porch lights were somehow still on, probably running on the same timer since her childhood.

It was not her father's watch in the ground next to Elisabetta Sottocornola's body. It was Colombo's watch, given to him by her father as a gift. She reminded herself of the situation for the fiftieth time, the shock of Colombo's audacity still just as strong as the first time she'd opened that box and saw the watch with the cracked face.

"Park in that spot there," she said, almost having to shout over the sound of the rain. "Furthest left in front of the garage. It's closest to the front door."

Marco parked and shut off the engine. Dante pulled up alongside them, his car rocking to a stop.

"Ready?" Marco asked.

She wasted no time, not waiting for Dante, running as fast as she could to the front door, Marco and Dante close on her heels.

They stood under the faint yellow light of the porch, watching the glimmering, simmering wall of water a meter away, spraying them with mist.

Dante shook his hair. His coat opened, revealing a button up shirt and slacks, dressed to impress even at one in the morning. The handle of his own firearm showed, tucked into his shoulder holster.

Dante motioned to the door impatiently.

She inserted the key and twisted the lock, swinging open the door. Dante walked in after her, then stepped into the house, flicking on the interior light. Marco stepped onto the mat, wiping his feet.

She shut the door behind them, quieting the chaos outside. Their shoes squeaked on the tile floor. Rain lashed against the entryway window, filling the space with violent tapping sounds. Muffled thunder shook the stones of the villa.

Dread filled her and she remained rooted near the door, not wanting to see the blood again. She held her breath as long as she could, then breathed through her mouth, not wanting to smell the stale death of her father.

Dante studied her, walking to the main hallway and flicking on the light there. "I had a disaster cleaning team come in yesterday. Any sign of what happened here has been removed. Including the couch."

She took a breath through her nose, noting the strong cleaning fluid scent, and stepped down the hallway, past Dante, and into the kitchen, allowing her eyes to seek farther into the house to the living room.

It looked strange with the large leather couch missing, the rug that used to lay beneath it gone, along with the television. It was not the house of her childhood anymore, just a vast, sterile space of earthen tile.

Ali noticed the meal that had been brutally paused mid-preparation, was no longer strewn about the counter. It looked like the place was ready to sell to the highest bidder.

That was fast, she thought. She was under the impression the investigation was far from over. That's why they were here.

Marco walked past the kitchen and into the living room, where it was darker. Lightning flashed outside, strobing the interior of the house, and a boom of thunder shook the villa again.

"Where's the watch?" Dante asked.

She reached into her jacket pocket and pulled out the box, handing it over to Dante.

Dante grabbed it with two fingers, carefully setting it down on the counter. He ripped a sheet of paper towel off the nearby roll and wiped his hands, then picked up the box and opened it.

His face remained neutral, but his hands were curious, plucking the watch from the velvet interior, twisting it in his fingers, studying the inscription on the rear of the casing.

"The note is tucked inside," she said, "right where we found it."

Dante pulled out the note, unfolded it, and read it silently.

She scanned the family room, looking so different to her without the couch. "Why did you remove everything?" she asked. "Isn't the investigation still ongoing?"

Dante kept his eyes on the note. "We documented everything."

Marco walked into the kitchen and leaned against a counter. "It looks like we said, right?" He gestured to the watch.

Dante seemed lost in thought, nodding gently. "So, Colombo saves your father's life, and your father gives him his watch. And then, later, Colombo gives him an identical watch, with this inscription on the back. As a clever joke."

"What do you think?" Marco asked.

"I think you're right." He looked up at them in turn, his eyes earnest.

Just then light slanted in down the hallway, traveling across the kitchen wall, as if somebody were pulling up outside.

"And I think it will be interesting to hear what he has to say about it." Dante set the watch down and walked toward the entryway.

"Is that him?" she asked, her heartrate jumping. She followed Dante down the hall toward the front door, reaching inside her coat, pulling her gun.

"Relax." Dante put out a hand to her, then continued down the hall to the front window.

"Relax? This watch here shows Stefano killed Elisabetta Sottocornola. Which means he killed my mother. Relax?" She felt the weight of the Beretta in her hand. She had never fired her weapon on duty. The old adage was never to pull your weapon unless you were prepared to use it. Would she use it on Colombo?

Over the thrashing rain on the windows, she heard the squeal of brakes, the thump of a car door.

Dante shook his head, looking back at her. "What the hell is he doing here? Did you talk to him?"

"No." Ali looked at Marco. She had taken a few moments in the bathroom of Chiara's apartment to change her clothes before they left. Had Marco talked to Colombo then?

Marco held up his hands. "Not me."

"He's coming," Dante said.

She clutched the Beretta tighter, keeping her finger out of the trigger guard.

"Ali, relax," Dante said. "Allow me to take care of this. Step back into the kitchen, both of you."

Ali and Marco ducked back out of view into the hallway.

The metallic rap of the door knocker echoed through the villa.

"It's okay," Marco said under his breath. His gun rested at his side.

Things were anything but okay, she thought. And what *was* Colombo doing here? She looked at Marco. He stood with his neck craned, hand clenching his gun, eyes wide and attentive.

The front door opened, and the sound of the rain filled the interior for a moment, a cold shot of air furling down the hallway and over Ali's face, raising goosebumps on her skin.

Something wasn't right.

"What the hell is going on?" Colombo's voice echoed down the hall. "What are you?—"

"Do you have your gun?" Dante asked.

The door shut.

"Give it to me," Dante said. "Slowly."

"What are you doing?" Colombo asked. "Where's Ali?"

"She's here. In the kitchen. With Marco."

The two men walked around the corner, shoes squeaking on the tile.

Colombo came into view first, wearing a long trench coat, sweatpants and sweatshirt peeking out from beneath. His hair was drenched, dripping water down his face, off his chin and onto the floor.

He stopped at the sight of Ali and Marco, eyeing the Berettas in their hands.

"Go on." Dante came into view, holding two guns now. "Move. Into the kitchen. Look at the watch Ali found, and the note that goes with it."

Colombo looked past them at the watch on the peninsula counter that separated the kitchen from the living room. His face remained unreadable.

"Go," Dante said.

Ali and Marco backed up to the kitchen sink counter opposite, their weapons half-raised and ready for any sudden movements from the second lieutenant.

Colombo slowed to a stop in front of the box, looking down, his arms by his sides.

"Go ahead," Dante said. "Pick it up. Take a look."

"I don't need to. I know what it is. I bought it for God's sake. I had it inscribed. I wrote the letter. I gave it to him."

"So you admit it," Ali said. "You gave that watch to my father."

Colombo said nothing.

"You gave him this watch because he gave you his," Ali said. "That's what happened, right?"

Colombo nodded. Rain dripped off his chin.

"Which means all this time it's been your watch in that grave up on the mountain," she said. "Next to the girl you killed."

Colombo shook his head. "I didn't—"

"And you killed my mother!" Her voice echoed in the space.

"No." Colombo shook his head and turned to Ali. "I swear to you. I didn't. I..." Colombo raised a hand to his forehead. He gripped his scalp with a claw of a hand, wiping down the side of his face, as if he were trying to ignore screams in his head.

"She had my watch. But I didn't kill her."

Ali frowned. "Why would she have your watch?"

"I gave it to her. For the abortion. She needed money." He turned around, slowly, looking in turn at Ali's gun, then Marco's, and the two in Dante's hands. "Oh, Ali. I'm sorry."

"For the abortion?" Dante aimed both guns at Colombo from his hip. "In case you're wondering, Ali, this man was screwing Elisabetta Sottocornola. Isn't that right, second lieutenant?"

Colombo said nothing, shame lowering his eyelids.

"And he got her pregnant," Dante said. "And he wanted her

to terminate the baby, so he gave her money. Sent her to the best doctor in town. Your mother. Elisabetta was supposed to go in, keep her mouth shut, and do the procedure, but instead she talked, didn't she, Stefano?"

Colombo shook his head.

"She talked about the important man, the cop, she was seeing. She saw the photograph of you and Dino hanging in her mother's office, and Elisabetta pointed at you and said he's the man. That's him."

Dante smiled, and then shook his head, the mirth turning to disgust. "And your mother, Ali, being the good person she was, didn't tell anybody. She could have told your father, she could have gone to the press, outing this important man, the great Stefano Colombo, who had just been promoted to marshal, the head of the entire region of the Carabinieri. But your mother wasn't motivated like some of the political jackals out there, who would have killed to get a piece of information like this, mind you."

Dante looked at Ali.

Ali frowned, seeing the strange look that had taken hold in Dante's eyes, like a petulant child who's been told it's time to go to bed.

"Instead, she went to him." Dante looked back at Colombo. "And she gave you an ultimatum. To do the right thing, of your own accord. To come clean."

Ali stood frozen, watching Colombo's eyes. It was all true, she could see. Her eyes flicked back to Dante.

Why *had* Colombo come here in the first place? Dante must have called him.

"How do you know all of this?" Ali asked, now acutely aware of her gun's position, aiming at the ground halfway between her and Colombo.

Dante's eyes flicked to her. "I've been this man's loyal

servant for twenty-five years, Ali. I make it my business to look out for him, to listen in on conversations, recording them, if need be, so I can protect him. It's good business for me, after all."

"So...you knew about Colombo and Elisabetta?" Ali asked. "From the beginning?"

"Of course."

Dante stared back at her. His face had changed, his upper lip tilted slightly, his eyes dead as a corpse. The two guns in his hand flared, booming in the confined space almost simultaneously.

She flinched and watched in horror as Marco and Colombo fell hard into each other, then onto the ground, both landing on the tile at her feet, their bodies convulsing, then slumping still.

The air was suddenly filled with acrid gun powder discharge, her ears whining in an angry high-pitched tone.

"I'm sorry, Ali." Dante moved like lightning, aiming both guns at Ali before she could even think to move. "I didn't want to kill your mother, but it's really this asshole's fault. He couldn't help but fill the local street walkers with his seed on a regular basis. And this one, this Elisabetta girl, he'd gone and fallen in love with, the sicko. He'd gotten her pregnant, and she'd wanted a lot more than a few bucks for a procedure at your mother's clinic. She didn't even want to have the procedure. That was the big problem. She wanted to keep the baby."

Dante chuckled, this time looking like he was enjoying the moment.

Ali's eyes stung, tears welling up. She looked down at Marco's inert form, unable to see a wound on his back, but he was lying face down. Dead still. Colombo's leg was twitching.

"And if she talked?" Dante continued talking, his expression manic. "If anything got out, especially at that time? I couldn't have that for my career. I'd spent years catering to this man's every whim so I could someday get to be where I am now. Colombo knew about me, too, Ali. And he accepted me. He was going to bring me along with him on his climb up the ladder."

Without looking down, Dante kicked Colombo in the side of the head.

"But now I don't need him. I've climbed high enough with him. He's dead weight." He snorted a laugh, his eyes immediately turning cold again.

Still frozen, her aim now on the two bodies at her feet, again she looked down at Marco and Colombo.

Blood streaked out from under Marco, following a grout line toward her shoe.

Dante continued to speak, but she heard nothing but the high-pitched tone in her ears as she stared at Marco's dead form.

She looked at Dante again, seeing a crazed look in his eyes, staring at her, both guns still pointed with unshaking precision at her chest.

"—and I am sorry," he was saying. "The girl was not trustworthy to keep a living child as a secret, and your mother? That's Colombo's fault, too. He shouldn't have recommended her. And he sure as hell shouldn't have given that girl the watch! If your father had learned about that, he would have put everything together eventually. And of course, that's why he had to die."

"You're not going to get away with this," she said.

Dante shrugged. "I shot Marco with Colombo's gun, and Colombo with mine. I'll put the gun in Colombo's hand and fire one into the wall. Maybe into your dead corpse. It will be the same thing that oaf did with your father. I'll be in charge of the investigation. It will all be Colombo's doing. Everything from your mother to her daughter, and everyone in between. I'll be just fine, Ali."

A tear flowed down Dante's cheek.

He smiled, wiping his face quickly with one sleeve, momentarily aiming one of the weapons astray, but just as quickly he returned to his previous position, both barrels pointed straight at her.

And here she was, still frozen stiff, every muscle in her body tensed.

She still had her gun, though. There was no doubt she would die, it was only a matter of seconds now. But something told her to remain still. To keep him talking.

"So you hired that man to kill my father," she said. "The man who attacked me."

Dante smiled, a sad, lifeless gesture. "I don't know if it was the same guy who attacked you. They have a lot of men on their roster. But I forgot to tell them about your father's left-handedness." He shook his head. "So stupid of me." He looked down at Colombo.

Ali tensed, wondering how fast she could raise the gun and shoot him in the head, evading the shots of the two guns at the same time. "Them? You forgot to tell them?"

Dante's eyes flicked back up to her. "Very bad men, Ali. If you need very bad things to be done, then you call very bad men. Now drop your gun."

A deep groan came from one of the men on the ground.

Ali looked down for a split second, then looked back up at Dante, knowing this was her opportunity. Dante's face scrunched in annoyance, his aim wavering downward.

Ali took her chance, ducking to the side as she raised her gun, shooting as soon as the tip of the barrel raked up across Dante's center mass.

The small space erupted in sound and light again. Both her and Dante's guns fired almost simultaneously.

Unimaginable pain punched her upper right arm, twisting

her as if she'd been sideswiped by an American football player. She collided hard into the edge of the counter, her gun clattering to the floor, her arm now useless, no longer able to grasp her Beretta. Her shoes slipped on the slick blood underneath her, and she landed on her side on the kitchen tile.

"Cazzo!" Dante grunted in pain, bending over, clearly hit.

She struggled to her feet, her shoes slipping again on the blood, gripping Colombo's foot with her free hand for balance. She could have sworn she felt movement of Colombo's leg muscles. Had it been him who made the noise? Marco remained motionless.

Dante's gun fired again.

She ducked, splintered wood behind her burrowing into her skin through her jacket.

He fired again, and she felt the bullet graze her hip, feeling like she'd been hit by a bullwhip on bare skin.

She got her feet underneath her and dove, colliding with the wall. Another gunshot missed her. She didn't bother looking for her weapon, there was no time, she just wanted to get into the family room, around the corner of the peninsula counter that separated the two spaces, to shelter from flying bullets.

She made it, rolling again, ignoring the flashing pain from her injuries.

Safely around the corner and into the family room, she still felt utterly exposed in the open space. There was no furniture to hide behind, no gun to protect her when Dante rounded the corner.

"Ah, you're dead, bitch. You're dead."

She heard his feet squeak on the tile. Frantically she searched the area. The brass floor lamp that used to stand next to the couch now stood alone. It was tall and unwieldy, especially with her good arm limp at her side. There was an iron fireplace poker and shovel propped next to it but moving across the room would expose her immediately.

Think!

She looked around frantically, her eyes landing on a shiny globe set in a wood cradle—a large marble her mother had purchased in Murano on one of their vacations—clear glass with an inlaid flower.

She picked it up with her left hand, hefting the weight. She could throw it like a ball at Dante when he rounded the corner. And do what? Give him a bruise? That wouldn't work, and that was even if she could hit him throwing with her off hand.

Think!

A bolt of lightning hit close outside, the searing light flashing in through the window next to her. She turned and sighted in on the glass, the ball clutched in her hand.

Without hesitation she reeled back and threw the marble.

With a loud crash a jagged hole opened up in the window, and as the glass tumbled in sheets down to the floor and out into the rain, Ali dove, fist punching, head ducking.

The glass gave way easily, her adrenaline running too high to feel any of the dozens of cuts that raked across her arm, scalp, and neck as she burst through. For a moment she floated, the tinkling of glass faint behind the rush of water that was suddenly all around her, then she landed hard on her side.

For an instant she lay stunned as cold water cascaded over her, staring up at the window she'd just dove through, now a half-covered opening into the villa a good two meters above her.

A blast of gunfire shattered the remainder of the window, and with glass falling on her, without consulting her body and the injuries that might or might not have been there, she rolled, got up, and ran alongside the house.

Another gunshot rang out, and she could hear a bullet slice through the rain next to her head.

She ducked around the corner, wincing and falling to her knees, feeling something sharp jabbing into her leg above the ankle. Had she been shot? No. It was a small, thin shard of glass that was jammed into her flesh, piercing the denim of her jeans.

She reached down and touched the fragment, clenching her teeth as pain shot up the inside of her leg. With a grunt she grabbed it and pulled, ignoring the head-swirling pain that pulsed up her leg as she threw the glass into the night.

She leaned into the exposed stone at the back of the house. The two stained glass windows of the living room filtered faint light above her. She looked up at them, waiting for a moving shadow, but no movement came.

The more she waited, the more dread took hold. Dante could be coming outside right now, rounding the house to pick her off. If only she could have grabbed her gun. She needed a weapon, but she stood on long grass.

"Shit."

The lakeshore, with its rocks she had used against the tattooed man, lay thirty or forty paces away. How about escape? The dock was barely visible through the rain, and she already knew there was no boat tied there. Not anymore.

She hadn't even driven here. Marco had, and the keys would be in his pocket.

Marco!

She needed to get him to help, or help to—

Her phone! She had purchased the burner phone earlier, and it was still sitting in her pocket. Damn it, she was thinking too slowly. She pulled it out, praying the water hadn't drowned the cheap device yet.

With a push of a side button the screen illuminated, and she dialed 1-1-3.

"*Polizia*, what is the nature of your emergency?"

"I've been shot. There's been a shooting." She gave the address, not pausing to let the man on the other line speak. When she was done, she left the phone call connected and put it in her pocket.

Dante was close, she could feel it. She hobbled to the front edge of the house, favoring her good ankle, snuck to the corner, and peeked out.

Another vehicle arrived, parked behind their cars. Hope flared inside her, but it was short-lived, replaced by horror as she saw the figure standing motionless in the rain near the front porch.

Lightning flashed and she saw the big man. His clothing was matted to his body, accentuating rippled muscles. He wore what looked like a neck brace. His attention was directed toward the other side of the house.

Her knees felt weak as she stepped backward.

"There you are!"

Dante's voice came out of the rain. He had snuck around the corner behind her.

She turned around and now they stood face to face, the barrel of his pistol no more than a meter away.

All hope washed out of her.

Dante's hooded eyes dripped rivulets of water. With bared teeth, his head was cocked against the driving rain, free arm pressing against his abdomen. He convulsed, and when he did his eyes went wild with fear. But the episode stopped just as quickly as it had begun, and he motioned with the gun. "Back inside."

She stayed where she was.

He shot the gun, aiming it to the side of her.

She didn't flinch, which surprised even her.

"Move!"

Ali stood her ground, deciding she would wait to join her mother and father with dignity.

But then something powerful gripped her from behind, yanking her backward off her feet. And then she was moving, carried under the arms, her feet dragging, hauled by a muscular arm painted with an Egyptian eye tattoo.

30

Ali landed hard on the tile floor of the entryway room, her gunshot arm hitting the ground with an explosion of pain.

She looked up at the big, muscular man. He was just as menacing, if not more, with the wound she'd given him the night before. He was rain-soaked, his chest painted with a streak of red, blood running out of the neck brace and down his shirt.

"Bring her into the kitchen!" Dante shuffled past her. His voice was a controlled grunt now, his abdomen wound clearly bad and getting worse. "I need her in there to stage the killing."

"She's soaking wet, with blood washed all over her." The big man's voice was hoarse, the only indication the stab to his neck had caused him any harm. "It'll look like she's been shot and ran outside, and that she came back inside."

"Shit." Dante stopped inside the entryway along the wall opposite her, his wild eyes flicking back and forth. "Okay, get the old man and bring him out here."

The big man stepped away from Ali to the hallway. "The

guy lying in a pool of blood? What's the angle you're playing there?"

"Just fucking do it!" Dante buckled over in pain, leaning into the wall as he dropped his gun onto the floor.

Ali watched the weapon skitter a few feet from Dante, but no nearer to her.

Neck Wound stayed where he was, looking between them.

Ali kept her head up, noticing the big man was now holding a gun at his side. Her neck felt like a hot poker was jabbed into it, something to do with the muscles tensing because of the gunshot to her shoulder, but she kept her head up, searching for any crack in the fate these two assholes were dealing her. The police had to be on their way. Minutes from arriving, anytime now. She had to stall and try to take advantage of the ensuing chaos.

You have to make your own fate, Ali. She remembered her father kneeling in front of her, his kind eyes twinkling as he wiped the tears from her cheeks that day. He was with her. So was her mother.

Waiting for outside help wasn't going to cut it.

"I called the police a few minutes ago," she said, deciding to bring the chaos to these men early. The panic in Dante's face made her smile. "That's right," she said. "They're on their way. They have to be close."

"What the fuck?" The big man shook his head, shuffle-stepping in place. "I'm out of here."

"No! Wait! An extra hundred-grand if you bring the man out here to me." Dante grunted. "Then you can go. Just drag him out here."

Ali focused beyond the big man in the hallway to the kitchen. Colombo still lay face down, clearly dead, all the blood that had been inside his body now on the kitchen tile. Marco was still there, still motionless, although it looked like he had moved positions significantly, turning his body a hundred and eighty degrees, as if he had tried to crawl his way out of the kitchen and down the hall but the life had drained out of him. Now he lay face down in the pool of blood, which was larger than ever.

She watched as Neck Wound cursed under his breath and walked to the kitchen. Just as he left, Dante reached over for his gun.

"Wait!" she said.

"What the hell do you want?" Neck Wound spoke fast, pointing the gun at her. "Shut up!"

"He's going to shoot you," she said, nodding toward Dante. "He's going to shoot you when you get back here. Look!"

Neck Wound stepped quickly back to the entry room, looking down at Dante.

Dante had been stretching for the gun, but the wound in his bloodied abdomen wouldn't let him reach it. He sagged back into the wall again, shaking his head. "Don't listen to that bitch. Get the old man."

"He showed everyone your file, you know that?" Ali said. "We all saw it. You're from Naples. We saw your rap sheet."

"Yeah, so what?"

Dante reached for his gun again.

"So you'll go into that kitchen and bring that dead man out, and then he'll shoot you, crawl over and shoot me with your gun, and put all the blame on you. You're a killer. You take the rap, and he gets away."

The big man looked at Dante.

"Don't listen to that bitch." Dante reached over, missing his gun again. With a loud grunt he finally tipped himself over, then clutched his weapon.

The space erupted in another loud boom as Dante's head

exploded onto the wall behind him. His body slumped to the floor.

Ali gazed at the service Beretta underneath Dante's lifeless hand, still an impossible distance away, knowing she would never get the chance to use it.

Big man lowered his smoking gun, squaring off to Ali.

"I told you, I called the cops," she said. "They're on their way."

He stared at her, putting a hand up on his neck, touching the neck brace gingerly. His eyes flared with hunger. "That's a shame. I would have liked to have some time with you." He raised his gun and aimed it at her. "Oh well."

"Wait!" She held up a hand. "Wait!"

"Not this time. Sorry."

There was another loud bang.

She shut her eyes.

And when she realized she hadn't been hit by a bullet, she opened them.

A patch of blood grew on the man's chest. He jerked rigidly, eyes widening, and then his expression went slack. His hand dropped from his neck. His gun clattered from his other hand to the floor. Then his knees buckled and he fell, head whipping down, connecting with the tile, sounding like a dropped cannon ball.

She lay still, listening to the sound of rain patter against the windows, and the growing sound of sirens.

She got to her elbow and focused over the man, back into the living room, to the smoking gun in Marco's hand.

31

FIVE DAYS LATER...

Ali's shoes clicked, the sound echoing off the marble and stone as she walked down the long hallway of the columbarium. Light from the gothic rose window behind her pushed her shadow ahead of her, Basso's and Chiara's shadows still a good distance back.

She passed crypt plates of varying degrees of elegance, carved inscriptions commemorating the deceased remains behind them. She decided at first chance she would tell those in her life to scatter her ashes out in a Tuscan field when she died—any field, so long as it was decent-looking—and, for the love of God, to not seal her into a tiny box in the wall of a mausoleum like this.

The urn containing her father's remains felt light in her hands, considering it contained an entire human body, albeit condensed down to a pile of carbon. The ceramic container was brown, with silver leaves on the top, the shape reminding Ali of an ancient Greek amphora, minus the handles. And she could have used the handles. Never had she felt so scared of dropping something, clutching the container with one hand against her body, the other unable to help as it hung limp in a sling hooked off her right shoulder.

Basso and Chiara's footsteps continued tapping in tune with hers, always remaining a few paces behind her.

Ahead, a panel had been removed from the right wall, creating a dark hole among a particularly floral section of cremation niches. A man dressed in a dark suit waited with folded hands and a somber expression, a bucket filled with cement at his feet, a trowel lying on a cloth on the floor underneath her parents' final resting place.

The man nodded, lowering his eyes.

Ali stopped, looking into the darkened space, and the urn that sat inside.

Light lanced off the polished marble floors such that the container filled with her mother's ashes cast a shadow behind it. It stood smack in the center of the shelf, with twenty or so centimeters space on either side.

She turned to Basso and nodded, and the man hurried over on silent feet.

With slow, deliberate, reverent movement, he took the urn from her tentative grasp, reached up, and placed her father's urn next to her mother's. She noticed the dust on her mother's urn had been buffed away, leaving hers brighter and shinier looking than her fathers. She smiled. It was just like real life. Her father had been no slouch in the looks department, but her mother turned heads.

She stepped back, looking at the two containers, tears flowing down her cheeks. She let them fall, the smile on her face growing as big as it could get.

"You two will have to work it out," she said. "I'll see you later."

She stepped back again, wiping away her tears. Chiara came

up behind her and put a hand on her shoulder. Basso stood on her other side and placed a hand, too.

The stone mason picked up his trowel, and with expert precision, put cement on the edges of the niche, lifted the plaque, and pushed it into place.

The crypt plate read:

Jennifer Falco and Bernardino Falco lie here, reunited in eternity.

A Falco Never Gives Up

32

The Valduce Hospital was a sprawling collection of sherbet-orange buildings. Taking up a good portion of real estate near the center of Como, the campus was tastefully landscaped with old trees and shiny, thick-leaved bushes bursting with fragrant flowers. Ali walked along the sidewalk, following the written directions she'd scrawled on a piece of paper pinched between the forefinger and thumb of her right hand poking out of the sling. In her other hand she carried a half-dozen sunflowers.

She reached a bronze sign hanging on the stucco telling her she'd reached the correct building and headed into the automatic glass doors.

Her slung arm twinged with pain as she transferred the paper to her other hand. At least she felt something. And at least she could move it. After the surgery the doctor had told her she'd been lucky to even have any movement or sensation at all in the arm, and that with a hell of a lot of work, she could eventually have eighty to ninety percent mobility back in six to twelve months. Of course, she would shoot for one hundred percent in half the time, and not accept failure as an option.

Because that's what Falcos do. And Falcos don't give up.

Inside, the receptionist directed her to room 502. "The inspector is up there in the hallway waiting for you." She pushed a clip-on badge across the counter.

"Could I ask you a favor?" Ali asked. "May I leave these flowers here? These are not for this visit. I'm visiting somebody else in another building after this."

The receptionist nodded and gestured to the counter in front of the glass. "Please. You can leave them there. I will guard them for you."

Ali set the flowers down, walked to the elevator, and rode up.

She felt oddly calm at the prospect of facing the old man.

On the fifth floor, she immediately saw the inspector and Carabinieri soldier standing in the hallway to her left, marking her destination.

Inspector Tedesco saw her coming. He broke off his conversation with the soldier and walked towards her. "Good morning."

"Hello."

"You're looking well," he said. "How's the shoulder?"

"Fine, thanks."

Tedesco nodded. "Are you sure you are up for this?"

She nodded again.

A young soldier stood at attention next to the hospital room behind Tedesco, his eyes watching her. Next to him stood a foldout table, a laptop computer opened with a pair of headphones connected to it lying on the tabletop.

"We're recording everything in that room right now, just so you know," Tedesco said, pointing to the computer. "We have a camera and microphone. He hasn't spoken a word to me since he woke up from his surgeries, other than to say he wants to speak to you."

She nodded.

"And he says he won't speak to you if I'm in there. So, I'll stay out here and watch. The bullet paralyzed him from the waist down. He's in pretty bad shape internally, too. So, there's no way he's going to try anything."

She shook her head. "I wasn't too worried."

Tedesco paused. "I also just want to make sure you're not going to..."

"What?"

"I just want to make sure you're not harboring ideas to try anything in there yourself."

"No. I'm not."

"Okay." Tedesco cleared his throat and stepped aside. "Whenever you're ready."

She opened the door and entered. The room was brightly lit, the window coverings pulled open. She stood motionless for a moment in the tiny entryway, while Tedesco pulled the door shut behind her with a soft click. She heard a faint beeping sound, the chuffing of a pump, a ticking noise that seemed to have no rhythm to it.

There was a tripod set up near the window with a camera affixed to the top of it. The television was off. Other than the medical machine noises, the room was silent.

She steeled herself and walked to the foot of Colombo's bed.

Colombo lay motionless, a large bandage covering his chest, tubes snaking out from under the bandage, a catheter snaking out from his sheets. His left wrist was handcuffed to the hospital bed. His eyes were open, staring at the ceiling.

"You came," he said with a dry whisper.

She said nothing.

His eyes lowered to look at her. They moved to her sling, then to her eyes. "I know what I've done is unforgivable."

"Which part?" she asked. "The part where you pretended

for over a decade not to know my mother was murdered so you could continue moving up in the ranks of your job? Or how you pretended not to know about your watch being found in that grave, allowing me and your inspector to continue investigating down a rabbit hole that almost got us killed?"

He closed his eyes.

"Or are there other parts you're apologizing for?" She shrugged, a gesture that sent a punch of pain through her shoulder. "What do you want from me, Stefano?"

"You have it wrong, Ali. I did not know your mother was murdered eleven years ago. And I had no idea what had happened to Elisabetta. I thought she ran away to have the baby somewhere. I've been wondering when she would show up in my life, along with a child."

"Well, now you know where she was," Ali said. "Is that it? Because I have another patient to visit. One of your inspectors who was almost killed because of you."

Colombo sighed, wincing. "I will tell you the truth, Ali. If you will listen. Will you allow me to give you that?"

"My father used to say never trust a liar."

Colombo nodded. The handcuff chain rustled as he gestured to himself. "I have lost the ability to move my legs. My career is through. My wife and daughter don't want anything to do with me. I have nothing left to lose."

"That's a shame."

Colombo leaned his head back, looking back up at the ceiling. "Twelve years ago, Dante used to work as an inspector with your father. I was head inspector. When the marshal retired, I was next in line and got the promotion. Your father was happy for me. We were both happy. He would become head inspector.

"But...it was then that Dante came to me with some recordings he had made. Of me. Me in compromising situations...with women. He wanted to be promoted to head inspector, even though he was fifteen years newer to the force than your father."

Colombo shook his head. "Dante was so young. Everyone questioned what I had done, even the former marshal and the second lieutenant, but I did it. And that, rightfully, angered your father. He felt betrayed for that. I could have fixed everything right then and there. I could have told the truth in that moment and confessed to your father why I had done it. None of this would have happened."

"But you were too weak," Ali said. "You were worried about yourself. About your career."

Colombo said nothing.

Ali went to a chair next to the window and sat down. "So, he was blackmailing you," she said. "And you were seeing Elisabetta?"

Colombo shook his head. "Elisabetta came later. But, yes, he knew about Elisabetta when I got her pregnant." Colombo looked at her. "I wanted her to get an abortion, but by a doctor, somebody who was competent. I sent her to your mother. Somehow your mother got the truth out of Elisabetta.

"That next day your mother reached out to me at work. She wanted to speak to me, so we met for a coffee, where she told me about what she'd learned—that I was the father. She told me Elisabetta had fallen in love with me. That she was young and impressionable, but she wanted to keep the baby, and wasn't going to go through with the procedure. Your mother knew I was in trouble. That I was doing Elisabetta wrong, and that I was doing my wife and child wrong." Colombo closed his eyes. "That I was doing everyone wrong."

"Your mother told me she would tell nobody while I figured out how to deal with the problem. She promised to keep quiet if I kept her informed on the situation. But after our meeting, I was certain your mother would tell your father. And my career was all but over from that point on. After all, I'd already done the Falcos wrong by promoting Dante over him.

"But your mother had kept her word. Nobody ever knew. Not even your father. She was such a good person, Ali, you know that?"

Ali glared at him. "And the night of my mother's death? Elisabetta was with her. She went back to my mother?"

Colombo nodded. "After my meeting with your mother, I convinced Elisabetta to have the abortion after all. I'm not proud of it, but I tried to take your mother out of the equation, thinking the girl might go through with it at a different clinic. I gave her money. I gave her my watch...because I wanted to give her something valuable. Something that proved I loved her. Something that would convince her to just have that abortion. If she would have just gone through with it, none of this would have happened."

Colombo drew his hands into fists, then relaxed them.

"But, in fact, Elisabetta took my money, and my watch, and went back to your mother. And that's when your mother called me. I was supposed to meet them in that parking lot. To discuss what we would do next, once and for all. But I was stuck with my family at dinner." Colombo blew air from his nose. "I'm sitting there with two other couples and their children at my house, having a dinner party, and trying to deal with this situation at the same time. I couldn't get away."

Ali said nothing, watching him speak.

"Finally, I did break away. And when I got there...when I got to that parking lot," Colombo closed his eyes, "I had no idea what was going on. There were emergency vehicles everywhere. Your mother wasn't there. Polizia were there. Carabinieri were there. Ambulances. But there was no sign of your mother and Elisabetta."

Colombo's voice went quiet.

"And then I learned. I learned your mother had gone over the edge. And I learned she had been alone in that car. That Elisabetta was nowhere to be found." Colombo shook his head.

"And then what?" Ali asked.

Colombo kept shaking his head, clenching his eyes shut. "I was so confused. I didn't know what had happened."

"What did you do?" she asked.

"Nothing." Colombo opened his eyes. "I did nothing."

The machines beeped. The pump chuffed again.

"And why was my father so upset with my mother that night?"

"It is true, he thought I was having an affair with your mother. Somebody saw us in the coffee shop, talking about Elisabetta, and told him. And then he looked in your mother's phone and saw we'd been talking. And when he asked her about it, she lied to him, saying we just saw one another at the shop and decided to have coffee together. She protected my secret, sacrificing her own happiness to let me have the space to take care of my problem."

"How do you know all this?" Ali asked.

"After your mother's death he came to me. He said he knew we were at the coffee shop, he knew we'd been speaking on the phone. He wanted to know why she was lying to him when he asked about it. And I told your father the same lie I told you—that your mother and I were planning a birthday celebration for him. I told him that your mother approached me because she was trying to get us back together, that she was plotting to rekindle our friendship, and she wanted to know how to plan a birthday celebration that could do that."

Tears dampened Colombo's cheeks. "Your father took the news badly. He told me it was all his fault that your mother had died. He told me about their fight. He told me he thought she was cheating with me. He put in his resignation and went down to Rome. I never told him about Elisabetta. I never told him the truth. I did nothing."

Ali shook her head. "And when Elisabetta was found? You knew right then my mother must have been killed that night, too. That it couldn't have been an accident."

Colombo nodded.

"And when my father killed himself, you knew it was murder, and you said nothing."

Colombo closed his eyes.

"And when they cleaned that watch from Elisabetta's grave, you knew it wasn't my father's watch, but it was the one he'd given you. And you still said nothing."

"I didn't know what was happening," Colombo said. "I didn't know Elisabetta had been killed. I didn't know who was doing everything...I didn't know it was Dante."

"But he blackmailed you before. He was doing what? Recording you? No. You had to have known. The guy was bad news. And you made him your right-hand man. And you watched our lives get destroyed while you got your power."

"I didn't know." Colombo shook his head, his voice barely audible. "I didn't do anything."

"And that's the problem, isn't it?" She stood up. "Now if you don't mind. I'm going to get on with my life now. And I'll let you get on with yours."

Ali walked out of the room.

Tedesco was pulling off headphones, clicking some buttons on his computer when she came out. "That was...interesting," he said.

"Are we done? I'm afraid I'll vomit if I stay here any longer."

"I'll walk you down," Tedesco said, hurrying to step beside her.

They got in the elevator.

"That recording will be a godsend for prosecutors," Tedesco

said, watching the doors close. "We can add it to all the Dante recordings we found on his hard drives. Did you hear about that?"

"No."

"We found hundreds of recordings on Dante's computer. He's had the offices bugged for years. He's got them all organized by politician, or by ranking member of Carabinieri."

She frowned, shaking her head. She'd been so wrong about Dante, and the grip on her heart tightened when she thought about it, so instead, she looked up at the numbers above the elevator door.

"When are you headed back down to Siena?"

"Later today. After lunch."

"Ah." Tedesco eyed his watch.

The elevator dinged, the door opened, and they stepped out into the ground floor waiting area.

"I was going to go see Marco, I mean, Inspector Vinci first."

"You haven't seen him yet?"

She shook her head.

No, she hadn't seen him yet. Not since that night. They had been put into separate ambulances and taken to the same ER at this very hospital. But Marco had been on a much more difficult path to recovery, taking a bullet to his abdomen area, undergoing multiple surgeries.

She could have gone to see him yesterday or the day before, having been released from another building within the hospital complex herself, but she had been preparing for her father's memorial service, and quite frankly she didn't feel like confronting Marco's fiancée. Or, rather, she didn't want to be present to witness the love between her and Marco, to be reminded what Ali still didn't have. Sure, she was grateful for Basso and Chiara, but the truth was she had been lonely in that hospital bed, not having a special someone at her side, holding her hand, waiting for her to wake up from her surgery, rubbing her forehead, or massaging her feet, or whatever lovey-dovey things people did at a hospital bedside.

She spent three days in the hospital bed after her shoulder surgery thinking about the embrace she and Marco had shared that night, before hell had broken loose. The way their bodies fit together, the way they squeezed each other...she hadn't felt a connection like that with somebody in over a decade.

And then there had been the rest of that night, sitting with Marco as they waited for the police to come, petting his face as he clung to life. Holding his cold hand.

"Well," Tedesco said, escorting her to the bouquet of flowers she'd left near the receptionist, "it will be nice for Marco to have another visitor besides me and Salvaggio. Without his fiancée around, he's been pretty lonely in that bed."

She looked at him. Keeping her tone casual, she asked, "Why is his fiancée not around?"

"They broke up. The day you two got shot. Must have been final. Because she never did show up to the hospital."

Ali stood frozen, computing the information. "Uh, well, I guess I'll go see him then."

33

Ali followed a nurse down a long, wide hallway. Through the open patient room doors, she saw peaceful people conversing and laughing or watching television. Building 8 of the Valduce Hospital campus felt full of optimism.

"In here." The nurse walked up to the door, knocked twice, and entered without waiting for a response. "Mr. Vinci, I have a guest for you."

Ali followed into a brightly lit room double the size of Colombo's. Three bouquets, dwarfing the clump of flowers in Ali's hand, were lined up along the window ledge.

"Who is it?" Ali lingered in the entryway of the room, hearing Marco's raspy voice before she saw him.

"Come in, woman," the nurse said. "Show this man your beautiful face. He needs some cheering up today. He's getting sick of only seeing his mother. Not that she isn't gorgeous herself."

Ali walked inside, a sheepish smile on her face. She raised the flowers in greeting. "Ciao."

"Ciao." Marco smiled, and to Ali it looked as if he were relieved to see her.

Ali smiled in return. She kept back a few steps, giving the nurse room as she circled the bed, checking a readout, gently squeezing an intravenous bag that snaked down to his arm, clicking the keyboard of a computer.

"Okay, looking good Mr. Vinci." She winked at Ali, then gave Marco a stern look. "You'll be good while I'm gone?"

"Yes ma'am," Marco said.

"Good." She turned to leave. "Marta will check on you in two hours. Press the button if you need anything. You know the drill." She closed the door behind her, leaving the room silent, save the faint beeping of Marco's machines.

Ali turned to face Marco. His normally sculpted dark hair was disheveled, his face covered in a few days' stubble, which somehow made his aquamarine eyes stand out even more. He looked somewhat pale, but vital, considering the large bandage covering his abdomen.

"How are you feeling?" she asked.

"I'm feeling good." He held her eye contact. "Grateful they passed the law against us using hollow point bullets." He smiled.

She raised her eyebrows, looking down at her shoulder. "Yeah."

"And you?"

She shrugged, wincing. She needed to stop doing that. "It hurts when I move it, but I'm lucky, they say. I should make a full recovery." It felt good to bend the truth to her liking.

"That's great."

She went to the window ledge and placed the sunflowers next to the other arrangements. She leaned in and smelled the other bouquet, discreetly checking the cards that hung from two of them, wondering if fiancée Valentina had sent him something. One bouquet was from the Tedescos, another from the Valencias. She couldn't read the other card without looking like she was snooping. Which she was. She straightened and turned around.

"I love sunflowers," Marco said. "We used to go to Montalcino as a family when I was a child. I remember there was a villa that had a field of them. I remember it vividly, the way they used to turn toward the sun. My father loved them, too."

"I love them as well, for much the same reason. Except we used to go to Siena for our family trips."

"Hence the reason you live there now," he said.

"One of the good reasons, yes." She looked around. "Your room is a lot better than Colombo's."

"You saw him?" Marco's eyes darkened.

"I did. Just now, before you."

"Tedesco told me he wanted to speak to you. What did he want?"

She shook her head. "To have his excuses heard, I guess."

"Well, I hate to say somebody got what they deserved by being shot through the spine...so, I guess I won't say it." Marco shook his head. "I'm sorry, Ali. I also heard from Tedesco you were having a service for your father. I wish I could be there."

"Don't worry about it. I already had it this morning. It was small. I didn't know who to invite, so I didn't invite anybody." She smiled briefly. "Which is how I'm sure he would have preferred it."

They descended into silence, Ali standing at the foot of his bed, unsure where to put her eyes, Marco keeping his eyes on her.

"Anyway," she said, "I'm sure glad you shot when you did. And I'm glad your aim was better than Dante's."

Marco nodded. "Me too."

"How are you doing with that?"

"With shooting the guy?"

"Yeah."

"He was going to shoot you. I couldn't be prouder of anything I've ever done."

"I suppose that's one way to look at it."

"I'm serious," he said, and his eyes told her as much. "If he would have killed you, I..." Marco looked out the window.

She followed his eyes outside, to the green mountains cutting a line in the azure sky, and the shimmering silver lake beneath it all. A line of kiteboarders raced back and forth across the lake, riding the wind through white powerboat wakes.

"It's a beautiful view," she said.

"It is."

"I'll miss it." She looked at him. "But I won't at the same time, you know?"

"Yeah," he said. "I do."

Ali moved a step closer to the bed, resting her free hand on the plastic footboard. She decided to get on with it and speak what she was thinking. "You broke up with Valentina."

Marco nodded, his eyes finally coming back to her. "It wasn't going to work out."

"That's a shame."

"Not really."

They held eye contact now, and Ali moved around the side of the bed. "May I?" She gestured to the edge of the bed and sat, not waiting for an answer. She sat on his right, putting her sling arm closest to him.

Marco reached up and touched her shoulder, the backs of his fingers barely grazing the spot where she'd been shot. "You were lucky."

"I was."

She looked down at his bandage, remembering the way the wound kept seeping blood while she held his hand in the kitchen that night, the way his hand had been cold and clammy.

"You were lucky," she said.

He smiled, dropping his hand. "I was."

She reached across her lap with her good hand and put it on his. His warm grip closed around hers.

"I'm leaving to go down south," she said.

"I know." He nodded.

"And if you're ever down in Tuscany I want you to give me a call, okay?"

Marco nodded. "And if you're ever up here..." he didn't finish the sentence. "But you're not going to be coming back up here, are you."

"I will, actually. To figure out how to sell the villa. After that...no. I don't plan on spending much time up here."

"You'll miss it," he said. "But you won't at the same time."

She smiled briefly, then looked down at their intertwined hands. "I don't really know you that well. But I think I'll miss you."

"I'll miss you too," Marco said without hesitation.

"Who knows?" she said. "Maybe if you ever get that Rome transfer, you could give me a call."

"What's it, two hours from Siena to Rome?" he asked.

"Two, two and a half."

They sat in silence, looking at one another, both of them coming to a silent understanding that the cards were stacking up against them.

"Well," she pulled back her hand, but he kept hold of it.

Marco looked at her seriously. "Aren't you going to kiss me?"

"Oh I...I thought I dreamed that. I mean, I hoped it was a dream." She felt her face going red. "I must have thought you were somebody else."

"Oh." He let go of her hand. "Okay, well. That's a shame."

She smiled, grabbing his hand, pulling it to her mouth and kissing the back of it.

He turned her hand over, pulled it to his face, and kissed the back of it, leaving a wet spot where his lips had touched.

She stood up, putting her good hand down on the pillow as she bent over, her hair tipping over her shoulder and landing on his forehead. Without hesitation she continued, her lips pressing against his, fitting just as perfectly as their bodies had during their embrace all those nights ago. She closed her eyes, feeling immersed in the moment that seemed to stretch for eternity.

When she stood up, she felt light-headed. She smiled at the way Marco seemed frozen, his lips still puckered slightly, his eyes open halfway.

He cleared his throat. "I liked that."

"Me too." She backed away, realizing at that moment they were somehow holding hands again.

She looked down at their intertwined fingers, squeezed his hand again, then let her fingers slip from his. "Goodbye, Marco." She turned and walked out.

"Goodbye Ali."

She turned, tears floating on her bottom eyelids.

"And good luck," Marco said. "You deserve it."

She smiled, letting the tears drip down her cheeks. As she turned and opened the door, for the first time in eleven years she knew in her heart Marco spoke the truth.

34

A bead of sweat dripped down Ali's arm.

Damn this sling, she cursed silently. With the tape and gauze wrapped around her stitched surgical wound, the way the contraption pressed her arm close to her body, keeping it immobile, she was already slow-roasting even though it was only eight-thirty in the morning.

The sun speared down the straight road ahead. Squinting against the glare, all but blinded, she could still bask in the familiarity of her walk in to work, feeling the cool presence of the thick vines covered in red flowers near the Madonna shrine built into the wall, inhaling a deep lungful of the fragrant flowers, taking in the scent of freshly baked bread wafting at her back, riding the southern wind.

A woman smacked open wooden shutters a few stories up, then began a loud conversation with someone in the building across the road. A man passed by, whistling the Song of Verbena, the Palio race upcoming in August clearly on his mind.

Ali was back in Siena, once again immersed into the life she'd created for herself over the last decade. When she had gone back to Como, she realized she had missed the lake and the surrounding mountains, but she knew now, as she hiked up the inclined street toward the Polizia HQ, she missed the hills of Tuscany more. She felt connected to this land down here.

She ducked into the next side street, and out of the blasting sunlight, finally reaching police headquarters tucked into the northern wall of this narrow slot-canyon road.

Returning for the first time in over a week and a half, having left under circumstances she'd rather forget, her stomach felt full of helium as she stepped up and opened the door. And yet she felt a steely resolve as she walked past the passport control office and up the steps.

Basso had told her on the drive down that the punching incident had been all but forgotten when Fabiano had been promoted to inspector instead of her. That tidbit of information had incited anger inside her, along with the feeling of being out in an arena, playing a high stakes game with cheaters. Cheaters who were twice her size.

As she walked up the steps, into the familiar scent of coffee, cologne, and body odor that permeated the hundreds-years old building, she left behind that feeling of helplessness, along with the second floor, as she continued past the squad room to the upper level.

"Ali." Clarissa lowered a cup of espresso from her lips as Ali walked into the upper-level administration offices. "I thought you were taking today off. You said you were coming in next week."

That's what Ali had told her at the end of their drive down from Como. But she had lied. And Ali had not mentioned this morning's plan either, not to Clarissa or Basso, because she didn't want to hear anyone else's opinion on the matter. She needed to follow her gut and speak her mind to Ferrari, before she lost the nerve and it was too late.

"I need to see Ferrari."

Clarissa's eyebrows popped. "He has a meeting this morning." She flipped open a notebook, running her finger down the page.

"Is he here?"

"Yes."

"Is he with somebody now?"

"No. But—"

"Then that's all I need to know." She turned and walked to Ferrari's door, knocking three times. Even in her determined state, she cringed inwardly at the volume of her knocks. She sounded like the Gestapo about to bash down his door.

"What?" Ferrari's voice asked from within.

"It's..." Ali shook her head and twisted the knob, pushing it open a crack. "It's me, sir. Falco."

"Falco! Come in!"

She walked inside as Ferrari exhaled a plume of smoke out his window, the cloud swirling away, reflecting bright in the morning sun.

"Close it," he said. "Close it."

She ducked in quickly and closed the door behind her.

Ferrari remained near the window, holding the cigarette, a shrug of resignation lifting his shoulders as he took another greedy drag. "I don't care. Life is too short to not have cigarettes in my own office."

After another drag, he flicked out the butt and faced her. "You look good. You look strong. You have color in your cheeks."

"Probably because it's hotter than hell out there already," she said.

Ferrari smiled. "It's good to see you, Ali." His face went serious. "I've heard everything from the Carabinieri and Basso. I know you must be sick of talking about it, so I won't make you go over it again. But just know that I am proud of what you accomplished up there."

"Oh. Uh, thanks." Curious, she asked, "Who did you speak to at the Carabinieri?"

"Tedesco? Was that his name?"

She nodded. "Yes. Inspector Tedesco." Not Marco, she thought. He was probably sleeping right now, still in his hospital bed. That kiss had been on her mind ever since it had happened.

"He was the only one available when I called," Ferrari said. "Everyone else was either dead or in the hospital." He shook his head, his eyes glazing over. "My God, Ali. I'm sorry about all that's happened to you." He bared his teeth. "The deception."

She nodded, saying nothing.

"I thought you were coming back in next week," he said. "That's what I thought we discussed."

"I was. But I was just coming in because I need to speak to you."

"What is it?" Ferrari gestured to the seat in front of his desk, then walked to his swivel seat and sat down.

Ali sat, moving with slow deliberation to keep the jarring of her shoulder to a minimum. "I wanted to apologize to you, sir."

"Oh?" Ferrari kept a neutral expression, eyes unblinking.

"Yes. I was completely out of line with you before I left town."

Ferrari gave a little twitch of his eyebrow and mouth, as if to say, it's old news now, let's move on.

She sat without speaking, feeling all the things she'd been rehearsing in her head over the last couple days boil inside, threatening to explode in a rush.

She stood up and began pacing behind the chair. After a lap to the window and back, she stopped. "I want to be an inspector."

Ferrari tilted his head back and to the side, eyeing her. "Okay."

"I'm sorry that I didn't tell you as much the last time I was in here. And I know I've blown my opportunity for this time around, but I just want you to know that I am gunning for the next position when it opens up."

"If it opens up," he said.

She blinked. "Right. I mean, *if* a position opens up." She emphasized the word, which made her balk. She hadn't considered an inspector spot never opening up again. She shook off the thought. "Whatever. *If* a position opens up, I want it."

"Oh, you do, eh?"

"Yes."

Ferrari measured her skeptically. "And you know now that punching that man out in the street was wrong."

"Yes, it was wrong."

"And you would never do that again."

She shook her head. "The man knocked over a child, hurting him badly, then smiled about it. That earns a punch in the face every time in my book."

Ferrari folded his arms theatrically, pulling the corners of his mouth down. "Okay."

"But hopefully, perhaps next time, my partner could stop me before I do anything too rash."

Ferrari smiled, then turned to the window behind his desk and laughed. He stood and looked out. "Oh, Ali." He shook his head, turning toward the sun and closing his eyes.

She stood at attention, her eyes remaining fixed on the back of his head.

A moment later he turned around. His smile had vanished. "Who told you?"

"Who told me what?"

His eyes narrowed. "Who told you? Because I was told they would be taking me to court, and if I told anybody about what happened they were going to sue my ass. Therefore, I have told nobody. Not even my wife. I need to know how you found out, and I need to know now. Was it Basso? Clarissa?"

"Sir. I swear to you I have no idea what you're talking about."

Ferrari's eyes relaxed. "You don't know."

She shook her head, her curiosity raised to desperate levels.

He flipped a hand. "Okay, you can have the position."

"*If* a position opens up."

"A position has opened up. Again. And you can have it. I'm officially promoting you to inspector, effective immediately."

Her mouth hung open. "What about Fabiano?"

"Fabiano is an ass, and always has been. He was never a good fit. My conscience couldn't take it anymore. I decided to do the right thing. I purged this building of the Fabianos."

"And now they're going to take you to court?"

He waved her off. "I've said too much. Don't worry about it. They have no legal basis." He unfolded his arms, putting his hands on his hips. "So, Inspector Falco. With what else can I help you?"

She shook her head. "Nothing, I guess."

"I want you taking the week off and report back next week. We'll assess your health then. If you need more time, you'll take it."

"I won't need more time."

He waved a dismissive hand, reached into his desk drawer, and put another cigarette in his mouth. "Don't play tough with me, Falco. Just go home and get some rest."

"Yes, sir." She turned towards the door, then swiveled back around, turning a full pirouette. "Sir?"

"What?"

"Thank you. I won't let you down."

Ferrari nodded. He pulled the unlit cigarette out of his mouth and pointed it at her. "Please don't tell anybody about what we just discussed, about your promotion, and certainly not anything about me firing Fabiano. I have a couple meetings this morning on the matter, and then I will make the announcement myself. So, when I say go home, I mean go home."

"Yes, sir." She turned toward the door.

"And Falco."

"Yes, sir?"

"You're welcome. I have to admit, before our conversation just now I wasn't sure you were right for the job. Now I know you're going to be great."

She nodded. "Thank you, sir."

She closed the door softly behind her as she left.

"Well?" Clarissa asked, leaning back in her chair. "Did he bite your head off? He bit my head off yesterday. Something is going on. I think it's something to do with Fabiano."

"He was fine. I'll see you later. I'm taking the week off."

"You came to your senses. I'll come by with a bottle tomorrow?"

"The doctor didn't tell me wine was part of my healing process."

"That's because it's implied."

"Bye." Ali left, managing to skirt past the second-floor squad room without being noticed. Now that she had been on her feet all morning, she had less energy than she thought to deal with Rossi, Patucci, and Basso. Even with the news she'd just received.

She left the building and weaved her way to Porta Romagna to the south.

This time of the morning was too early for tourists, too late for workers to be out having coffee and the bench along the south wall was free.

She sat alone, unbuttoning her jacket. The sky was cloudless, tinged with a limonata-yellow haze from a scirocco coming in from north Africa, over the Mediterranean, hitting her now with warm air that licked the sweat from her body.

The hills were still green, though crisping brown under the relentless summer sun.

She remembered the photograph on her father's screen saver, of Ali and Clarissa sitting on this very bench, telling a story, in the throes of laughter.

Ali stood and moved to the railing, looking down the slope. A car swung lazily around a switchback turn where her father must have parked his own car and saw her, snapping his camera with a telephoto lens. How had he seen her? How had he known she would be sitting there that day, at that particular time?

Because Ali was here most days, that's how.

She sat back down, smiling to herself. Her father must have lurked nearby countless times if he knew her routines. How had he done all that without her noticing?

Because he was a good inspector. One of the best.

She leaned back, stretching her good arm across the back of the bench, allowing her mind to trace forward to an exhilarating future.

"And now," she whispered, "I'm going to be just like you, Papà."

Thank you so much for reading The Como Falcon, and I hope you enjoyed the story. My wife and children are dual citizens of the United States and Italy, and we often travel to the areas featured in this novel.

It has been a long time coming to explore something

outside of the David Wolf Series, which I've become so fond of and so comfortable writing.

If you enjoyed the story, I hope you'll consider leaving a review on Amazon, as it helps so much with other people discovering the book, sales, helping my family buy more pizza.

—>You can Leave a Review for The Como Falcon by Clicking Here.

And I also hope you'll consider sharing this book with friends, loved ones, strangers with obvious hankerings for international mysteries, and anyone else you think might like the novel.

You can contact me at jeff@jeffcarson.co (no "m"), and you can sign up for the New Release Newsletter by clicking this link — https://jeffcarson.co/newsletter/ (Sign up to receive a free story sent to your inbox.)

ALSO BY JEFF CARSON

THE DAVID WOLF SERIES

Gut Decision (A David Wolf Short Story)– Sign up for the new release newsletter at http://www.jeffcarson.co/p/newsletter.html and receive a complimentary copy of the David Wolf story.

Foreign Deceit (David Wolf Book 1)

The Silversmith (David Wolf Book 2)

Alive and Killing (David Wolf Book 3)

Deadly Conditions (David Wolf Book 4)

Cold Lake (David Wolf Book 5)

Smoked Out (David Wolf Book 6)

To the Bone (David Wolf Book 7)

Dire (David Wolf Book 8)

Signature (David Wolf Book 9)

Dark Mountain (David Wolf Book 10)

Rain (David Wolf Book 11)

Drifted (David Wolf Book 12)

Divided Sky (David Wolf Book 13)

In the Ground (David Wolf Book 14)

High Road (David Wolf Book 15)

**NEW! Dead Canyon (David Wolf Book 16)

THE ALI FALCO SERIES

The Como Falcon (Ali Falco Book 1)

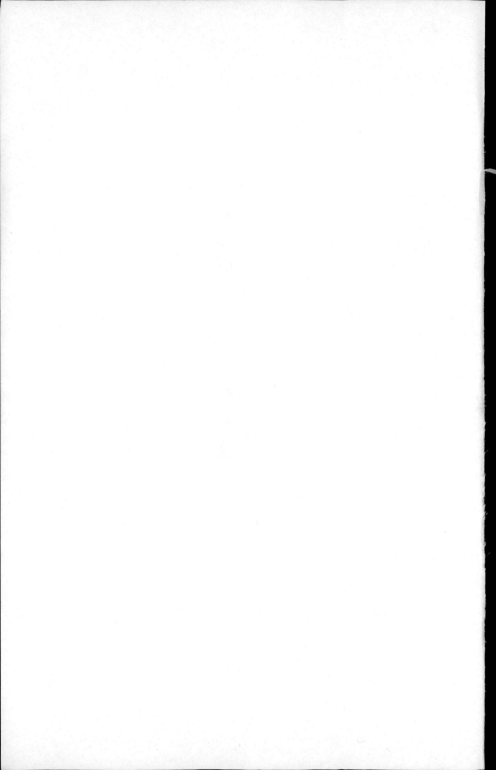

Made in the USA
Monee, IL
30 June 2022